Shrouded

Carol Anne Davis

snowbooks

Proudly Published by Snowbooks in 2006

Snowbooks Ltd.
120 Pentonville Road
London
N1 9JN
Tel: 0207 837 6482
Fax: 0207 837 6348
email: info@snowbooks.com

www.snowbooks.com

British Library Cataloguing in Publication Data

A catalogue record for this book is available from the British Library.

ISBN 1-905005-32-6

ISBN 13 978-1-905005-32-1

Shrouded

Carol Anne Davis

PROLOGUE

The boy awoke—was wakened. Shadows slipped and slithered round the room. Down below, he heard the settee squeaking. Each creak broke the stillness—a rhythmic groan. His little church-shaped clock read ten thirty, which meant they hadn't gone to bed after all.

Now he could watch *Fear on Friday* with them. The other kids at school got to see it every week.

'Tate's not got a telly!' three of the tougher boys had started to chorus most days. But he did, he did. Only sometimes Paul said that a programme was bad for you, or dangerous. That you shouldn't watch TV when eating, or on Sundays at all.

So he'd read instead, running his torch along the lines of print as he huddled beneath the covers. Sometimes he told one of the quieter boys about the adventure stories he'd read. Even then, when his classmates discussed Friday's werewolves and vampires, he couldn't compete. Unless...

Slowly, slowly he slid one foot out of bed, wincing at the coolness. Stretched it out, out, past his slippers to the floorboard nearest the chest of drawers. This was the friendly floorboard, the silent one, the one that would never tell. If Paul heard him in his room or on the stairs, he'd hit him and even kick him if his mum wasn't looking, then send him back to bed.

Douglas breathed slowly, shallowly, hands searching the air in front of him like a sleep-walker. If he made it safely into the living room, there was a good chance mum would let him stay up.

Shivering, unable to find his dressing gown in the dark, he tiptoed forward. Held his palm flat against the door, and edged it open by a quarter of an inch at a time. Almost, almost... As soon as the gap was wide enough, he turned sideways, slipped through it. The landing was in darkness—Paul said it was wasteful to keep on unnecessary lights.

'He gets scared. Don't you, love?' his mum had said when Paul first married her and introduced the No Lights Rule. She'd made the gesture that felt like she was polishing his hair.

Paul's small brown eyes had focused on Douglas, narrowed like those of next doors tabby.

'If he's done nothing wrong, if his conscience is clear, then he should be able to sleep.'

But he couldn't sleep—he couldn't. He'd rather sit and watch girls screaming at vampires, than lie in his divan alone in the uncertain dark.

Onto stair one now, clutching the banister, not breathing. Stairs two, three, four: the settee's creaking growing louder step by step. Were they jumping up and down with excitement, like he did when it got to the scary bits? Paul rarely cuddled his mum the way new husbands did all the time on TV.

Maybe he was liking her more cause she'd had her hair curled pretty? Maybe he'd start to like Douglas, too. Taking two steps at a time now, soles light as whispers, he reached the living room door.

'Mum?' He was just about to say it. She'd turn and see how cold he was, how lonely, how small. And would snort 'Look at him!' and hold out her arms, and take him on her lap. Then Paul would say 'He's eight years old, Alice! He's much too big for that,' and she'd set him down again.

'Let him watch the film, Paul,' she'd plead, putting her head to one side and pursing her lips together, 'He's not doing any harm.'

And Paul would say 'He's your son', and turn away from them, thin shoulders hunching. His mum would ruffle Douglas's hair and give her high pitched laugh and all would be well.

Inhaling, Douglas peered round the door. Where were they? No blonde and brown heads sticking out from the back of the settee. Alice might have gone into the kitchen to make a cup of tea, but Paul said that that was woman's work, that men were the thinkers. He looked harder, closer, choked back a laugh.

Paul's bum—he could see Paul's bum! He was moving up and down on top of his mum, very quickly. They did this on TV, did couples: it meant they liked each other lots. His skin prickled—he knew he wasn't supposed to be watching this. In the movies they took the phone off the hook or put Do Not Disturb signs on the hotel room door.

'We won't be down for breakfast tomorrow,' the man would tell the receptionist, and his girlfriend would turn away, smiling. It was pretty clear they wanted to be alone.

Afterwards they were nice to everyone—even strangers. They smiled and joked with people, and if it was a musical they burst into song.

In the films, though, they spoke, said 'I love you.' Paul was just pushing, pushing: his mum's eyes were open, her head facing away from the door. All Douglas could see of her was her face and naked shoulders. He changed his position slightly, and noticed her feet sticking out from under Paul's. She'd painted her toe-nails a deep glossy purple. Her fingernails, resting lightly against Paul's back, were long and red.

She was nice like this, thought Douglas—gentle, peaceful. He hated it when her voice went all high in the corner shop as she told the owner a joke. And the Gas Man stared at her when he came to read the meter. And she giggled, even if he hadn't said anything, and walked funny when they passed the men digging up the road.

'Uh. Uh,' Paul was going now, still pushing forward. His bum was even smaller than it looked in jeans, 'Make an effort,' he added, and seemed to shift position slightly. Eyes still open, staring into the distance, his mother opened her mouth.

'Uuh!' she said: her voice was flat, like when she got too tired to be angry, 'Uuh. Uuh. Uuh,' she kept saying, in this scary, haunting voice.

'Mum?' he said, stepping forward, suddenly afraid for her, 'Mum? Are you alright?'

His mum jerked her head towards him, shouted 'Douglas!' She sat up really quickly. Paul was thrown back.

'Little bastard.' He got to his feet, started towards

him. Douglas turned and fled towards his room.

Mistake. Paul would get him there. He should have stayed near his mother.

'Mum! Mum!' he screamed, racing ahead. His mind broke the speed barrier, searching for exits. Paul was leaping behind him, gaining step by step.

He caught him before they reached the bedroom door, carried him on into it. Threw him down on the bed, held his back as he pulled his pyjama bottoms down.

'No!' Paul had spanked him before—much worse than the cuffings. He tried to cover his flesh, but Paul pinned both hands back with one of his own. And reached for something on the ground. Douglas tensed, waiting. Paul had said to pray for guidance. Douglas prayed. Paul's hand whizzed down. Douglas screamed, cried out. Bucked, tried to twist over. Pain shot down, down.

Twisting his head round, he could see Paul using Douglas's own slipper on him. It was small, but had a hard plastic heel.

'Paul?' His mum stood in the doorway. Douglas gazed at her through his tears, already crying so much he couldn't speak.

'He deserves this, Alice.'

'I know. It's just...' She looked away from him.

'I only wanted to see *Fear on Friday*,' he sobbed.

Paul gripped his arms more tightly, as if planning to break them: 'You were told you weren't allowed.'

Douglas stared at his mother. She'd put her blouse and underskirt on again. Her hair was coming out of its band, wisps reaching her shoulders like it did on Hallowe'en witches. One hand clutched the door jamb, red nails on white paintwork. She was breathing hard, and so was Paul.

'Mum?' he sobbed again. His bottom was hurting. His stepfather was gripping him tightly, his own bare flesh against the man's.

'You shouldn't have come down, and you shouldn't have been watching,' his mum said sadly.

'Alice. Bring me my dressing gown and my belt,' Paul said.

So it was over, over. Douglas continued to sob at the unfairness of it all. But Paul was going to go back downstairs, and watch the film, so his heart stopped thumping quite as hard. Tomorrow at breakfast Paul would pretend not to notice him, and his mum would give him extra cornflakes and shake her head.

'Don't you think he's had enough, Paul?'

He stared at his mum, not understanding.

'Do what I told you, then get into bed.'

His mum went. He heard their bedroom door open, her footsteps returning. She handed Paul his navy blue dressing gown, and he let go of Douglas to put it on.

Free. The boy put his stretched wrists beneath him, and rolled over to the side of the bed, rolled off it. As he fell, he grabbed the top cover and pulled it over his nakedness.

He could sense his mum still standing there, unmoving. Douglas closed his eyes. *Please make Paul go away.*

'And the belt, Alice.'

He heard his mother say 'Go easy on him.'

'I'll be through later,' said Paul, 'Get into bed.'

Then sounds of the bedroom door closing, and the springs on his bed protesting. *Paul had stayed. Paul had stayed. Paul had stayed.*

'Right,' said Paul. There was the sound of something hitting the mattress. Then Douglas felt himself being grabbed under the armpits and dragged back onto the bed.

'We can do this the simple way, or you can make it difficult,' Paul said. Pushed flat again, Douglas stared at the blanket. Its turquoise background had never seemed so bright. 'You can take your thrashing like a man, or make a noise and I'll give you more. Then you'll really have something to cry about.'

He knew he'd cry out—he knew he would. Even the spankings made him scream and shake. It was so scary, those big hands coming at you... Was Paul really going to hit him with a belt?

'I didn't mean to peep. I didn't,' he screamed, trying to get his hands free, 'Paul—I'm sorry. Don't hit me. Don't! Don't!'

'If you won't learn...'

The first lash felt like when you burnt yourself on the cooker.

'Do what you're told... Respect your elders... Know your place...'

Douglas was screaming, scrambled words and shouts and wailings. His mum would come. The neighbours would come. Someone would. The pain stopped. Paul stretched out. It must be over. Then Douglas felt the smooth dryness of cotton shoved against his mouth. *His pyjama top. Paul was pushing his face in his pyjama top.* He felt something tighten round his head.

And now he was still screaming, but it was just coming out like the TV did when you had the sound right down. Yelling, promising. But no one could hear—except Paul.

Please God, make him stop, he kept saying at first, inside his head, like a nursery rhyme. Please, please... But the torment went on and on. Everything felt scalded now, blazing. Acid rose in his throat, water blurred his eyes.

'Is this what you wanted?' He felt Paul's palm close round his private bits. Warmth enveloped them. No one had touched him there before. 'Like that, do you?' Paul was stroking, teasing. Douglas swallowed, glad that the beating had stopped. And whimpered and rubbed to increase the new sensations—then screamed and screamed. For Paul was jerking his privates upwards, outwards, pulling harder, faster, more and more and more.

'Did you want to see your mother and me at it?' Jerk, jerk—Douglas felt sickness start in his belly and keep rising, sour as curdled milk. 'You dirty little bastard,' Paul was shrieking, 'Did you want to see her tits?'

His hand was doing terrible things: worse than the thrashing. Sharp pains jerked and juddered up Douglas's groin.

'I'll show you how to buck,' Paul said, picking up the belt again. Pain and pain and pain and pain and pain.

How could there be so much hurt, when you kept promising things? When you swore in your head you'd do exactly what you were told? Agony and torture and torment and... there weren't enough words for it. He couldn't breathe, see, think, act—could only feel.

Red mists. A far away voice.

'I hope you've learned something,' Paul said, getting off the bed, 'Now don't move.' Douglas heard his footsteps go to the door. He heard him pause as he reached it. 'I mean it, you little bastard. One more squeak from you tonight, and I'll really tan your hide. Don't you as much as blink without permission. You stay just where you are.'

Stay, stay. Douglas lay there, staying. His arms prickled, but he kept them exactly in place. He could feel the cold air as it slid over his fevered flesh, making him shiver. Don't move, Paul had said—which meant the blanket stayed out of reach.

He tried to get his shattered brain round the words 'don't move', fighting the urge to curl into a little ball. Don't move meant he couldn't relieve himself. Don't move meant he had to leave the pyjamas top where it was. Paul had taken it away from his face when he started retching, and now its acrid smell soured against his nose.

Don't move, don't move. He concentrated on keeping his eyelashes as still as possible. Through a watery fog, he could see Lucky, his goldfish, staring back.

Don't move, he thought, as the fish swum round, then upwards. You could rely on Lucky: she never blew smoke in your face, or giggled in your ear. *Stay still*, he begged, as liquid ran from his mouth's corners. *Stay still, still. Don't make Paul mad.*

And so he lay there, not moving, as his church clock ticked away the seconds, the moments, the hours. And though his buttocks swelled and throbbed he kept the rest of his body immobile and found a measure of peace.

CHAPTER ONE

Peace. There was peace to be had here, amongst the uncomplaining. Gently, he helped Terry lower the female corpse onto the waiting metal board. Cold flesh touched cold surface.

'Cue passport!' grinned Terry, reaching for an identification tag.

As his colleague wrote the woman's name on a yellow label, Douglas stared round the Preparation Room. All Funeral Parlours had one—but did they all have a Director as coarse as Terry was? For the older man, dead bodies literally equalled laughing matter. He had a collection of World's Worst Death Joke Books, and came up with a new variation almost every day.

Adrian, who was brighter and should know better, could be just as flippant. But with his squash and his backpacking and restaurant-going, he at least spoke of other things. He'd come into the business after his father, so knew its history. Terry, Douglas suspected, would be just as happy working on the buses or driving a van...

After all these years Douglas still felt uneasy whilst working with him. Even in the still, calm beauty of the Chapel of Rest, he was loud.

Not that there was anything beautiful about the Preparation Room, Douglas admitted wryly. Except its current occupant, of course. Her dark eyes stared at the future from a face as pale as her nightgown. With some feeling of regret, he put his fingertips to her lids to make them close. Even that made her different, for many people's eyelids closed of their own accord when they slid into oblivion. Running a palm over them was a movie myth...

'Sign 'er in!' Terry handed him the book, and he added his signature. Two directors signed in each body, to avoid identification mistakes. Not that there could be a mistake about this one. The hospital had phoned first thing, so she was the Funeral Home's first admission of the day.

A car crash. He looked more closely for signs of injury. After securing his funeral directors diploma, he'd done the two year embalming course. Terry hadn't, for embalming was optional. As a result, he couldn't expertly conceal a wound.

'Quick lipstick and powder?' Terry asked, indicating that the corpse needed minimal attention, 'Want me to...?'

'No, you do the forms,' Douglas said.

Uncapping his pen with a flourish, Terry left the Prep Room. Douglas could hear him whistling as he strolled along the corridor to the office, which backed a waiting area with a Reception Desk. This area Douglas was in now—the Prep Room and outlying Chesting Area—was the part of the Funeral Parlour the public would never see.

He always wanted to apologise for this bit—it was

so spartan. To say: 'You're worth better than this. I know. I understand.' But Terry or Adrian might come back and do their 'talking to a stiff?' bit. Better to communicate in silent calm.

He stared down at the waiting woman, then brushed her fringe back from her forehead. Her brow had gone wonderfully smooth: only the tiny creases that had once been furrows remained. Death did that with most of them, at least for a few hours. This was the tranquil period, the ultimate relaxation after life ebbed away.

Bath time had left her sweetly scented: the nurses had washed her. Used cotton wool to plug her rectum, her vagina and mouth. Otherwise, fluids would seep out, and spoil her perfection. If only she could stay as she was right now...

Why did some people resist the idea of burial at sea, he thought distractedly. All flesh reverted to water in the end. Organs broke down, liquefied. The stomach and its contents began to rot away.

Why, for that matter, were sailors so desperate to off-load a dead body into the water? Why was it considered so unlucky to have a corpse on board? If you had to bring the body back to shore you were supposed to make sure it left the vessel before the sailors, the living cargo. Douglas snorted: he'd come to no harm spending year after year with the dead.

He looked down at his dead client: she was still beautiful. It was his duty to keep her that way for another two days. Her husband might want to see her, say goodbye to her. Some mothers wanted to see their adult children for the last time...

Thoughtfully, he teased out her hair till it flattered her features. It was surprisingly glossy, still springy, still invested with life. With practiced ease he tilted her face and tucked a chin rest under her lower jaw. The little prop brought her lips together, gave a pleasing certainty to her mouth.

Douglas stood back to admire his handiwork. She looked tranquil, younger than her twenty eight years. Twenty eight. The same age as he was. He wondered what it would be like to lie there like that...

'Phone call from Liberton. Male. Eighty.' Adrian was speaking even as he walked into Prep. This part of the building was soundproofed, set slightly apart from the rest. Outside, where you might meet mourners, you had to look funereal. You had to walk slowly, and not smile at anything. You had to be quiet and respectful at all times.

'I'll be finished by the time you get back,' Douglas confirmed quickly. Adrian liked to get through the work, to get home to his still newish wife, 'Help me chest this one,' he added. Together they carried the woman's body to the mahogany coffin, and lowered her in.

A nice coffin this, towards the top of the range. People went into the ground in boxes ranging from two to eight-hundred pounds. Douglas indicated the nearest space in the metal coffin frame which stretched almost to the ceiling. It could hold twenty coffins, and currently held ten brought in over the past two days. Automatically he raised his eyes to the cooler which sat on top of the frame. It was functioning perfectly. She could rest now, well preserved.

Smoothly the two men slid the coffin into its chosen section. Carefully, Douglas laid the lid with its nameplate and inscription on top. That was all there was to do for now: Rest In Temporary Peace. The coffin wouldn't actually be sealed till funeral day.

'I'm off to Liberton,' Adrian said, looking at his

watch, 'I'll take Terry too.' It required two men to lift each body. One seriously overweight corpse had required three. 'There's kids there. The son wants the old man out of the house before they notice grandpa's not talking,' added Adrian. He disappeared into the box room for a concealing body bag. Later the family could choose a coffin from the little booklet of wooden options. There was no time for now.

Time, though, for Douglas to disinfect his hands, and go to the staff toilets to wash his face. There was a funeral party due any moment. He wasn't dealing with them direct, but they might see him, however briefly. Perfection was all important in this line of work. Tangled hair or a not-quite-straight black tie was enough to upset some mourners. It made them think you didn't care...

As he always did, and as Terry had teased him about, Douglas took his time studying himself in the mirror. Did his face look fat—or strong and certain, as his horoscope said?

His hair, cut close because Reevon's—and, in earlier years his mother—liked it that way, could be described as dirty blonde, though he washed it every morning, and rinsed it lavishly. His skin had the pallor of someone who stayed indoors all the time.

Even when he was little, he'd looked blanched, anaemic. Alice had ferried him to the Children's Concerts in the park, and left him there for interminably long days. She'd collect him bearing a tan, her latest boyfriend would have a tan, so would the Concert Presenters who stood half in the shade of the stage. The sun had beaten down, down on the seated Douglas: but he'd still remained pale.

Douglas cleared his throat, knowing his voice always sounded more strained then he expected it to. Low, too, even when his spirits were reasonably high.

A door slamming made him glance at his watch: it was 2pm. Just enough time to go to the office and complete the paperwork before the next body was brought in. Both extremes of summer and winter led to a glut of corpses. He was checking the relevant documents when one of their hearses drew up carrying another load.

Quickly he began to fill in the cremation data, stating whether or not a funeral service would be held at the crematorium. Then came the address of the officiating clergyman, details of the hymns to be sung, where the ashes were to be disposed...

'Time you were off, isn't it?' asked Reevon himself, striding into the office.

'In a moment,' said Douglas, glancing at the older man. Though Reevon owned four funeral parlours in the area, he worked alongside the other men in this parlour, his first. Rarely pulled rank, did exactly the same tasks as everyone else.

'Parents got everything packed and ship shape, have they?' the owner asked, half seating himself against a corner of the table. The bright office lights picked up the glimmer of scalp beneath the rapidly receding brown hair. Still the man's eyes were lively, interested. What to say?

'Alice keeps adding things to their packing list,' he said reluctantly, wishing he didn't have to think about her. Reevon seemed to expect something more, so he added: 'Wants to take tins of soup in case she can't find Paul's favourite there. You know what she's like.'

Reevon did. When Douglas had first been taken on at the undertaker's as an apprentice, Alice Tate had come in, bringing her son bars of chocolate or a bakery-bought cake.

'Loves his food, does Doug,' she'd say, offering some round to the other men. Terry had laughed and kidded Douglas, but Reevon had steered her out as soon as possible, a look of both anger and pity in his eyes.

Pity for Douglas and anger at his mother: it was an unusual combination. Their neighbours faces had shown wonder that so energised a woman could produce such an insipid boy. That was before she'd started taking the tranquillisers, of course. Before Paul...

'Got your accommodation sorted out?'

'Bedsit,' Douglas confirmed shyly, 'I've been moving my books in during the last few days.'

'Quite a change for you,' Reevon said. His mouth looked thoughtful.

'It's long overdue,' muttered Douglas, looking away.

Twenty eight was a ridiculous age to be leaving home for the first time. Where had the freedom years gone? Several months of unemployment after leaving school, then a swift moving from office clerk to delivery boy to salesman as he tried to find something he'd like to do or was good at. By the time he'd gotten the trainee funeral directors job he'd been all of twenty three. He'd saved some money in that time, of course, but not enough to furnish a flat even if he found one for a single person. Then the apprenticeship, on spartan wages, had taken two years...

Still, he should have gone two years ago, when his wages stabilised. But as she'd said: 'You've got everything here, son. You've turned your room into a little palace, so you have.'

And he had—with a Baby Belling cooker and a teasmade and a toasted sandwich machine. He was fine there, as long as they left him alone and didn't make too much noise...

'I'll finish off here,' Reevon said, bringing him back to the present, 'That coach won't wait.'

****

People were supposed to hate goodbyes—to cry and cling to each other and not eat for a while. Douglas looked at his mother and then at his watch.

'I knew I shouldn't have worn that black underskirt,' she said, catching hold of herself in the bus depot's window, 'See, Paul—it shines through.'

'Take it off in the Ladies, then.'

Paul was still a man of few words, thought Douglas, walking as far away as possible from the smaller man, and refusing to make eye contact.

'Oh, you!' said his mother, and playfully slapped at her husband, as if he'd made a suggestive remark.

She turned to Douglas.

'You'll remember to change the lock on your bedsit? I saw this woman once on *TV Trials*. Just moved in when the previous owner came back one night. Raped her, he did—walked straight into her bedroom. Just used his key...'

'I've already taken care of it, Alice.'

He'd fitted new window locks too.

They walked to the ticket kiosk.

'It'll be strange for you without us,' added his mother. Her eyes trailed up and down him, as if looking for a loose thread, missing button, unflattened lock of hair she could comment on, 'It's not as if you have aunts and things. That's the trouble with my being an only one...'

She stopped some yards from the ticket seller and Douglas and Paul stopped beside her.

'I'll be fine. Really,' Douglas said, feeling perspiration start to trickle beneath his arms. He felt heavy, awkward, like a teenager forced to go on holiday with its parents. He didn't know where to look, what to do, what to say. He wished that he could be anywhere but here, alone again. He was sure people were staring at the three of them.

It had been years since he'd sat with them, eaten with them, been a real son. Now they'd be on the opposite side of the world, in what his mother called 'Neighbours Land'. He watched as she pushed Paul forward to pick up the Reserved envelope containing the tickets.

'It's hot here. Just think what it'll be like out there!' she exclaimed for the hundredth time.

It was August here—didn't that mean it was winter in Australia?

'The human body can adjust to most things,' he said.

It was what he knew best—the human body. You couldn't mould it and plug it and arrange it every day and not know. Know how it broke down, discoloured across the lower abdomen. Know its sights, its smells, its early precious quiet...

'Maybe I'll fight the flab there,' added his mother, smoothing down her pink satin skirt suit. They followed Paul to the depot's Waiting Room and took scratched plastic orange chairs. When she leaned forward to set down her bag the material clung to her, flesh folding over the fitted waistline like pleats.

He noticed that the freckles on her upper cheeks were prominent again: she'd been trying to fade them with lemon juice for as long back as he could remember. Still, her blonde hair, in its inevitable bouffant, brightened her features, helped make her look younger than her fifty two years.

The bathroom cabinet paid testimony to the hours she'd spent dyeing it. When he'd been at school he'd hated that hair. It was a parody of a tart, of a fifties good time girl.

'Last time I'll do this on Scottish soil,' she mouthed now, reapplying her lipstick without the aid of a mirror.

Bet you do it again on the coach going down to London, he thought wearily. Bet you do it at least four times in the airport lounge.

'If God had meant us to have deep pink lips we'd have been born with them,' Paul said, like a broken record. He took out a cigarette and lit it. Douglas swallowed hard. If God had meant us to smoke he'd have made us with cigarettes hanging from our mouths, he thought wearily. He'd made the mistake when he was seven of pointing this out...

'Hope I've got everything,' his mother said loudly. She'd said that before every date, every weekend break over the years. 'You'll write?' she added, turning to her son, 'Airmail's fastest.' A pause, 'You get them from the Post Office.'

'Alice—I know.'

Even now, he felt nothing—nothing. Maybe the sadness would come when they got on the coach, or if they phoned from the airport before boarding the plane?

'Hope these sandwiches stay fresh,' added his mother, sniffing inside her carrier bag. It seemed hours before the London-bound service arrived.

'Bye, love.'

She cried, as he had known she would—she cried easy. Paul hesitated for a moment, then shook his hand. The older man's flesh felt dry and slightly flaccid in his own large palm. Douglas thought about tightening his grip, then didn't.

Couples were boarding the bus, talking, laughing. He stared as they stepped onto their Noah's Ark. A girl slapped her thigh at some unheard joke, her bracelets jangling. 'Give her one from me!' yelled a youth in dungarees to his departing mate.

Noise everywhere—he'd had years of it. His mother's radio, Paul's television, their voices, hoarse or shrill. Now, at last, silence, silence. At last he'd have a room where he could dream.

And plan. There was ample space in his personal computer. He could take up a new hobby, play some intellectual game. They'd gone, gone—and he could do anything. Anything! Life began at twenty eight.

Didn't the psychology books say some people were simply late developers? Maybe he could... his imagination failed. Whatever he decided, Alice and Paul would no longer be around to spy on him. He'd been set free. Maybe the men at work would take him more seriously now, treat him as an equal. Maybe Shelley the receptionist wouldn't glare. She might even smile at him the way she did at the others. Trembling with potential, he walked towards his new life.

CHAPTER TWO

'So that's them off, then?'

He was half way up the stairs to his new room when she appeared on the landing, huge grey bulk of shadow blocking his path. Eleanor Denning: he remembered her from his previous trips to the rooming house. Five foot eight of curiosity in a large white dress. Her calves were planted apart now as if nailed to the brown-green carpet. *Thickset* his mother would have called her, before she herself put on weight.

'They caught the coach—yes.' He didn't know what to call her. Didn't fancy first name terms, know what her prefix was. Would Miss or Ms be appropriate? He could see she wasn't wearing a wedding band. He automatically checked for them nowadays: he'd struggled to remove so many from the fingers of the deceased. Strange how a widow often wanted her husband's wedding ring. Married till death us do part.

He wanted to take a step forward, but his new neighbour was still in his path, looking him over. Her brown hair was so dry in places as to look almost grey. With dead people, the hair and nails kept growing for a while: he trimmed the latter. Pressurised gases could cause the deceased's penis to erect. A gradual process, was molecular death, the body refusing to let good protein go to waste...

'It'll be a big change for you.'

God, she sounded like his mother.

'I was planning to move soon anyway,' he lied.

He breathed in, waited for the pain of loneliness to start. There was none. Yet they'd told him so often they were all he had. I could have done this years ago, he thought exultantly. Could have formed a life free of trivia and noise.

'The cooking's a hassle, with the kitchen being down a stair, you know.' She'd already told him that on both his previous visits. 'Jenny—who had your room before—and I used to take turns about.'

Staring past her, he nodded. If only she wasn't situated so near him on the top floor. Only the narrow bathroom they were to share separated their bedsitting rooms. He wished he could afford a full-sized flat.

'They're getting a nice day for it.'

He blinked: 'Sorry?'

'For all their travelling, I mean—it's nice and warm.'

'Oh... yes.'

He couldn't talk to women like her, didn't want to. Hard, though, to be rude: it wasn't his way.

'You'll be watching the telly hoping for a glimpse of them.'

She let out a coy, girlish giggle. He stepped back, curled his fingers into his palms. She named some programme he'd never heard of, presumably an Antipodean one. He shrugged.

'I must...' He leaned forward again.

'So—is this near your work?'

He began to breathe faster, heartbeat speeding. She'd be bringing him sandwiches next.

'My work is everywhere.'

That was elliptical without being anti-social. Her lipsticked mouth opened, freeze framed, as he'd hoped it would. *Go, go.* His head started chanting imperatives as it had for as long as he could remember.

'Well... I'll better let you get on with it,' she said.

Alone at last. He took the stairs with unusual speed, feeling reckless. Unlocked his door, entered and locked it again. Walking in a straight line took him to his computer, its companiable screen and reassuring buttons. Quickly he powered up, entered the 'Find Out' file. *Check temperature in Australia in August,* he keyed in. *Find correct way to address female of unknown status (neighbour, informal but remote).* He stared at the neat white print, wishing he had more data to give. *Try library for books on geography and etiquette,* he added in bold underline.

Then he quit the document and moved on to his Engagements Calendar file. Carefully he deleted *Mother and Paul to coach station* from the list. *Replace sandwich toasting machine,* he typed in, remembering that his own had started crackling. Eleanor had said he could use her toaster in the kitchen but... He shivered, hating her familiarity. She'd probably see a shared toaster as proof of domestic bliss.

At home he'd managed to fit most things into his room—now it was vital. There he'd known that at elevenish his mother and Paul would go to bed. He'd bring a take-away or ingredients for a toasted snack in with him at six or so. Then he'd have something more substantial downstairs when they retired for the night. He didn't go to bed himself till 3am or later. Loathed the uncertainty of the time before sleep arrived...

But now—fixtures to fix, plans to be made. He keyed in a careful inventory of the room on his computer, noting which areas of the cornice needed retouching, which parts of the skirting board would benefit from a paint-honed brush. *Sugar soap, undercoat, emulsion* he keyed into his shopping list, *disinfectant, furniture polish, something to clean carpet with*.

For what seemed like the entire evening he paced the room, checking things and logging them. At last he looked at his digital waterproof watch. Still only 9pm. Of course, he'd left work early for a change. Reevon had told him just to go home after seeing off Alice and Paul.

Home—this was home. Douglas lay down on the bed, and stared at the ceiling. He'd put the divan in the centre of the room, so he could leap from all sides. That way if there was a fire or... something... he'd be able to escape from it. You had to think of such things in advance.

Don't think of the stain on the ceiling now, when the DIY shops are shut, he told himself, mind speeding. Don't worry about whether the house has a ladder to help you do the repairs. Forget that the other tenants might play loud tapes and radios. Forget that Eleanor Denning could appear at your door.

Think calm, think less, think nothingness, he told himself edgily. Gradually his breathing slowed down.

Once this had been hard to do—but no longer. Once every muscle had screamed against lying this still. But if you didn't move, you didn't bump into things—it was safer. You couldn't get told to watch your step or slow down. You didn't get over-tired: it was peaceful. The peace of the corpse—the ultimate unchallenged rest.

Yet he wanted some kind of connection—something that would be there for him. Some kind of caring that didn't shout or inspect or instruct or nag or pray. He thought back to his childhood years—the simple goldfish. Always there for him, watching calmly and uncritically all the time.

He would get one—no, two, three, four, a huge tankful! He could have a series of tanks, an aquarium from wall to wall. He'd come here and cook his meals and... dream a little. Read psychology books and biographies far into the night.

Amazing that he hadn't left home before, he reflected now, listening to the stillness. He'd used up so much energy just keeping out of their way. Like a prisoner too depressed to apply for parole, a fearful hostage. As the books explained, the cautious stayed with what they knew...

He loved his books—their reasoned wise awareness. His only sadness about Alice leaving Britain was that he had no place to keep several cases of his tomes. He'd stored his favourite quotes on disk, and taken the rest to a second hand store which paid reasonable prices. One day he'd have his very own library, a proper home...

But for now, his own bed, his own room, unshared possessions. At last he was an independent man. Slowly flexing his limbs, Douglas slid off the divan, and crossed to put the light off. The bed was thankfully larger than the one he'd left. Once he'd knelt, at Paul's insistence, to say his prayers each bedtime. God bless Mummy and Paul—there hadn't been anyone else. God, please send me a puppy or a kitten. God, please don't let me be picked on again at school...

Moving quickly now, he undressed and got under the

covers. Alice had always knocked on his door, then called a cheerful goodnight. Now there was no one to answer to—no one. Now he could set up an aqua-system: maybe design and build his own over several weeks.

Check floorboard strength and water weight, he reminded himself tersely. Consider shelving versus a cabinet-held tank. Some of the homes he entered as a funeral director contained aquariums. Pity he hadn't examined their glassy contours instead of concentrating so thoroughly on the dead.

His eyelids lowered slightly, feeling heavy. Fish species, he thought... computer... key in prices of tanks. The underblanket felt warmer than ever, he was descending into it. He snuggled down on his side, pushing the pillow away from his head.

Headstart... brown hair... he floated in twilight, increasingly absorbed in its images. Cool as dignity, with slim, pale limbs. Sleep clasped him and pulled him deeper into its currents. A long day. A long and eventful day...

Night. Breasts like moons, the tiny blue veins accentuating the whiteness. Waist burgeoning out to full, rounded hips. His fingers reached out, sliding, stroking. Found warmth and curves and lips and tongue and hair.

The dream woman moaned. He woke up, whimpering. *Bad and bad and bad and bad and bad.* Lay there paralysed, except for his groin's wild pulsing. *If only she'd stayed quiet, stayed still.*

God, but it hurt him, this throbbing, this needing. How long was it since he'd last given in? No Alice now, though, to interrupt his thoughts by calling goodnight to him. No Paul saying 'You'll go to hell' with each knowing look.

Shivering lightly, Douglas rolled over onto his stomach. Pressed down against the mattress, hands overlapping like protectors across his head. *Get it right this time—control what's happening*. Same woman, same song, dancing to his particular tune.

Or not, as the case may be. God, he hated dancing. Didn't ever want to flail, out of control, to some wild and primitive beat. His dream woman wasn't allowed to dance—he wouldn't let her. It spoiled things if they laughed and moved and spoke.

Sweet scent of soap, of satin. *Closer*. He brought her back into his head. *Too long, too long*. Aching, wishing, wanting—needing. Sliding, stroking, sensing—push and push.

Eyes shut fast, he moved more urgently against the mattress. Thought and throbbed and built and tightened and swelled. Sparks turned into heat and a steady pulsing. He thrust and thrust, ascending all the time. Breathless images: a model holding a pose as he pressed the camera. Computer keys existing solely for his every touch.

Soon shrieked the pulsing, pressing promise. Hands still holding his head, he rubbed and rubbed. *Soon, soon* screamed his soaring scrotum. Something contracted as his dream girl grinned and moved.

No—stay, stay said his need, too often unheeded. His legs itched fiercely, his brain stilled. 'Stop her,' shouted a voice somewhere beyond consciousness, 'Keep going. Hold her down.' Down, down...

The fantasy was receding, his flesh shrinking. Desperately he reached for a new image, where the girl was still. *Stay down, down*. In his thoughts he pushed her hard against the wall till she stopped grinning. Down, down... Her head hit the ground: she stayed and stayed.

Satisfaction guaranteed. His thought-self knelt and entered her. *Yes* shrieked sensation, begging for release.

Almost, almost... God, it was going to happen. That incredible release felt too few times.

Free, free, shouted the long-withheld sensation. And when it rushed to escape from its captors, he let it through.

CHAPTER THREE

'... decided that as we live in a flat, it wouldn't be fair to keep a dog or cat,' finished Marjorie. She took a deep breath, and smiled at the shopkeeper, eyes scanning his face.

'Fish sound the perfect choice,' agreed the man, returning her wide smile with a smaller one, 'We can supply you with your basic set-up today.' He took a business card from a plastic display box on the counter, and handed it to her, 'You'll find our opening hours on this.'

Aqualand. Proprietor: Michael Meer said the card, in embossed black letters, *Exotic Fish and Accessories For The Discerning*.

She looked up to find him levering himself slightly away from the counter, one eyebrow partially quirked. His hair had that somewhat faded look some men got at forty or so. That made him thirteen years older than herself. She'd seen this programme recently on Summer-and-Autumn style relationships. A psychologist had said...

'Tropical, coldwater or marine?'

'Sorry?'

To hide the fact she'd started blushing, she turned to scan the tanks on the nearest wall.

'Which type of aquarium set up do you intend to install, Miss? Tropical, coldwater or marine?'

'Oh.' They all looked equally colourful, lively. She turned back to him, including the assistant in her shrug, 'You're the experts. I'm flexible. Whatever you think best.'

The two men looked at each other.

'Most fishkeepers think tropical's easiest,' said the assistant with a shrug. Michael Meer edged past him and walked into the body of the shop. 'If you come this way, I can show you what we've got...'

She followed, bending down to examine the mollies and guppies and tetras he pointed out.

'They're gorgeous.'

She made stroking movements with her index finger against the unsmudged glass. Noticed belatedly the signs saying not to touch the tank as you could frighten the fish. Her face, looking rounder than she remembered, was reflected back at her, surrounded by thick brown curls.

As she stared, a snail made its unexpectedly speedy way along the gravel. Lidless piscine eyes stared at her, mouths silently opened and closed.

Marjorie turned to the proprietor: 'I'd like two of those little black ones, and a yellow one, and...'

'Em,' the shopkeeper cleared his throat and looked at the floor for a second. 'It's best if you come back for them in two or three weeks.'

'You mean they're not for sale?'

This was a big disappointment. She'd wanted them now, to love, to take care of, to show Simon. It would be something to tell the neighbours during these awkward encounters on the stairway, news to convey to her mum when she phoned.

'No, I mean you should buy your tank today, set it up with plants and gravel, and leave the water to mature for at least a week.'

He said something about biological systems, priming the filter, talked about nitrites and nitrates. She nodded, said 'Oh, I see' even when she didn't.

'... Then people come back and blame us when the fish die,' he finished. She hoped that she looked intelligent, smiled and smiled.

'I didn't realise there was so much to it.' She toyed with the cardigan she was carrying, wondering if her dampening underarms showed against the lemon cotton of her dress, 'As you can see, I'm new to all this. I've never had a pet...'

The door swung open again, admitting a fair haired man. Marjorie included him in her smile before turning away. He was quite tall, of a chunky build, walked slightly awkwardly. Men close to her own shape like this always made her feel more secure.

She turned back to the shopkeeper: 'I'd love to see some tanks, then, something big.' She spread her arms out, looked belatedly to make sure she wasn't close to hitting anybody. She'd always been so accident prone... She pulled out a piece of paper, and handed it to Michael. Simon had measured the space in their lounge corner and written the measurements down. 'Something like this,' she added, 'If that's easy to provide.'

He studied it, nodding.

'A two and a half feet one will allow you to stock several varieties, with space for them to grow.'

Good—at least she'd done something right.

'And you said I needed plants and gravel as well as a heating device...'

'Vallisneria grows freely in various temperatures,' said Michael Meer calmly. He preceded her to an open glass tank, with a small waterfall beside the tropical section. Light streams of water trickled over the various plants. He pointed to one with twelve inch long leaves. 'That's your vallisneria. It'll thrive providing you give it enough light.'

'How many should I buy?' Marjorie asked, admiring the foliage.

'Try six, and see how you get on.'

Taking her to different tanks, he pointed out natural and coloured varieties of gravel.

'The natural looks better, if you ask me. People tend to buy the coloured variety—along with the sunken wreck ornaments and plastic seahorses!—for their kids.'

'Well, I don't have any.' She ran a self conscious palm over her permed curls, 'Natural's fine.'

'John—can you get the lady another two bags of this?' Michael called back. Marjorie watched the assistant as he hurried past her. Thick-framed glasses drew attention to his ruddy complexion, slightly jowly face. Nice shirt, though, and well fitting jeans...

'I appreciate this,' she said, when he set the bags of gravel at her feet, 'Have I got everything now?'

'No. You need an aerator and a filter.' The boy walked back to the counter and brought out some boxes, 'These are our most popular makes.'

Wincing at the complexity, Marjorie bought one of each of them. She hoped Simon knew how to fix them up. The other customer had walked to the coldwater section and was kneeling by the lower tanks. With an effort she looked away from him: 'Do I need anything else?'

The assistant shrugged again. 'You could buy some stones for decoration, and maybe a cave for shy fish to retreat into. Oh, and a backdrop to stick to the rear of the tank.' He ducked down behind the counter and came up holding two long rolls of paper, 'It makes the fish feel more protected, and it gives your aquarium visual depth.'

She nodded as he unrolled the pictures they called backdrops. 'Only I'll have to keep the cost down.' Mentally she totalled up the bill, then laughed, to show she was a girl on a budget rather than a cheapskate, 'I'm spending my birthday money on this.'

Money from her mother, given each Christmas and birthday. Simon had given her a book on yoga and a painting-on-velvet kit.

'Is your car parked right outside?' asked Michael Meer, returning with the plants wrapped in cellophane, 'If not, it'd be easiest to drive it up to the door.'

'I don't drive.' She looked at the tank and various accoutrements with dawning realisation, 'Oh, I see. You thought...' She'd just assumed they delivered everything to your door.

She took a deep breath. Now came the moment when they'd look more kindly on her, forgive her for any earlier nervousness, 'I'm not allowed to carry lots of things or in any way over-exert myself. Asthma, you see.' Sometimes, when they didn't look concerned enough, she added 'Doctor's orders,' with a shaky laugh.

'John—can you help me drop these off tonight?' asked Michael Meer, raising his eyes towards the younger man. The assistant nodded, looking back. 'It's amazing what these tanks weigh,' said Michael, shaking his head.

He pushed a white paper bag towards her. 'If you just want to write down your address...'

Slowly Marjorie did so. She was vaguely aware of John going to serve the well-built man.

'If I'm out I'll arrange for Simon to be in,' she said, printing neatly, 'He's just a flatmate, though, so I can't take up too much of his time.' She looked at Michael, but he was gazing into the distance. 'Cost of the rent and all that,' she said into the void.

John had come up beside her with the fair-haired customer. The man was holding a tank of about eighteen inches by fifteen. *Talk to him. Say something. He won't bite you.* Simon said that to her all the time.

'For a child?' Marjorie asked, taking a deep breath. She scrunched her fingers into fists and hoped he'd say no. It didn't matter that she was never going to see him again: these days every married person seemed to be silently telling her she'd failed.

'It's a quarantine tank.'

The man had neatly sidestepped her question.

'Oh.' She nodded helplessly, 'I see.'

'As a precaution,' he continued, 'It's a good idea to isolate new fish. Some diseases take a few weeks to show up.'

He sounded like a teacher giving a nature lesson. He had a shy face, a wary face. She spoke again: 'Aren't you going to buy a fish for it?'

She kept her voice casual, tried not to smile too much. She'd known she'd blown it with Michael the second he got that strange, distant look, stopped making eye contact. Yet she only wanted a special friend...

'No, I want to fill it with water then leave it for a few days. Gives the chlorine a chance to dissipate.' The man briefly made eye contact with her, 'And micro-organisms are born into it which help the fish.'

'Chlorine burns their fins,' Michael added, looking at Marjorie. The three men nodded at each other and smiled.

Marjorie smiled at the customer. He had nice thick hair and was at least six inches taller than her own five foot four.

'You're obviously an expert,' she said, pulling in her stomach.

'No, I'm buying my first set-up today.'

Maybe we can exchange notes. She wanted to say it. Wanted someone to talk to when Simon went out for the night. But if she suggested something she'd see his gaze shift away, see him shuffle, change the subject. She got the banknotes out of her purse and handed them over one by one. Counted everything out like a shop assistant, feeling silly. But mum said that by doing so you avoided confusion and mistakes.

'See you tonight, then,' she said to the other two, trying to sound as if she made such arrangements every day.

She could have stayed on longer if she'd had a cheque to write out. But when you were unemployed the banks saw you as persona non grata, and wouldn't give you a cheque account.

'Around eight o'clock,' called Michael as she swung open the door into the sunlight. She nodded, then caught sight of the poster on the outside. Should she? She was always writing down the details of social events but hardly ever plucked up the courage to go.

'I'll take a note of this club here, just in case,' she called back. No one answered. Scrabbling to undo her shoulder bag clip, she searched through it for a pen and old shopping list. Heartbeat quickening, she wrote down the address and meeting date of the *Fish Are Fun* club. It was only a half hours walk away.

Go. Go. There was nothing left to delay her leaving. Letting the door swing shut, she walked out into the street. Two workmen eyed her bust, and she started to put her white cardigan on again. Buttoning it fully, she scurried to the other side of the road.

Judging by the lack of a queue, she must have just missed the bus again. Still, she was in no hurry: it was only 6pm. Nothing else was scheduled until Michael and John came round at eight with her aquarium. It wouldn't take her long to make them a cup of tea.

For a moment her heartbeat speeded again as the aquarist's door opened to expel the fair-haired stranger. John held the door open, the tank taking up both the customer's hands. As she watched, the man nodded towards the *Fish Are Fun* details, and the assistant disappeared back into the shop. Returning a moment later, he said something, laughed, and dropped a leaflet into the empty tank.

Well, almost empty. From across the road, Marjorie could see the glass rectangle also contained a bag of gravel, some kind of sponge device and a blue plastic lid on its side. Was he going to cross the road, to speak to her? Their builds were similar—together they would look just right. And he'd heard about the asthma, would hopefully be considerate and kind.

She could ask him what fish he planned to buy, what sort of aquarium he'd install eventually. *Come and speak, come and speak, come and speak.* He might even want to come round tonight and watch Michael and John install her aquarium. Get some tips, have some tea. She felt the familiar ache of lowness as he walked away down his own side of the street, blind to her lonely, questing presence. He was yet one more man who she'd never see again.

CHAPTER FOUR

NO PETS said the sign: his stomach tightened in either irritation or disappointment. He never could work out what he was feeling, despite all these 'know yourself' books. Seemingly you could get a computer psychiatrist nowadays. It was so good most people couldn't tell the machine from the real thing...

'Morning!' As he washed up his breakfast dishes, he heard a voice behind him. Wincing, he turned slowly, but it wasn't Eleanor, it was the landlady, Val Browne. 'Browne with an E,' she'd said, when he'd first gone round about the room, and been interviewed. It had seemed important to her, so he'd noted it in his computer in a separate section to the one reminding himself what to pay her in rent and when it was due.

'Hello,' he said now, willing himself not to start blushing. He'd done it as long as he could remember: a Pavlovian response. His mother would say 'Look at the colour of him' and most of her boyfriends would look away quickly. Only Paul had kept staring. Paul said that it was bloody pitiful, so it was.

'If you've any questions, just ask them,' Val said now, stooping to put a new liner in the pedal bin. 'Dustbin men come today,' she added, grinning some more. She seemed very energetic given the hour, he thought curiously. Almost hyped up.

She looked round the kitchen, and he used her distractedness to stare at her lids, heavy with matt purple shadow. Pity she blinked so much and kept jerking her head. Nice lips, full and well-shaped, with a touch of gloss in the centre. If she'd just hold them open like that...

He wondered how old she was, would like to be. Even at the funeral home it could be hard to assess a person's age. Often he'd said fifty, only to check the chart and find it was a forty year old or even younger. Pain, if it was prolonged enough, advanced the years...

Val was still standing there, small blonde head to one side, as if waiting.

'About the no pets sign,' he said. She nodded, and he pulled his arms in close to his sides, as if to contain her refusal, 'I'd have liked to keep fish.'

The lipsticked mouth relaxed. 'Oh, fish are alright! It's larger creatures—one tenant kept a guinea pig in his wardrobe, would you believe? Well, you can imagine all that straw, the smell and everything. I mean, he didn't even have a proper water bottle for it, and it kept knocking its bowl over and wetting its bed.' She lifted her eyes towards the ceiling, 'I suppose we're just lucky it didn't gnaw its way through the wood, and breed.'

Breed with what, he thought distractedly, nodding as she made each point in quick succession. He was so busy wondering what to say next, he forgot that he should smile.

'I'll just put this away,' he said, turning to put his plate and cup in the wall-mounted cupboard.

'You're lucky you're tall,' she said, 'I can never reach.'

She had her own kitchen downstairs, so presumably didn't have to. He smiled: 'My father was tall.' It was the kind of thing his mother would say, and that the neighbours would agree with: people liked you to say simple things like that. He didn't really know what size his father had been. Paul was tiny, and he definitely hadn't been like Paul—couldn't be. No, his natural dad had been a strong and upstanding kind of man.

'We're all petite in my family,' said Val. She twisted slightly on her soles and gave herself a little hug, 'Still good things come in small packages, so they say.'

'Which is why I'm going to buy fish.' He felt quite pleased with that—it rounded things off nicely.

'When I first took in guests after my husband died,' said Val, 'I let the middle floor to a woman with a Pekinese.'

Dead dogs were often burnt in heaps, sent on from various veterinary practices. They didn't take them at Reevon's, of course, but he'd read about it in a book. His cup and plate tidied away, he wondered what to do with his hands and finally settled for his pockets. The black trousers and long black coat that were his work clothes made him look slimmer than he really was.

'Attacked the meter man... yapped when the tennis was on TV... hairs all over the place,' Val was saying. He longed now to look at his watch. Other people found it so easy to say excuse me, must be going. Why not he?

'Excuse...' He opened his mouth.

Val pointed to the no pets sign: 'If I didn't have *that* someone would bring in one of those... you know... designer pigs.'

'Vietnamese pot-bellied pigs,' he said automatically.

She raised her eyes: 'Do you work with animals, then?' As he shook his head, she focused more closely on his morning suit, 'Oh, silly me—I forgot. You said what you did.'

His laugh sounded weak, stunned by the length of her monologue. She'd gone on till the words hurt his head inside. Fascinating, though, in a way, the talkers ability to keep going. Didn't they ever monitor themselves, edit out the trivia before it reached their mouths?

'A funeral director's work is never done,' he said now, smiling. She meant well, wouldn't interfere like that Eleanor woman next door...

'Busy day?' she asked, stepping aside to let him past.

'They all are,' he confirmed.

Did that sound abrupt? Rude? He didn't mean it to. He was used to just saying a few words—a very few words—to the men at work. Shelley, the receptionist, was equally hard to talk to. She had this way of staring that made him sweat. Her hair was blonde and waved, and looked hard as concrete. Her breasts were small and firm beneath her plain pink blouse. Maybe he just disliked changes? She'd replaced Reevon's elderly mother as receptionist only last year.

He looked back as he reached the doorway.

'See you tonight,' he added, striving for casualness.

'I've Holiday French on tonight,' she called, as he turned towards the stairs.

'Au revoir, then,' he retorted, reddening slightly.

He heard her laugh.

A days work, then chips from the nearby cafe and a brisk walk to the Aquarists. Letting himself out of the rooming house, he keyed his plans into the data base in his head. He'd already got a book out of the library entitled *Setting Up The Aquarium*, and had measured the free space in his room.

Tomorrow he'd find out which tank sizes were available. Then lots of versions of Lucky, lots of... Something pulsed at the edge of his mind, its blackest contours. Something about his goldfish, about...?

He shook his head, forced himself to count the passing buses, the cyclists. If it was important, he would have remembered it by now. Walking on, he thought of Val's lips, Shelley's breasts, of the girl in the Aquarists passive limbs and smiling devotion. Yes, he liked that curly-headed girl the best.

He pictured telling her to lie still, spread her fleshy legs wide apart. He'd do anything to her, then—*everything*—if only she didn't cry out. She would look unfocusedly into the distance, forever mute and accessible. It would be like it was in his collection of magazines.

CHAPTER FIVE

Male eyes were staring down at her, pointing. Model-like women, their lips curling in disgust, were turning away. This happened in accidents—you read about it, feared it. You lay there bleeding at the roadside and they hurried on past. Wait, whispered Marjorie, but the sound couldn't travel to her voice box. Something was crushing her, like a house-sized boulder of molten lead.

Led away... Too many potential friends at school, at work, led away by more sophisticated, more entertaining comrades. The more you needed friends, the less you seemed to keep. Mum didn't have anyone. She didn't want to be like her. Mum said all she'd ever wanted was dad, but she'd only said that after he was dead.

Awful to die and have no one attend your funeral, or cry for you. Weight, weight: heaviness hurting her head. Popular girls dancing past her, with their princes. Girls and boys who knew what to say, how to look, what to wear.

'Marjorie Milton—always keeps her kilt on!'

That chant, that chant, that bloody stupid chant she thought she'd never hear again. Yet now she was lying on the ground and the passers-by were singing it. Had been singing it all these years, waiting for another chance to taunt her, skipping from the school playground through the last decade until...

So they'd caught up with her, and she still hadn't done it. Still hadn't undressed for a boy like the other girls had. Oh, they'd had such stories to tell, of stolen moments in parental living rooms, of secret rendezvous at midnight in caravans and garden sheds. Big brothers' cars and small sisters' Wendy houses and the back row of the cinema. One girl said she'd been impaled on her boyfriend's lap when her father walked in.

'We were fully dressed, like. Just kept talking to him. Georgie was wettin' himself!'

Marjorie found it hard to imagine, even now.

Found it hard to breathe, just thinking about these things, far less picturing them. What did you do? Or say? How did it feel when he...

'Mar hasn't gone far... hasn't done it in a car... has her legs glued shut with tar...'

Her name had produced rhymes for even the least imaginative of her classmates. *Such hatred, just for not being asked out by a boy.*

Not my fault, she wanted to say: she didn't have the right clothes, the right labels. Boys wanted the girls with the right hemlines, and Marj's were too low. But mum bought the skirts, so mum decided how long they were. Mum bought the blouses, which meant plain white cotton rather than embroidered denim shirts with metal buttons like the other girls had. Almost everyone else had had carved wooden clasps in their hair, or a psychedelic gypsy head scarf. She, Marjorie, had had to wear a thick white Alice band that made her look even more plain.

Wrong clothes, wrong hair, wrong weight, wrong words, wrong voice tone. 'Milton smells like Stilton!' Stupid phrases day after day after day. And, God, the hatred in these cold, cold eyes, the way they looked at her. Such hatred for not managing to be the same...

Crush her, they wanted to crush her. To squeeze her in till she was the same shape as them. To pull her up by the hair roots so she was equally tall. And then they'd push their fingers between her thighs, and take her hymen, tear a hole in it until it resembled theirs. Strip her down and dress her in the regulation denim and shortened skirt. Take away her briefcase and replace it with a canvas sports bag bearing a designer name. Remove her sensible lacing shoes and substitute clumpy black ones with heavy thick soles.

But they couldn't do that so instead they'd annihilate her. Take the biggest boulder in the world and press it down on her chest. Press and press, all of them sitting on the stone to add to its effectiveness. Crushing, crushing, squeezing out her differentness, her very life...

Her eyes flew open. Just a dream, just a dream. But the feeling was still there, the leadenness. Head pounding, can't get enough air, can't think. Oh God, she was having an attack—a bad one. *Breathe, breathe... find help, find help, find help*.

The duvet felt like an iron sheet wrapped in cloying cotton. With effort she pushed it back, out of the way. Realised she couldn't swing her legs out, couldn't find the momentum. Turned on her side instead, rolled herself over and out of bed.

Keeping one steadying arm on the mattress, she

knelt by the bedside cabinet, pulled the door towards her. Grabbed her inhaler in a fast-numbing hand. Press canister... God, she'd forgotten to breathe in, breathe the mixture. Try, try, try again...

The walls of the room swayed a little. She fought desperately to find lung space for the air around her. Can't exhale...

Stand, stand. She pulled herself up, staggered to Simon's door, knocked on it weakly. He must be out. Oh, mum, mum—help! The older woman had been here the one other time when the inhaler hadn't been enough to halt the asthma. Just her presence—any presence—had helped calm her. Must... get... to the... phone... as... soon... as...

A tunnel of grey. Sliding to the floor, Marjorie began to crawl towards the phone, reached the phone chair. Pulled herself half up, pressed out the familiar number with a wavering hand. Heard her mother say 'Hello?', heard herself wheezing, gasping.

'Marjorie! Are you at home?'

'Ye... yes.' Her throat was drying, cracking.

'Try to open the front door. Do it now. Just hang up the phone. I'll sort everything out.'

Door, door. Now she had an objective to concentrate on. Breath trickling in as if syphoned through a straw, she edged her way along the wall to the outer door. Opened it, and sank down on the threshold and waited. So tired, so alone...

Voices: male. Was she slipping back to her dream again?

'Mum?' she wheezed, trying to open her eyes.

'Your mum'll meet us at the hospital.'

Meet us, meet us. Meet who, and when, and why...?

She woke to hear her mother saying something about new treatment.

'We've given her oxygen,' said a voice.

Marjorie opened her eyes.

'Ah, so you've joined us again,' said a man in a white coat, in his forties, 'You were exhausted—needed that sleep.'

She was in hospital: could vaguely remember the stretcher. Voices that were kinder than normal. Men that smiled.

'I phoned for an ambulance,' her mother said, stretching a hand out as if to touch her and then withdrawing it again. Mum's face looked softer than usual, less disapproving and annoyed.

'We'll have a talk about strengthening your medication,' said the forty-something man, still looming in the background, 'When you're feeling more like yourself,' he added as Marjorie tried to sit up and focus on his face. People were liking her, were interested in her, were caring. Settling back against the pillow she closed her eyes.

CHAPTER SIX

Conscientiously Douglas vacuumed out the contents of the old man's bladder. The disinfectant around the sluice was losing the battle, for already the Prep Room had begun to smell. Garbage smelt sweet, and vomit acrid, but bodies smelt differently from each other according to age and season. What they'd died of, what they'd eaten, when and where they'd been found all helped to determine the stench.

'How's the new bachelor life?' Adrian asked, finding one of the man's arteries and beginning to feed in arterial fluid. The man was of Italian extraction. He was going home.

Douglas watched through his protective glasses as the liquid disappeared down the plastic tube like a drip feed. Most bodies held four litres, but this corpse was smaller than most.

'Bedsit's fine,' he said, watching the formaldehyde do its embalming work. Now the body wouldn't putrefy for at least two months. 'Big room,' he added, 'Rectangular, with a built in wardrobe.'

'A view?'

'Onto other houses, at the back.'

'I was thinking more of Salisbury Crags, or the castle—some landmark. Some of those big old houses have panoramic views. You should see this place where Terry lived after his divorce.'

'Oh.'

He'd never understood the attraction of green fields and brown brickwork. Alice used to exclaim over views on the TV. He'd asked her once why she liked them: he'd been genuinely curious. She'd said 'Oh, you,' and shook her head.

'Salubrious?'

Adrian liked to have extended conversations. He'd been to College and it showed.

'Passable.'

Douglas made a mental note to himself to look up *salubrious* in the dictionary—by paging the thesaurus in his word processor he learned similar words. Alice said he had more words in his head than he knew what to do with, but looking new ones up made him feel as if he was bettering himself, could get more in future out of life.

Adrian asked about the rent, the laundry, how he paid for his electricity. Douglas answered, wondering why anyone would want to know. He felt a moment's satisfaction as the last of the fluid found its way into the once-pale corpse. The man looked healthier already, a robust pink.

Removing his rubber gloves, Douglas walked to the metal sink and washed and disinfected his hands minutely. Then he removed the glasses, worn to ensure the body's fluids didn't splash into his eyes. Reevon had assured him that undertakers lived as long as the rest of the community, but it was prudent to take care.

'Any highlights, then?' asked Adrian, speaking with his usual agility. When the mourners came, he had to slow his speech right down.

'Highlights?' Douglas raised a curious eyebrow. Extensive vocabulary apart, Adrian was guilty of using a language all of his own.

'Talent.'

'Oh... women.'

'Or men, if you're so inclined,' said Adrian, and stared.

Terry had hinted at much the same thing in Shelley's presence. Refusing to rise to the bait, Douglas looked away. He began to wash down the surfaces with cleaning granules and steaming water, scrubbing at each tiny stain.

'Well, there's Mrs Browne, the landlady.' Irritated, he noticed the large container of cavity fluid wasn't in its usual place. This was the poor man's liquid. In ancient times men had filled the cavities of their Kings with cassia and myrrh...

'Age? Weight? Looks?' asked Adrian intently.

'Forties. Seven stone. Blonde,' Douglas said. Quickly he swung the container from the sink unit to the hollow under the trolley, its normal home.

'Blonde,' whistled Adrian, who for some reason had married a brunette. He joined Douglas at the sink, and began to wash his hands, using his own special nailbrush, 'A looker, or what?'

Douglas thought quickly. In sculpted form she'd look desirable. But with that voice, those flailing arms...

'No,' he said, 'She's...' There weren't really words to describe it, 'She... tries too hard.'

'I know the type,' said Adrian, 'Sizing you up as husband number two.'

Was she? He had a vision of her laughing, turning, eyelashes blinking, pendant bouncing against her chest on its heavy chain. If she'd only stay still like a snapshot, forever perfect. Existing to be looked at, her own eyes looking away...

He'd seen some incredible photographs both at school and in the jobs he'd had before coming to Reevon's. One of the other boys was always bringing magazines in. Heads arched back, exposing necks ready for the kissing. Nipples pointing skyward, arms stretched above sleepy-eyed heads.

For a while he'd thought about becoming a photographer: lessons at school had proved he was good with a camera. *Oh, to look and look and look.* To stare at those airbrushed curves, that waiting fleshiness. To gaze at an image and imagine, stroke and touch...

Adrian signalled to him, and together they got the old man ready for despatch. The airlines wouldn't take a body unless it had been embalmed.

'Anyone else of interest at your new abode?' asked Adrian off-handedly.

Douglas thought of Eleanor Denning, and winced.

'No.' He paused. That wasn't quite accurate, 'Well, I haven't met everyone yet. There's an older man and a teenage couple on the second floor.'

'A teenager, eh?' Adrian smirked and made his eyes much rounder, 'Sweet sixteen?'

Shrugging, Douglas followed him from the Prep Room. Adrian and Terry were always making remarks like that. He tended to leave work later than they did, was trusted to lock up the place. He preferred the quiet times spent there before going home. But a few times he'd shared part of their journey on the bus.

'Alright?' they'd muttered, nudging each other as new girls sat down, stood up, disembarked. Shoulder bags were swung and hair tossed, manicured fingers and pointed toes tapping as the made-up eyes flickered and blinked. He shuddered. Give him his photographs. It wasn't wrong to gaze on a woman's image if she didn't know.

He'd received the first airmail from his mother today, spidery violet ink on pale blue paper. She seemed nicer somehow, more peaceful in print. Temperature. Foodstuffs. She'd given the kind of information people gave on postcards. He wondered if she was fully aware that this trip was for life. They'd needed all that competition win to convince the Australian authorities to take them in the first place, plus they'd sold the house and Paul's car to raise extra funds.

He had a sudden vision of her arriving back in Scotland, ready to claim her baby. He could never live with her and Paul again. Hurrying to the office, he bent his head over the funeral estimate forms. The very act of renting his own place had made him feel more confident and self assured.

And now he was going to join an aquarists club, and learn about the inordinate number of fishes available to the hobbyist. He'd gotten some idea from the library book, but had only fully realised the choice when he reached the shop.

Coldwater. He'd stay faithful to Lucky's memory for now and buy coldwater. Stay with what you know, what's sure. Coldwater fish were relatively easy to care for. They'd cost less too, as he wouldn't be using up electricity heating a tropical tank.

That reminded him... Reaching for his wallet, he walked into Reception. Be nice to her, smile, try to act the same way that Terry does.

'Shelley.' He couldn't bring himself to call her 'love' like the older man did, 'Would you... I mean could you give me a pound of change for the phone?' Her eyes remained uncomprehending, blank: he rushed on. 'There's a coinbox at my new place, and I have to make a few calls tonight. So I thought...'

'Oh.' She disappeared into the main cupboard and came back with the petty cash box. 'There you are,' she said flatly, counting out a stack of coins. The inevitable cotton blouse tightened slightly with each of her arm movements. She wore a blue or pink or lemon blouse every day. That, teamed with a navy or black skirt, was her version of a uniform. Except when she changed at five thirty to go to her aerobics class, of course.

'Phoning for furniture?' she asked, accepting the pound coin he proffered.

'Mmm? No, for aquarium prices. I'm setting one up and want a few quotes.'

Her features became slightly more animated, though the red-painted mouth never softened.

'Oh, my Sean had one—just a little tank in the kitchen, you know. We got it when he was one and it died last year, when he turned four.'

'Goldfish can live for over twenty years.'

If you don't suffocate them in tiny living quarters he thought and felt his stomach contract.

'Twenty?' Shelley put one hand to the front of her head, and patted the wave that was sculpted across her forehead, 'You'd be pretty bored with it by then.'

He looked at her, and thought of building an aquatic

community, aquascaping a tank, even breeding its occupants—all the things you could do to avoid becoming bored. He didn't realise he'd been staring till she began to flush, and looked at the Reception counter. Her lipsticked mouth turned down.

'I... hope you get what you want,' she said.

'Mmm?'

It took him a moment to realise she meant a fair price for a tank.

That night, almost sure he could hear Eleanor Denning pacing behind her door and listening to his movements, he went to the phone and called the various local aquatic dealers that stayed open till eight. Michael Meer had said you wouldn't find cheaper than the tanks he made himself, but you couldn't trust anyone nowadays.

Thoughtfully he took the information back to his room, and keyed it all into the computer. Made columns for prices and measurements and the cost of the tank hoods that accompanied them. Created another page for plants and rocks and ornaments, everything from models of mermaids to plastic skulls. He grinned, feeling his own skull beneath the now-dampening blond hair. Strange how little boys thought that putting a skull in the water made them seem tough. The skull was the emblem of finality, yet their own lives were just starting out...

Or not. You couldn't be sure. No one could.

'Makes you live for the day, working in this place,' Adrian often said. But it didn't with him, Douglas—at least, he didn't go out most nights like Adrian did. Maybe seeing the hours after the death agonies made him more determined to have a little peace whilst he was still alive. After all, you didn't know what was coming next—what trials. Paul's Armageddon or Alice's angels, or the forever chomping of the worms. If there was a soul, the head was supposed to be its dwelling place. In the early days he'd looked for answers, not finding them in these long-vacated skulls.

After a while, you saw Death everywhere: were trained to see it. Saw it in the people around you as they aged year by year. Saw it in your own skin, as it dried every so slightly. Saw it in the few more hairs that nestled in your comb.

Yet he didn't care enough to do anything about it. Knew that you lived longer if you ate slightly fewer calories than you needed each day. Still brought in pizzas and pies and chips and ate them in his room, with the window closed. Stayed up late reading psychology books and playing computer chess.

Prices of sunken submarines, ancient mariners. He keyed the information into his data base, knowing he'd never buy such things. Still it was useful to make comparisons, find out if some shops were more expensive—and one day another fishkeeper might appreciate the information he could give.

He paused, considering a world wide network of fellow fishkeepers. The girl who'd been in the shop would be having her aquarium delivered around about now. For a moment he stared beyond the monitor, remembering. She'd listened quietly the whole time he was talking, she'd smiled and smiled. He'd appreciated how respectful she'd been, how yielding. He shivered. He'd liked her insipidness. Liked it very much indeed.

CHAPTER SEVEN

Marjorie stared at the powerhead. Could you really submerge it underwater and not set the house on fire? And which way was she supposed to slot in this filter? And the tube leading to the aerator seemed too tall.

She wished, not for the first time, that she'd waited for Simon. Only she had nothing else to do, and the diagrams made setting everything up look okay. Pity Michael and John had been in such a hurry to get on to some meeting. She could have cooked them supper if they'd stayed around to help.

'The free delivery's our dead strength,' Michael had said, when she'd suggested it, 'It's all yours.'

Shame that they hadn't had time for the cake and chocolate biscuits she'd planned. She'd bought them in especially when she got off the bus earlier tonight, but now they remained, unopened and unshared, in the fridge.

She stared at the wires that sprouted from everything, and lay in coils along the floor. Unless she could loop them all together, she'd spend the rest of her life being tripped up every time she walked past the tank. It wasn't as if she could ask Simon to come home early. He'd said she should phone him at work if someone was hanging around or something was worrying her, but that she mustn't keep calling for a social chat.

God, but the time passed slowly when you were on Invalidity Benefit. Oh, well, she could at least wash the gravel, now lying in a corner of the lounge.

'Rinse it till the water runs clean,' John had said, dumping the polythene bags on the carpet, 'Do a half bag at a time.'

Glad of something simple to do, Marjorie shuffled into the kitchen with the first bag, took it over to the sink by the window. Immediately she opened it, dusty gravel poured into the basin, dust clouding the air before her and coating the basin's sides.

Wow, it *was* dirty. She turned on the cold tap in full, spattering her dress and arms, and knocking the washing up liquid bottle to the floor. Hastily she turned the pressure down, retrieved the liquid. Michael had said something about running your hands through it to loosen the particles. She poked a tentative finger through the detritus.

Three rinses and the first half bag looked reasonable. Quite pretty, really, pinkish pebbles and brown ones and little green ones visible in the shiny grey and white stones. Pouring the washed gravel into a bucket, she put the second half bag into the sink, and gave it another three rinses. Still another two full bags to go.

She wondered how the customer in the shop was getting on with his isolation tank. She wondered if she'd see him again when she went back to buy her first fish.

Still, for now, two rinses would probably do this gravel. The water looked clear enough: the dust on the surface was easily rinsed away.

Picking up the bucket containing the washed stones, she lugged it into the lounge, and looked at her leaflets again. Damn, she had to put this undergravel filter in before she could pour the gravel on top. She squinted at the impossibly tiny diagram, turned the leaflet over, finding instructions in German, French, Dutch... Ah, English, tucked away in the corner. The plastic board should be slotted in thus...

Angling it in, and pushing it down as best she could, she spilled the dripping stones on top of it. Went back to the kitchen, got another batch, and did the same.

By the time she was finished, her throat felt tight, and the air didn't seem to be getting down to her stomach. She sat down on the settee for a few minutes then got up again. It would be great to have things up and running when Simon came home. He was such a 'be all you can be' type. He'd be impressed.

Levering herself up, she walked to the kitchen and filled a bucket with water from the cold tap. Walked back, and poured the contents into the tank. The leaflet had said you could put a plate down to stop your gravel being disturbed unduly. But she could just poke in a stick or something afterwards, and rearrange her gravel till it evened out all right.

Buckets and buckets and buckets. Back and forward, back and forward, back... It hadn't occurred to her the tank would require as much water as this, that each bucket would feel quite so heavy. Breath accelerating, she looked over in the direction of her bedroom, wondering if she should go there just in case. Her newest inhaler was nestling in the bedside cabinet: it was stronger than her last one. They'd given it to her at the hospital after that awful night.

Resting her hands against the sink, Marjorie looked out of the window into the September evening. She'd seen Dr Ashford the day after her recent hospitalised asthma attack, but now she wished she'd mentioned the dryness of her hair. Seemingly hair problems could signify the onset of something serious. She could quite fall for Dr Ashford, she admitted to herself, smiling slightly. He was attractive, in a slightly aloof kind of a way.

'What can we do for you this time, Marjorie?' he'd say, smiling as if she were much younger. Still, he'd known her since she was a little girl. Knew her mother, too—had probably even known her father. Could she have inherited his heart weakness? These things were often hereditary. She should ask.

Hard, though, to concentrate when he was taking her pulse or asking her to breathe in certain ways for him. Lucky Mrs Ashford, having such a caring, sensitive man. She'd seen the woman in Church once—mum had dragged her along because the TV cameras were in recording a *Songs of Scotland*. Mrs Ashford had stared straight ahead beneath her fuchsia hat, and never ever smiled. Was Dr Ashford happy with her? Could he be? She, Marjorie, smiled at him all the time and always collected the prescriptions he took the trouble to write out.

She'd be back tomorrow at this rate, suffering from a strained wrist or back from carrying all these buckets. He said exercise would help her, but mum wasn't so sure. And as mum said, she'd been around longer than Dr Ashford had. These doctors knew all the theory, but it was real people like mum who had lived and seen what could happen for themselves.

One bucket to go. She cheered inwardly as the last few drops took her up to the tank's water-line. The water looked almost opaque: a dirty brown. The tank hood's inner tray defeated her: again it seemed slightly too big to clip into its fitting. There was a plastic stopper stuck fast where the hole used to feed the fish should be.

Trekking back to the kitchen, Marjorie took the bag of cakes from the refrigerator and put the bag on a plate. She'd been thinking of their delicious fillings since the men left. Pity mother wasn't due until tomorrow. She'd be impressed at so large and sumptuous a range.

Making herself a cup of tea, she carried her tray into the lounge and switched on the television. She'd just have a meringue, or maybe two, as a reward for trying so hard.

She paused, then reluctantly wrote the two cakes into her food diary. Mum had bought it for her, checked it weekly, insisting some foods could make asthma worse. Only by noting down everything you ate along with your symptoms could you find out which caused your illness. Dr Ashton had said she could do it if she wanted to: she'd checked. He'd added that moderation in all things was usually healthier. 'This'll be a great help to the doctors one day,' Mrs Milton had proclaimed.

She was half way through the last éclair when Simon came in. He whistled when he saw the aquarium in the corner.

'Have you done all this yourself, then? I'm impressed.'

He was wearing his white jacket with the blue stripes, the one she thought of as his Andy Pandy jacket. His blonde hair was mussed, as if ruffled by the September breeze.

'I couldn't do the wiring,' she admitted, going over to stand beside him, 'And these bits don't seem to fit.'

Simon picked up a leaflet.

'I'll work it out later. For now, I'm going to have my tea.'

'I could've made lasagne if I'd know you'd be in,' she said pointedly.

'I've got one of those microwave curries,' Simon said.

She wondered where he'd been shopping this time: they virtually never went to the supermarket together. When she'd complained that she ended up buying all the cleaning fluids, he'd set up a jar into which he put a weekly amount to pay for them.

Which hadn't been what she wanted, really. She'd liked the idea of someone else sharing a trolley with her for a change. Nice to say 'Shall we have this?' or comment on new products and rising prices. Great to have someone to go to the cafe with afterwards for a cup of tea. Instead, she walked past the tables of tea-drinkers and sandwich nibblers. Walked alone to the bus stop and had her refreshments in solitude at home.

'Looks like that tank needs a good clean already,' said Simon, coming back from the kitchen followed by the low hum of the microwave. Michael had said her tank wouldn't need cleaning for some weeks. He'd told her to change a third of the water at least once a month depending on the number of fish and the amount she fed them. Marjorie smiled, anticipating the task. Her mother would phone, expecting her to be killing time, and she could say: 'Phone you back later. I'm cleaning the aquarium out.'

She stared at the TV, a documentary. Something about too much fat in food. Simon backed out of the room as the microwave bell rang in the kitchen. As he left he said: 'Tomato-based curries are great.'

Marjorie wished she dared try Indian and Chinese

cuisine, or a Turkish restaurant. On the few occasions when she'd been out with Simon's work she'd always chosen from the European Menu most places had. Too many years of mum spouting on about foreign rubbish, too many years spent eating bacon and eggs.

'It's only curries made with cream that are lethal,' Simon added, returning with a plate from which he was already forking up cucumber slices and rice and sauce. He knew a little about everything, Marjorie thought tiredly. Sometimes she didn't know whether to be irritated or impressed.

'Michael and John brought this lot round for me.' She indicated the fish accoutrements, and Simon raised his eyebrows, and smiled.

'Michael and John, eh?'

'The owner of the shop and his assistant. Well, I could hardly carry this lot home.'

Simon nodded. 'You know I'd have been happy to collect it for you.'

'Oh, you're always at work...'

Simon seemed to turn away from her slightly and looked more intently at the television.

'Anyway, it was on their way home,' she said. There was a pause. 'I almost had to use my inhaler today,' she added into the silence, 'Too much rushing about with buckets of water, I think.'

'Still, you're fine now,' said Simon, looking at her closely.

'Seem to be, though I'll better see Dr Ashford about a couple of things.'

She waited for Simon to ask which things, but he picked up his cup of tea and started drinking from it. If he had asked she would just have said 'woman's trouble.' He couldn't make light of what was happening to her body then.

'So, what's this Michael like?' Simon asked, nodding as the TV voice said something about the fast food industry.

'Oh... old,' she said.

'And the other one?'

'John? Oh, he's just a kid.'

That reminded her.

'Simon... there's this fish club meets in the city centre.'

'Uh huh.'

He looked at her, giving nothing away.

She took a deep breath; 'Will you come with me, just for the first time?'

Watched him sigh, forkful of food held in mid air.

'Marj, you'd be better off on your own, you'd meet more people.'

'You'd like it, though—the poster said they have films and talks.'

'Anyway, what do I know about fish that isn't wrapped in batter and sold with a pickle?'

'Exactly—you could learn!'

Watched him smile, thought she might be winning. Winced at his next words: 'Remember that Dream Analysis Workshop? You said...'

'I know. But everyone else looked so much more confident. I was the only woman without lipstick, and the tutor kept giving me funny looks.'

All her promises to talk to others had deserted her. She'd stayed by Simon's side throughout the entire Saturday, even standing outside the Gents whilst he went in.

'This would be different, though—I know it.'

'If you went on your own you'd have to talk to others, Marj. You must see...'

Her heart was beating very fast now: she could feel it. She couldn't walk into a strange hall on her own.

'Just go in with me, then? You could leave after half an hour.'

He sighed again. 'It's really not me.'

'We could make a night of it, maybe go for a pizza before, and get some chips for after.'

'You've got it all thought out,' he said with a shake of his head.

Did she? It was hard knowing what to ask for sometimes. Mostly he was nice, but if he got irritated he could be unkind.

'Two hours isn't much to ask, is it?'

'I'll take you there and pick you up at the end, Marj. Believe me, that's best.'

Oh well, she'd try again later... Glancing at her watch, she got up and went over to the aquarium, peered in at the still murky depths.

'We'll better wire this up if it's to run overnight.'

Simon picked up his cup again. 'Who's this communal *we*?'

'I've tried to do it—but I don't understand.'

His eyes got that narrow look she recognised.

'I'm just in, Marjorie. You know I've been working overtime. I promise I'll do it tomorrow night.'

'But if we do it now, I can buy my fish a day earlier. The filter needs to mature, you see.'

'One more day won't make any difference.' Simon said evenly.

'Not to you, maybe,' said Marjorie, tightness closing in on her throat.

Not for him, when he had a brilliant job as a deputy editor. Not for him, when he had friends and a social life.

'Sorry,' Simon murmured, but he didn't sound sorry.

'I'm going to bed,' said Marjorie shortly, 'I don't feel right.'

She made a lot of noise pulling open her bedside cabinet, hoped Simon realised she was getting her inhaler out. He'd feel remorse if she woke up in the night with breathing problems. She wouldn't be the first woman he was close to who'd died...

Frustration and rage and hurt welled over into tears that were fuelled by thoughts of how boring her life was. *All she wanted was to love and be loved.* She'd be such a good wife, so caring, so devoted. Her husband would be well fed and he'd always have a clean shirt and ironed socks. She'd be cuddly and amicable and talkative. She'd be anything he wanted her to be.

She lay awake, staring into the tepid darkness. She'd thought she was tired enough for sleep, but, as was often the case, little nagging uncertainties kept her awake. Think of something nice, she willed herself, as she had time and again when she was little. But there were no party invitations for the likes of her.

Think pleasant thoughts, she urged again: it was what her mum would say. She dwelt briefly on images of chocolate and double cream. But she didn't want to spend her life with a tray of food—not alone, leastways. She wanted a little more than that. Finally, she thought of the fairy tales her gran had told her when she was tiny. And she prayed that she would soon meet the man of her dreams.

CHAPTER EIGHT

She was in remarkable shape for forty, must have exercised almost every day. Still, a slim figure couldn't guarantee an unclogged artery, didn't dissolve the embolism waiting to stop you in your tracks.

All her trying was over now, her quest for eternal youthfulness. She could relax in an elm coffin rather than an ivory tower. Douglas combed out her hair, his thoughts turning inwards. The Zoroastrians in India had had Towers of a different kind...

Towers of Silence. Literally. Burial in the sacred earth was taboo as far as they were concerned. Ditto cremation, which contaminated fire, another element. Disposal in water was equally forbidden.

The sect had seen dead bodies as unclean, tainted. So much so, that its followers in India had built special towers for their dead on far away hills. These buildings were deliberately built without roof or windows, giving the vultures ample access to their next fleshy meal...

Douglas stared at the woman, considering. He felt

the world was more contaminated by the living than the dead. The September streets he'd just walked were full of their pizza boxes, their fish and chip wrappers, their empty beer cans. They filled up their minds, too, with gambling and pointless sports. Talked too loudly and too often and carried radios and made false, braying laughs.

It was wonderful to wake without mother calling to him. Alice, he reminded himself: she'd asked him to call her Alice when he was nine years old.

'I'm too young to have such a big boy for a son,' she'd said, smiling her lipsticked smile as he stared up at her. Paul had sat there, saying nothing, looking pleased.

This morning he'd woken up to see his new fish swimming amicably through their plants and hollows of bogwood. He'd fed them, then gone to the cafe on the corner to feed himself. Brave new world: he'd ordered an espresso. He'd seen people drinking it on a poster on his way to work.

'Can I help you?' the waitress had asked, and her breasts had pushed close to his face as she bent forward. Breasts in a soft pink jumper with a little flower on each lapel.

This one was bound for the crematorium. He wiped a small smear of liquid from the side of her mouth and wondered if she'd usually worn lipstick. Bright leotards and kicking feet and hectic breathing: he wouldn't have liked her when she was alive.

Still, cremation was so destructive, so ungiving. No gradual breakdown to nurture the surrounding soil. Carbon-containing tissues soon burned away, and gallons of body water evaporated. Five pounds of ash was all that remained.

'Done the needful?'

Terry walked in and briefly interrupted his reverie.

Together they lifted the nightgown-clad woman into the waiting chest.

'Big game tonight,' said Terry, walking back into the Prep Room and picking up the disinfectant.

'I'll clean up,' said Douglas, 'You go.'

'All work an' no play.' Terry was half out of the door already. Douglas wondered what it would be like to tackle someone and win the ball. Did you apologise if you shouldered them? Were you allowed to show pain if you twisted a limb?

He'd got hurt the first time he played rugby at secondary school. 'Never liked sports meself,' Alice had said, that night, seeing his taut white face. The next week she'd written him a note, unasked, saying he had a verruca. He'd kept using the excuse until the teacher examined the sole of his foot.

'Seems to have cleared up.' He could still remember the coldness in the man's eyes, the way his lips quirked strangely at one corner, 'We'll see you on the field a week today.'

'A good game of rugger'll make a man of him,' Paul had said, overhearing him tell Alice that he needed his sports kit. So he'd lined up with the others the next Thursday afternoon.

Sights and sounds and colour and blurring motion. Boys pushing, pulling, sly elbows striking, feet kicking, scraping shins. Heat and noise and sweat and fear and pain in a frenzied maelstrom. Socks and shorts had swum closer, shouts and screams and fast expulsions of breath as boys hit the ground. Up again, running: for a few seconds he seemed to see the soles of everyone's trainers as they sprinted into the action. Saw them fade to grey, heard the murmuring of bees as he went down, down, down.

Hospital lights. Nurses padding past in starched white uniforms. A doctor holding up fingers, asking him to count them out loud. Alice beside his bed, with Paul, saying 'He's never done this before.' Then they'd moved him into a wheelchair, taken him to a little room, with charts.

There another doctor had shone beams of light into his eyes, said something about reflexes. Then picked up an implement, aimed it at his knees. He'd tensed up, then, knowing he'd scream, waiting for Paul to hit him for not being manly. But it was only a rubber hammer which didn't hurt at all.

They'd let him go home, then, and Alice had been nicer to him than usual for the rest of the day. Paul had said he was 'a big jessie', though, when the tests came back and showed there was nothing wrong with him except nerves. Afterwards the gym teacher had gotten him to help carry the bat and ball for rounders or put the nets up for netball. He'd been encouraged to just observe the rugby. No one had insisted he enter the scrum again.

Forget it—forget them. Still it was hard to stop your mind from wandering from present to past. Here today, gone tomorrow: like this newest woman would be. It took a few minutes to conceive a body, nine months to grow one, a mere one and a half hours to cremate...

Hindus believed that cremation was necessary to prevent the spirit from staying near the corpse, presumably enjoying its familiarity. The ashes were sent to India to be sprinkled in the Ganges, if circumstances permitted this. Some higher ranking Hindus preferred to be buried, though. Dust to dust.

Douglas looked towards the coffin frame that now held the corpse of the woman. When he'd first got this job, several of Alice's neighbours has asked him if he wasn't afraid of being alone with the dead. Some older women had had relatives die at home, had left the windows and doors open to let the deceased's soul escape easily. Others had turned every mirror to the wall, believing that the soul might snatch a mourner's reflection and take it with him for company in the Afterlife.

After death, many relatives showed a strange ambiguity towards the corpse. Loved it, sometimes, for who it had been, but feared it for what it was now or might become. Thus some brought flowers and ornate wreaths, appeasing gifts.

In ancient times, Chinese Emperors had been buried with armies and realms of slaves, carved from stone. It was believed that they'd come to life when their master was resurrected, would serve him in some other world.

Douglas shook his head slightly, as he finished cleaning up the area around the sink unit. Once the sacrifices to the dead would have included a wife burnt on the funeral pyre. It seemed the kind of thing Paul would do with relish. He could just hear the man's earnest voice; 'If the book says so...' Had the book told him to go to Australia, hopefully to die?

He wondered if, when his own time came, he'd have some precognition. So many mourners had told him that the deceased had seemed to be in perfect health. Yet suddenly he'd made a will, put all his affairs in order. Sorted out old grudges—then died as soon as he'd put his world to rights.

This was right—he, tending the newly dead, the recently departed. How could you fear someone who lay so still? These arms and legs wouldn't reach out to strike or kick you, that placid tongue wouldn't shriek insults or make a mocking laugh.

All that they were shrouded in now was their burial shrouds—often the suit or dress they'd loved best. They literally had nothing else left to hide behind. Even the covering of fabric could be removed.

Whereas the living remained shrouded by their hypocrisy, their self-deceptions. Paul hid his stupidity behind the rigid barriers of his religion. Terry hid his fears and angers behind a series of jokes. As for Adrian... he didn't yet know what Adrian was hiding. He, Douglas, hid more openly from the world.

And Alice. He shuddered, glad that this more sensible coffined female was now here for him. Alice had hidden behind so many shrouds that he couldn't even begin to peel them away. She'd hid behind motherhood, refusing to work or have hobbies. Yet she'd never really been there for him as a mum. She'd also hidden behind the respectability of wifedom, though there had been nothing respectable about the way Paul treated her or her son.

Had she even hidden behind pregnancy all those years ago, creating a child to hide the fact that her sexual union with his father wasn't meant to be anything more? Douglas sighed, feeling smaller. The skin of his face felt hot and dry. He saw too much deceit and evasion. Saw and despised and shrank from it, even as a part of him yearned to inherit that outward calm.

Still recognisable as human, but without the mortal failings: that's how he liked them. For a few hours the perfect silence and preservedness of the recently dead ruled supreme. Then... well, a buried adult could take ten to twelve years to break down into something unrecognisable. A child took half that time. Heavy clay and peat could preserve the corpse almost indefinitely: water would speed its decay.

Douglas sighed. Nowadays, people died more slowly, lingered. Had a more gradual withdrawing than the deaths of their ancestors had been. Yet their disposal was still swift: almost indecently so. In theory, if the death certificate was issued immediately you could be buried right away. In practice, the cemetery usually required notice to prepare a grave, and the funeral director needed time to deal with the administration, though the process was speeded if you'd paid for a family plot of land.

Imagine, first Paul—he hoped—then Alice, then himself being buried like the tiers of a wedding cake. He'd have to make sure he went to the next life, or to oblivion, alone.

He shuddered, contemplating his own mortality. He feared dying, but not death. Death was painless, noiseless, stressless. Death brought superiority, an 'I know something you don't know' mode of thought. Those pale limbs hopefully went somewhere else in a disembodied form, went somewhere so seductive that they never felt compelled to come back.

Back to basics, to filling in her crematorium form. Very environmentally friendly, those gas heated cremators were. Feed the fire, fan the flames: Paul's Catholic creed had ensured he had hated the notion. Combustion carnage houses, both controllable and cheap. Controllable and cheap... He stopped, inhaled deeply. The thoughts were coming again, coming strong.

Strange that he could go from thinking about work or school to thinking about... *other things*. Curves and crevices and textures, sights and smells.

Scarcely breathing, he walked into the corridor and listened for human sounds, living sounds. He and Terry had been the last in the building and now Terry had gone.

Silence. Slowly he retraced his steps into the Chesting Area. It wouldn't be wrong, surely, to say goodbye? She was all alone now, trapped within layers of cool wood and satin lining. Tomorrow she'd be ashes raked in the soil.

Dig the dirt. Breathing quickly, he walked back towards the metal frame with its precious cargo. Tilted her coffin half out and held it in place with his chest. Swallowing hard, legs itching fiercely, he pulled off the unsealed lid and put it on top of the neighbouring coffin. Blood racing at her willingness, he lifted her out and carried her back to the Preparation Room.

Beautiful. Accepting. Revealing. He slid a tentative finger down the long curve of her neck to where it reached her neckline and held it there. He'd lingered this long before when putting on their make up. Skin so soft, so silky. His hand went down, down, down to the first button that held her nightie in place.

'You'll go to hell,' said Paul, as he always did. His words floated in and out of Douglas's head like the tune of a pop song. But Paul had gone, gone: had abandoned him. He had a room of his own now: he was an adult, a grown man. And men... *It wouldn't be wrong to touch, just to touch her.* His hand slid beneath her modern shroud, and stayed.

CHAPTER NINE

She didn't feel so exposed now it was cooler. September sun was more muted, kind. It didn't illuminate the swell of her bust so much, the puffiness where her short sleeves ended, the uncertain shifting of her size sixteen hips. Boys and girls had gone back to school rather than out to play now that the Summer vacation had ended, which meant fewer pseudo wolf whistles and sarcastic remarks.

Marjorie crossed to her bedroom wardrobe. She could wear her brown pinafore dress and a white jumper and not feel an unseasonable frump. She could put on tights again without looking unsummery. In a week or two she'd be able to hide inside her beloved baggy cardigan and not get the underarms damp.

Today she was going to buy a fish—maybe even two of them. The filter had matured by now, or whatever it was supposed to do. Marjorie looked at the alarm clock: it was 10am. If she had breakfast immediately and made her shower a quick one she could be there before twelve. Which meant she'd just get in before the lunchtime crowds: all those suits and briefcases. All those tall sure women with neat, nyloned legs...

For days she'd peered into the tank, hoping some kind of life form would appear, maybe just a water beetle or snail which had gotten in on the plants. It would be nice to have something to watch, something to show Simon. So far her mother had only said she hoped the thing wouldn't flood.

Sitting down again on the side of the bed, Marjorie slowly pulled on her tan tights. Asthmatics shouldn't do too much first thing in the morning: it was a difficult time. What with house dust mite, and pillow allergies, and that early tight-throated feeling... She brightened: nothing that breakfast couldn't put right.

Still in her underskirt and jumper, she went into the kitchen and put some oil in the frying pan. Whilst it was heating she put three bacon rashers, some potato slices, five mushrooms and an egg on a plate. It was tiring walking these days: she needed the nourishment. As her mother said, a good breakfast set you up for the day.

Right on target, the phone rang. Mum picked up her pension at this end of the town once a week and often came round. Hurrying into the hall, Marjorie picked up the receiver, murmured her number.

'Can an old woman wheedle a cup of tea?' said her mother's voice.

'Mum, of course—I'm just about to cook breakfast.'

'I had mine at seven,' her mother said. Her voice dropped slightly, as it always did when there was a moral coming up, 'Early to bed, early to rise, that's what I say.'

She said it every week.

Drawing a little cottage on the telephone pad, Marjorie made agreeable noises down the receiver. As ever, her mother went on to complain about the tiring bus journey to the post office, the litter on the pavements, the heat.

'Why not transfer your book to a post office nearer you?' she asked every so often, knowing the answer.

'Got my pension at that post office since your father died and I'm not changing just cause the council saw fit to move me,' Mrs Milton would say.

Which wasn't quite fair to the council, Marjorie thought, staring at the message-free telephone pad. After Marjorie moved out Mrs Milton had told them the house was too big, so they'd arranged for her to be moved to a neat little flat.

'Come round, mum,' she said, stomach rumbling, 'I'll put the kettle on now.'

Returning to the kitchen, she added the breakfast ingredients to the smoking oil. Walking towards the bread bin, she felt her thighs rubbing together, feeling hot. That did it—she wouldn't have buttered toast with her meal. For some months now she'd been getting heavier and puffier. It was probably hormonal: Dr Ashford should be told.

She'd mention it on her next visit: he might want her to go for tests or something. She must get round to making an appointment soon. Now that the summer was passing, she'd get out and about more. Maybe mum would like to go to the zoo.

Mum wanted tea and biscuits: at least she usually did. Glad of someone to cater for, she put on the kettle, rinsed the teapot under the hot tap, poured milk from the carton into a cream jug. The older woman hated beverages served in a mug, hated biscuits from the packet, hated powdered milk.

She looked around, knowing her mother would notice any stains on the work surface, any slovenliness. The place looked fine, neat even: Simon usually tidied up in his wake.

Marjorie hoped her mother wouldn't stay long. She'd decided to go to the aquarists before lunch. Or to *an* aquarist. She paused as she carried her tray into the lounge. She didn't think she could face Michael just yet, not so soon after he'd realised that she fancied him. It made her cringe to think about it. He hadn't wanted to know, didn't even want to stay for a cup of tea after delivering her tank.

Setting down the tray on the coffee table, she reached for the remote control, switched the television on. She could go to a different shop for her piscine purchases this time. Later, if he proved to be the best stockist, she could return to him. By then she'd be able to talk knowledgeably about nitrates, about why fish were fun.

Heartbeat speeding, she speared a piece of bacon and a chunk of potato with her fork, and added a slice of mushroom to form a breakfast kebab. She'd look up her options in the *Yellow Pages* as soon as she'd finished this. At least this time she knew a little about conditioned water and aerators. Michael must have thought her so dumb...

The doorbell rang just as she scooped up the last of the egg yolk. Marjorie hurried to the kitchen and threw her tell-tale plate into the water in the sink. Mum thought eggs were death by cholesterol, wouldn't have them in the house. Not that she did everything mum said: that was the reason she'd left home in the first place. Mum's favourite saying had been: In my house you live by my rules.

Marjorie prepared a smile as she walked down the hall, opened the door that led to the landing.

'That stair needs sweeping,' said her mum, with a sweep of her hand.

'We've got a man comes round, mum, and washes it weekly. Each flat pays him 65 pence.'

Her mother wiped her feet on the mat, then strode in, towards the living room.

'Well, he's not coming round often enough if you ask me.'

'Tea coming up.'

Leaving her mother to find her own seat, Marjorie hurried to the kitchen and poured water into the teapot.

'Nothing in that tank yet?' Mrs Milton said when she came back.

'No. I thought I might go today, pick up a fish or two.'

Taking the armchair facing the older woman, she stretched over and switched on the glow of the electric fire.

'Watch you don't catch anything,' Mrs Milton said. 'Slimy things.' She looked at Marjorie, then added 'Toffs are careless!'

Following her gaze, Marjorie realised she still hadn't put her pinafore on.

'I was just getting dressed when you phoned,' she lied quickly.

Like most of her clothes nowadays, the garment cut into her at the waist, so she liked to put it on just before she left the house.

'Don't mind me.'

Her mother had the kind of demeanour you had to mind. Grey hair like teased steel wool—which she often hid behind a head scarf—topped the kind of face you saw on peasant women in Romanian films. Not that you could blame her: she'd been widowed in what she called the prime of her life and she'd suffered with her health for years.

'So, post office busy, mum?'

They'd been having these same conversations for months now, ever since Marjorie had had to give up her cleaning job and go on invalidity. Most pension days they went over the same ground on the phone and in person. Better, though, than the quietude of a library book, the false gaiety of breakfast TV. Anyway, having a visitor gave her something to tell Simon about, made her feel less alone.

'Same as usual.' Her mother touched her large tan shopping bag with her foot as if to reassure herself that her pension was still in it, 'They were running low on change.'

Silence. Marjorie nodded belatedly, searched for and failed to find a new conversation piece. Leaning forward, she poured two cups of tea.

'Been using your inhaler?'

'I haven't needed it since the hospital.'

'Just don't get complacent Marjorie, that's all.'

As if she would, with the memory of these attacks at the office. They'd robbed her of her work, her workmates, what little confidence she had. Gasping, coughing, her chest feeling tight, tighter. The other girls staring, pinkness draining from her boss's face. Brain asking 'what's happening?' even as she tried to speak, to reassure them. Then fading out into nothingness, coming round in dizzy stages, feeling sick, scared, confused.

'You've got to be careful with animals, Marjorie. You know—allergies.'

'That's fur, mum—not fish.'

'Just the same. You don't know where they've been—imported, probably. You'll not touch them, will you?'

'No, they come in a bag of water. You can just tip it into your tank.'

At this rate, mum wouldn't want to go with her to the aquarists, which was good, really: on her own she'd have a better time.

'Want to come with me?' she asked, knowing the answer.

'Me? I've no time to go gallivanting about.'

It was true really: she'd spent years watching her mother in action. Ironing a blouse could take fifteen minutes in itself, each item of clothing sprayed with tepid water then pressed to perfection. Blouses and skirts were hung in the wardrobe just so.

Cooking and cleaning took equally long, each step made slowly and methodically. Every corner was vacuumed till the carpet showed signs of wear. Tables and chairs were polished with the zeal given to a newly won trophy. The windows in her ground floor flat gleamed like the sun.

'No, I've got another appointment at you know where.'

Mrs Milton referred to the Dental Hospital that way all the time.

'Dentures still not right, mum?'

'Not right? The things are completely wrong.'

They'd been wrong since her original dentist made them, didn't fit tight against the gum, moved when she ate. The dental technician had filed them and filed them and filed them. He'd referred her to the Dental Hospital in the end.

'Maybe they'll sort it out this time,' Marjorie said hesitatingly. A smile was trying to force its way through her tight closed mouth. It must be awful to feel your teeth could jump out at any time!

'Anyway, you just go and enjoy yourself,' said her mother, 'I can fend for myself.'

****

Marjorie peered uncertainly in the aquarist's window. She liked to know the set-up she was going into, exactly where everything was. That way, she was less liable to fall down a step or go into the wrong part of the building. Once, during her old office's annual night out, she'd ended up in the Staff Quarters, in the Gents.

She tried to squint round a poster advertising terrapins. She wanted to walk straight to the fish and spend some time looking round. Too often, assistants in shops led her to where she wanted to go, then stood beside her, tapping their feet till she either bought something hastily or fled. This time she wanted to look round before anyone asked if they could help.

She'd chosen this shop from the *Yellow Pages*. Its lists showed there were aquarists everywhere. After some thought, she'd copied out this address about twenty minutes walk away from Michael's shop. There'd been a drawing of a smiling sea lion beneath the lettering. The advert promised a good range of small pets and fishes and birds.

Unfortunately the window was full of cat baskets and cages. Realising that her view of the inner shop was blocked, Marjorie took a deep breath and stepped in. A bell rang above the doorway. Budgies were chirping, hamsters were rustling: there was a sawdusty smell.

Walking forward, parallel to the counter, she began to look at the animals ahead and to the other side of her. She could sense the male assistant watching but he didn't speak. She walked past rats and mice and gerbils in floor-based hutches. Saw lovebirds and cockatiels in larger cages further up the walls.

Ask to see our snakes said a cardboard sign, pinned

against the plywood. *Fish House* proclaimed another sign pointing to a recess further back. Quickening her step, she went there, stepping over a sack of foodstuffs and a small metal ladder. It was darker here, but the musty smell had gone.

Twenty or thirty tanks lined the walls, all teeming with occupants. Oscars, Catfish, Platies, Sticklebacks, Carp. After a few minutes, she realised that the unheated tanks were on one side of the room, furthest away from her. This here must be the tropical side. She began to concentrate on those.

'Can I help you?'

She'd been there for ten minutes or so when the man appeared beside her. He had a gruff voice, looked like he'd been running his hands through his hair.

She pointed: 'I'd like to buy two of those neon ones.'

She tried to keep her voice measured, confident, wanted to seem as if she bought fish all the time.

'Two neons coming up,' said the man jovially. His belly, in a short sleeved white shirt with a blue stripe, hung over his trousers. Quickly he netted two of the fish and put them into a water-filled bag. Then he looked her in the eyes: 'We've got some lovely flame tetras and cherry barbs and coolie loaches in. See for yourself!'

Pink and silver and red and lemon and golden. She stared, enraptured, as he pointed out the qualities of each. Some of the fish were quite little and her tank was a big one, as Michael had pointed out. Surely there was space?

'I suppose I could have two of those,' she said hesitantly. The man didn't try to stop her, didn't talk about bacteria like Michael had.

'Good choice,' he replied, 'Peaceful little fish.' He paused, 'By next week the loaches will be gone.'

She'd hesitated some more. 'I just set up my aquarium.'

'Loaches don't take up much space, love. They stay around the floor of the tank, you know.'

She hadn't. Still, he presumably knew what he was talking about.

'I thought I could only buy one or two fish at a time,' she said, 'Some fishkeepers say...'

The man snorted. 'If you listened to some fishkeepers, you'd never get round to buying anything.' He shrugged his shoulders, 'It's up to you, of course. All I'm saying is, they'll soon get snapped up.'

So she'd snapped them up herself—well, had them netted. Walked home with a total of eight fish contained within two polythene bags. The man had put the polythene bags inside a brown paper carrier with two strong handles. Still, she felt too self conscious to take it on the bus. The water sloshed around and was surprisingly heavy. She could feel the fish nosing energetically at the sides.

Only soon they'd stopped nosing, and had hung in the water, as if suspended. A still life: it seemed a contradiction in terms. A few hours later most had flailed their way upwards and stayed there, open mouths pressed against the surface of the water like suction caps.

Swim. Play. When she tapped the glass they flinched and swum away weakly, fins barely moving. Returned within minutes to gasp at the surface again. Worrying vaguely about blood sugar levels, she dropped in more tropical flake food, winced as they stared at it then drifted away. *Eat something*, she whispered, the dread building up inside her. *Do something*. Hour after hour, movement began to slow within her tank.

CHAPTER TEN

Marjorie was obviously having another lie-in. Feeling slightly guilty, Simon reached for the slices of toast he'd made for her ten minutes before. It was easy to be nice to her at this time, when he had the whole day at work to look forward to. Easy to be nice when you'd have intelligent office discussions, have fun thinking up daft magazine ideas.

He sighed as the stillness of the house continued. More and more nowadays, he knocked on Marjorie's door and she grunted something and went straight back to sleep. Easy, once you did that, to slide into a heavy-headed depression. It had happened to him as a student during vacation time when he first left home. Still, he'd had the University swimming pool and gym at his disposal. He wondered how she passed the hours when she eventually faced the day.

By eating, probably: she was always nibbling. She shopped a lot for crisps and cakes and sweets. He'd bought her a book on yoga, casually mentioned that the community centre ran classes. But she was timid when it came to trying anything new.

Take food, for example. When he'd first been given the room in her rented house, he'd taken her on his work nights out with him. Egon Ronay style evenings, sampling as many dishes as they could. But she'd sat there with her omelette whilst the others passed round the Chinese banquet. She'd eaten fried haddock in The Bengali whilst they heaped the table with plates of beef madras, tandoori prawns and saffron rice.

Not that choosing a different meal was enough to isolate one: the vegetarian female in their party ordered disparately. But Marjorie dressed differently too, in a brown-leaved print dress more suited to someone her mother's generation. And she had so little to talk about most days...

Simon poured himself more tea, and the inevitable pity swept through him. Parents were diverse in outlook, and she'd drawn the short straw. To Mrs Milton, life was an accident waiting to happen. When she asked how you were, you could tell she hoped for 'not so good'.

Worse, she seemed to relish Marjorie's isolation. 'I was always a loner myself,' she'd said in Simon's hearing more than once. As if that settled it—an inheritance. As if Marjorie had to exist in exactly the same way. Simon bit into his third slice of toast more savagely, felt thankful that the older woman lived some distance across town. As such, she tended to phone in the evenings rather than visit. When she did call, she usually made sure he'd be out.

Still, her influence was destructive, pervasive. She'd trained her daughter to think of life as being about getting a man. Simon had watched the girl gaze hungrily at his colleagues during these long gourmet evenings, seen her increasingly desperate attempts to win a date. Marj had chatted up sales reps and plumbers, the forty-something guy who came to read the meter, his friends.

He'd watched them panic slightly, flounder. For the first few weeks after becoming her flatmate, he'd felt that panic himself. Then he'd rationalised it: what was she going to do to him—rape him? She was simply lonely, unwanted, unfulfilled.

She hadn't been the first person he'd known to get this frightened. *It could be fatal if you just turned away.* Someone had to befriend the Marjories, encourage them, risk receiving embarrassing amounts of gratitude coupled with hostility and rage. For dependents held more than their share of anger and bitterness. They always turned against their providers in the end.

He stared down at his cup. It was inevitable, really. If you failed to meet just one of their requests, they had no one else who'd comply and this resulted in a child-like level of frustration. Hence Marjorie's occasional tight voice and door-slamming escapes to her room.

He replaced the lid on the marmalade. He just knew she'd been the fat child of the playground, the teenager who couldn't make eye contact, the one typist the boss never flirted with. She'd been brought up not to expect too much—invited little. Sometimes she received even less.

Time to go. Brushing crumbs from his jacket, he stood up and cleared his plates away. She always offered to do it, but it wasn't fair. If only he could find some way to ensure she used up her hours productively, got a job or a hobby. There was a brain in there, behind the fear.

His stomach tightening slightly, he looked over at the aquarium. Saw the side-floating evidence: another fish had died. He contemplated removing it before she awoke, but that was pointless. She knew how many remained.

He wondered if she'd bought incompatible ones or if she wasn't feeding them right or something. She had some tropical flakes and some granules, both in tubs. Maybe she'd given them too much to eat or too little? She meant well, but tended to rush things and get them wrong.

Shaking off the sadness, he let himself out of the house, and started off down the road, arms and legs swinging. If he kept up this speed he could walk to work, about forty minutes away. He wondered if Marjorie would buy herself replacement tank dwellers this afternoon. He hoped she wasn't going to embarrass the men in the shop. There'd been absolutely no need to have them deliver the aquarium in the first place: he could have driven her home with it any Saturday.

At least neither of them had tried to take advantage of her friendliness. It was one of the things he feared. There was something so naive about Marjorie, so innocent. He'd already gently suggested she shouldn't bring strangers back to the house. Or invite meter men to stay for a cup of coffee and an Eccles cake. Or ask the plumber if he'd like to stay for tea.

Nympho. That's what the tabloid across the hall from his office would have called her. *Come up and see me some time: Mammaried Marj offers all.* But she wasn't sex-obsessed, far from it. She wanted someone to cook for, to go to the cinema with, to love.

Edinburgh was getting busy now, couples traipsing out of houses, holding hands and kissing. Sun-happy hormones: he might ask Sue, their PR Officer, out. Simon walked on, mentally planning where to take her. It might be best to let her choose the venue herself. He wondered when Marjorie's prince would come and save her. He hoped for her sake it happened soon. Meanwhile, he'd take her to her blasted fish club and spend the evening there with her. It was the least he could do.

CHAPTER ELEVEN

Suicides had once been buried at the crossroads, with a stake driven through their bodies to stop their ghosts walking but this one was going to the cemetery at the other end of town. Douglas examined the hesitation marks that lay diagonally across her wrists: she'd held the knife there, trying to psyche herself up for some time, before opting for hanging instead.

A slow death, by asphyxiation. If you jumped at the right angle from a height you broke your neck and avoided the hangman's jig. Still, it wasn't the kind of thing you could practice, make perfect. When instinct took over, you clawed and gouged at the rope. Often they found rope fibres under the person's nails, proof that they'd tried to loosen the constricting knot. Others, who'd handcuffed themselves to the wheel of the car then sent it headlong into the river, were discovered with fingers bloody and raw from pulling at the metal restraints.

What did you see, feel at the final moment that made you change your mind, he wondered. Was it purely an innate struggle for survival or did some message suddenly tell you that this was wrong?

If he killed himself, he'd do it with whisky and paracetamol. He'd decided that long, long ago. Not that he liked scotch; he'd tried some of Alice's and found it sour and burning. He'd hardly touched alcohol since seeing her drunk. Seeing most people inebriated didn't affect him. But when it was your own mum...

Tablets was usually the woman's way, the next favourites being suffocation with a plastic bag or drowning. Men hung themselves, used poison or exhaust gas—death by drowning was rarely their first choice. More women tried to commit suicide than men, but more men succeeded. He'd always known he'd be able to do it right.

You had to go someplace where no one would find you. The tablets and alcohol eventually did the rest. Rest, rest... according to the bigots, you went to purgatory. Or limbo, or somewhere equally punitive and on edge.

He'd leave a suicide note, he would. Otherwise the coroner tried to put accidental death on the certificate. They liked to play happy families as much as the rest of them, hated to admit that some bastard had had enough. Sinful to take away what God had given you. Even if God had given you parents who wore you into the ground.

For years he'd fantasized about killing Paul and making it look like suicide. That would shake up the bastard's Church. The man presumably wasn't a bright young thing to start with, but his religion had made him infinitely worse.

And Alice, she was just as bad, attending services with him because 'it was a woman's place' to do so. He, Douglas, had stopped going as soon as he left school. Listen, repeat, listen, repeat, listen. Rituals that were the antithesis of thinking for yourself...

He thought now of all the ways history had disposed of dead bodies: executed prisoners used to have to be buried within prison grounds. At one stage, the corpses of executed murderers were always given over to the surgeons for dissection, punishment both beyond the grave and instead of it: they were never given a burial site.

Still other bodies had come back from their coffins with the aid of the resurrectionists. Such thieves gained Burke and Hare style profits, public hate. Undertakers had also sold corpses to the body-snatchers, weighing the empty coffins down with stones instead.

Her upper body was still perfect, though her face wasn't. Contorted, but in a mesmerising way. Minuscule thread-like red veins peppered her hairline and forehead, the whites of her eyes. Not that they were so white any more...

He looked down at her calves, a blackish-purple. The blood had pooled there whilst she hung. Asphyxiation removed the oxygen and made the blood darker, black as her last remaining thoughts.

He pressed a finger below her knee, and released the pressure. The discolouration was permanent now, for the fluid had congealed in her lower limbs. Too late to massage it away, to make her pale and interesting. With Reevon's help, he dressed her in a full length dress which concealed all ills.

'A sad case,' said Reevon, studying the female, 'According to the police, it was her younger sister went into the flat.'

Douglas nodded: 'Adrian said so. Was speaking to a neighbour two doors away who heard her screams.'

Silently they lifted and chested the body. If her

parents decided they wanted to view it, Douglas would give the corpse a facial mask. They used them for bad road accident victims, for features that had gone malignant or turned yellow, for people who'd sustained severe burns to the head.

'Doing anything special, tonight?' Reevon asked, as they returned to clean up the Prep Room.

'Not really.' Everyone seemed to expect him to lead a wild life since he'd left home, 'I've been painting the cornice,' he added awkwardly.

'A difficult area,' Reevon said.

Silence, bar the slight friction of cloth on metal. Douglas finished scrubbing the surface, and picked up the brush to sweep the floor. There was a cleaning woman came in early each morning and made things pristine. But by afternoon he felt compelled to clear the worst of the day's spills and stains and grime.

'Believe you've set up a fish tank.'

Adrian or Shelley must have been talking about him again. He nodded, knowing Reevon never judged anything until he understood it, was a thinking man.

'Believe it's quite difficult to do properly,' added the older man, 'Have you done it before?'

Yes. No. Sort of. He wondered if Lucky counted in adult eyes.

'Just a goldfish in a bowl when I was little.' He shivered slightly, remembering being little, 'But I've got a proper aquarium this time.'

At his boss's prompting, he told of the tank's occupants and furnishings.

'Like to see it sometime,' Reevon said.

Douglas looked down, reddening slightly. A visitor. He'd never had a visitor before. What did you say after you showed off the aquarium? Did you offer tea or wine?

'Just once you've got it all set up, of course,' Reevon added, into the silence.

'In a month or so I'll be fully stocked.'

It was the nearest he could get to issuing a full-blown invitation. He had to think about this. He had to be on his own.

'Terry wants to come round with his rod, of course,' the older man quipped, making a line-casting motion. But he said it in a we-know-what-he's-like kind of voice, which made Terry the odd man out.

When he got home that night, Eleanor Denning was fishing for information. Again she trapped him at the midsection of the stair.

'Getting everything ship shape, are you?'

'Yes, thanks.'

He'd done that the day he arrived.

'I was thinking.' She seemed to expect acknowledgement for this one phrase. He nodded awkwardly. She went on. 'We should have some sort of lounge or something—you know, a TV room.'

He winced. 'I don't watch TV.'

'Oh... well, I don't much either. Just the wildlife programmes, you know. And the news.'

He could tell she was lying. Alice's hands also flapped about and her face got that too-still expression when she was lying. He leaned forward to indicate that he'd like to walk past.

'I mean, you could just sit and talk there. Or... or read.'

'I like to read in my room.' He kept his voice light, even. He didn't want to make an enemy: he just wanted her to leave him alone.

'It's not the same though, is it?'

She had on a pale blue coat today: a sort of cape-like thing. She adjusted her shoulder bag, and he smelt a faint odour of long-stored clothes, and sweat.

He shrugged. 'I'm fine as I am, thanks.'

He had been, until now.

'I thought I'd see about our rights, phone the CAB.'

Our rights. *God*. His legs started to itch, his scalp prickled. He'd come home to relax, and she wouldn't even let him into his room. He made a sudden decision, turned sharply. 'Bye.'

'Thought you were coming in?' she asked tautly.

'Change of plan. Places to go, people to see.'

He'd heard Adrian use that: it sounded good, purposeful. He smiled as he hurried back along the road. Yes, he was going places, all right—well, to one place. Only the people he was seeing wouldn't be seeing him...

Or would they? According to Mohammedanism the soul remained in the corpse for between three and forty days, was worthy of reverence. Islam avoided cremation, as a result. Many religions were equally antagonistic towards the all-consuming flames, thought them fit only to destroy the clothes lepers had worn.

The early evening streets were full of traffic horns and ghetto blasters. Sirens. Shouts. Singing. His breathing only really calmed down when he closed the door to Reevon's, and locked himself away. It was nice here at 7pm: cool and collected. Chances were he wouldn't be disturbed.

Going into the office, he checked the answering machine was switched on. It gave callers one of the director's home numbers to ring. If the machine went into action, he'd do likewise out of the front door. It meant there was a good possibility that two of the men would show up with a corpse within the hour.

For now, tranquillity. He went into his staff locker where he always kept at least three books, took out the one on preventing fish diseases and sat back in the big chair. He felt a growing sense of pleasure: this wasn't really his chair, was the one Shelley kept for special visitors, or for herself.

Fungus... leeches... He studied the text for twenty industrious minutes, moving his bookmark from page to pristine page. To avoid fish illness you quarantined new purchases for up to three weeks. You also syphoned out uneaten food and other debris to improve the water quality.

Quality of life. That was the psychologists buzz phrase, the doctors buzz phrase, the phrase of presenters on TV. He put the book on the table, and sighed. Forget them. Nothing wrong with a quiet three score years and ten. Eat three square meals, mind your manners, stay out of trouble, keep your head down, survive.

Still there had to be superior moments—*something*. Something to take the tension from days such as this. Like... well, even fish drove each other into the reeds, pushed and nuzzled. Even fish pursued and wooed a mate.

But he didn't want... God preserve him from girlish, sad and witless chatter. Imagine getting home and having to stay with one of them every hour of the day. He wanted a more elevated comfort, wanted...

He wondered if the suicide had changed colour again, or texture. Fascinating, really, the hues the body was capable of. Green, yellow, purple: he'd seen them all, their swollen interweaving. Had watched, over days, as the skin changed from pink to purple to black.

With interesting variations. The skin beneath a belt, for

example, stayed pale, though the rest went pinkish. Same was true for other tight clothing and ropes. Sometimes you could strip a corpse and still know the kind of garments she wore. *Or he. Or he.*

Noise quality also varied. Depended on what they'd eaten, their gender, their age. Some gurgled and groaned and made occasional hissing noises. Others seemed more resigned to the longest sleep.

The suicide was one of the silent ones: he was glad of her repose. There was a quietness about depressives he adored. Even Alice had been subdued when popping the pills—such transitory pleasure. How old had he been then? About twelve or so?

He'd just been starting secondary, learning Shakespeare and Hardy and Lawrence. He'd been proud of his first grown up essay, had looked up from the fireside after finishing it.

'Alice, can I read it out?'

'Don't bother your mother,' Paul had replied, glaring, 'Can't you see she's not herself?'

It was only then that he'd noticed the vivid purple patches that stained her face at both sides.

'It's just nerves,' she'd said, 'Just me getting in a state about growing old.'

Paul had said he'd take care of it, but his cure of God and Masses hadn't helped.

The tranquillisers had: she'd taken lots of them. Though it was the anti-depressants that had actually made her limbs and belly swell. She'd been sedate then, talked little in a low voice. He'd felt calm around her for a while.

Then Paul had found something in his teachings that mitigated against medicine, flushed all her pills down the toilet, said she wasn't to go back. After that, the high voice again, the jerky movements. Hate and hate and hate.

Think love. It had been twenty years or so since he'd loved her, loved anyone. Twenty years of just getting by. But now, a room of his own—if only Eleanor Denning would go away, and he could enter it. *Enter, enter...* His collar suddenly felt tight.

He'd just go and see his girls—find out if they'd changed any. Captivating the way redistributing gases could cause a corpse to twitch. Even after death, they kept changing. Even he, for all his hesitancy, couldn't stay the same.

Same time, same place: he'd been here before of an evening. No Terry, Adrian, Reevon or Shelley: just him and her. Communicating beyond words, beyond intellect. He just sat with them for an hour or so, held their hands. He was respectful towards them, even reverent. Even Paul couldn't have disapproved if he had known.

CHAPTER TWELVE

'It's a bit dry, and I've not been sleeping right, and I thought...'

Dr Ashford raised his eyes and pursed his mouth into a rueful half grin. 'Alright, Marjorie. Slow down a little. Let's take it from the top.'

Where to begin? When she was more organised, she brought a list of symptoms along to the surgery and read them out to him. She let him keep a copy for his notes.

'Well, my scalp feels dry—a bit flaky. Mum said it could be the first symptom of something worse.'

'Did she now?' Dr Ashford stood up and walked to the side of her. She blushed slightly as he parted and examined her hair.

'Nothing that some careful rinsing won't help,' he said evenly, 'It would aid matters if you cut down on sweets.'

'For my weight?' She sucked in her stomach defensively. Sometimes he got the nurse to weigh her, and the scales pointer soared up and up.

'Well, that too, but it'll help clear your dandruff. It's

caused by a fungus, which feeds on sugary foods.'

A fungus. She'd have to get a book on hair care out of the library. Obviously her system was out of synch...

'Now, you said you weren't sleeping,' the doctor prompted, returning to his seat, and swivelling it sideways to face her.

'I'm not. I lie there for hours and watch the clock go round.'

Dr Ashford picked up his pen again. 'And when do you get up most mornings?'

She thought back, realised. 'Uh... well I've been sleeping through the alarm.'

'Why do you think that is?'

'Habit, really. During the summer I felt tired in the heat so I just stayed indoors.'

There hadn't been much to get up for so she'd slept later and later. There still wasn't!

'There's your answer,' Dr Ashford was friendly and cheerful as always, 'Get up early tomorrow morning and stay up till your usual bedtime, even if you feel tired long before. You might like to get someone to give you an alarm call the next day. You'll be back into a routine in no time at all.'

She stared. He was always so calm about everything, so dispassionate. If only he'd look alarmed for once, seem to care.

He was closing her folder, the way he did when the consultation was over.

'Don't I need a prescription?' she asked.

He smiled in what she supposed was a fatherly way, though her own father, when he'd been alive, hadn't often smiled. 'What for, Marjorie?'

'For...?' Because it would be something new to tell

her mother. Because Simon would be more likely to stay home if he thought she was ill.

'My weight's gone up again. I thought maybe a thyroid problem?'

'We ruled that out last year. The tests were fine.' He looked at her composedly, 'Remember, if you've been sleeping longer and sitting about indoors, you're not burning up so many calories. Even if your eating hasn't increased, your weight will have.'

Nodding, she stood up and tried to smile back at him. 'Thank you for your time.'

Clutching her shoulder bag more tightly, she left the doctor's office. Wondered if she could be going premenstrual: she felt close to tears. She'd planned to walk to Princes Street, to Boots the Chemist. Browse in the newsagents whilst they made her prescription up.

Now? She began walking slowly towards home, thinking of alternatives. The fridge was well stocked, her library books were new and she'd bought in snacks the other day. Mentally she went through each room of the house, trying to think if it needed anything. An air freshener, maybe, or...?

Of course—more fish for her aquarium. Only one cherry barb remained. Michael had been right about not overstocking: two days after letting them into the crystal-clear water, the first coolie loach had died. The other fish had started to eat its tiny cadaver. Feeling sick and shaky, she'd removed the remains.

The next morning, she'd gotten up to find one of the tetras floating on its side, on the surface. She'd cried, then: *please God, let the others pull through*. The next day they'd all been floating, lifeless, except for the remaining barb.

Even he looked a bit weak, a bit lethargic. Maybe a little friend would cheer him up? Steeling herself for the encounter, Marjorie began to walk towards Michael's shop. Experience had now proved that he'd given her good advice, so she couldn't bring herself to tell him she'd gone elsewhere and bought all these other fish. She'd just admit to purchasing the one barb, explain it was looking lonely. She'd ask for something compatible. She'd do what he said.

Simon had been as upset about the deaths as she had. He'd promised to take her to the fish club that very week.

****

Lunch coming up. Douglas snipped the corner of the bag and live daphnia poured into his net and floundered there. Carefully he rinsed them under the tap, then walked to his aquarium and tipped them in. Live food was good for fish: they enjoyed chasing it. Enjoyed its nutrients, its fresher taste.

He thought back to Lucky, his original goldfish. As a child, he'd fed the creature dried food each day from a little tub. He'd asked Alice in the beginning if Lucky shouldn't have variety.

'It's not like us, love,' she'd said, 'It's just a fish.'

Just a fish. He should have known not to trust her. He knew now that fish deserved a varied diet as much as anyone else. In the sea they picked around all day, finding plant and animal debris. He could emulate that by giving them flesh foods, live foods, vegetables, even wholemeal bread.

Fish that enjoyed a diverse menu had a special sheen to them. They were chunkier, more dynamic, less given to minor ills. He watched now as his Fantails swum quickly after the tiny water fleas, snapping with their round mouths until the entire bagful had disappeared.

Going to his plastic tidy box, he extracted the pH Test kit. Held the empty tube in the aquarium until it filled with water to the water line. Then he unwrapped a tablet from its foil coating and dropped it into the tube, putting the cap on before shaking it hard. In a few satisfying minutes the water would turn to light green or palish blue. If the pH was too low, it would indicate yellow. Too high was shown by a deep purple shade.

As he waited, he netted a brownish piece of plant stem from the water. You had to remove such flotsam before it rotted, polluted the tank. He intended to prune the plants weekly and take cuttings as necessary. He'd bought a magnetic cleaner to keep algae down.

Douglas smiled to himself as he gently wiped the outer glass of the tank to keep it pristine. This was what Sundays were about: putting the world to rights. He looked at his pH Test, gratified to see that the colour was exactly as it should be. Michael Meer had said that Scotland seldom had problems with its water, but you couldn't be too careful, couldn't presume...

He looked into his isolation tank, where a Moor goldfish was swimming. It would be ready to join the two Fantails in the main aquarium any day. He'd got the little tank looking cosy, with a home made backdrop, a large white shell and a floating elodea plant. It seemed a pity to move the Moor at all.

Still, the thought of a perfect community tank was even more attractive. And when the Moor exited the isolation tank, a new fish—even a shoal of White Cloud Mountain Minnows—could take its place. And there were other possibilities still to experiment with, like freshwater mussels and clams and apple snails. He could even set up a special tank for breeding nest-building sticklebacks.

Douglas looked round the room, measuring, assessing. If he installed an extra shelf on the corner unit, he could put a second aquarium below the first. He'd have to leave the artificial lights on slightly longer, of course, for the area was shady, but could use more plants and caves to give the fish places to hide.

Then, perhaps, a third tank against the other wall, say on a long coffee table. A tank with perhaps one big fish, or a few which were coloured especially bright. Sharks were popular nowadays: he'd seen some beauties in Michael Meer's shop. They'd been in elongated, heated tanks.

Elongated. Heated. The world was full of opportunities. *At last, he could do anything he liked.* He wondered how difficult tropical fish keeping would be, how expensive. He would go to the fish club and find out this very week.

CHAPTER THIRTEEN

Simon smiled at Marjorie as she stood before him, holding out the skirt of her green print dress.

'What do you think?' Her eyes flickered uncertainly till he nodded.

'It's nice.'

There was nothing wrong with the outfit: just the occasion. She was too dressed up for a hobby meeting, where the others would be wearing things like jackets and jeans. If he told her that, though, she'd lose confidence, start tearing through her wardrobe and bringing things out to show him. Still he felt guilty that he'd lied.

'Don't tell them about the deaths,' she pleaded now, for the second time.

Simon settled back in his armchair, and picked up his glass. He took a deep breath, trying to keep his voice friendly, casual.

'Hey, I doubt if I'll be saying anything to anyone,' he said.

Already she seemed to have forgotten her promise

that he could just get her settled then leave again. One of her remarks had suggested he might be a fishkeeper's friend for life.

'No one will be judging you, Marj,' he said softly.

She frowned uncertainly: 'It's just that I don't want them to think I don't care.'

She did care: cared too much, if anything. He wondered if he could arrange some voluntary work for her to take her mind off things. Hospital visiting, maybe—no, the hypochondria put paid to that. It was hard to know who'd help.

'Believe me, they'll be glad of a new member,' he added now, sipping from the remaining half inch of his Southern Comfort. He smiled. 'It's supposed to be enjoyable. Just ask questions, or listen, okay?'

He seldom drank like this at home in the evenings. But he'd had a long day at work, needed a boost to get him through this fish club thing. He'd hoped to meet Sue for lunch in the cafeteria, but a meeting had held her back...

He looked up to see Marjorie staring at her body sideways in the mirror as though she'd never seen it before.

'Fishkeepers come in all shapes and sizes,' he joked, smiling to show he was on her side. But she didn't smile back.

The *Fish Are Fun* club was held in a Church Hall close to the city centre.

'Sorry. We haven't yet persuaded them to leave the heating on,' the man at the door said as they filed past.

'I'm warm enough.' Simon smiled and Marjorie muttered something unintelligible. Simon noticed the man said the same thing to the people behind them as well.

They walked through the foyer into a cavernous room

with a wooden stage which had a table on it. Rows of plastic seats were grouped in circles: it looked like a Sunday School. Only the circle nearest the stage was occupied and it still had vacant seats available. Simon walked towards them, giving Marjorie an encouraging smile

'You do the talking,' she said, as they got nearer. He forced back the irritation. She was just scared.

They sat down next to each other, choosing from four untaken chairs grouped together. The other seven they'd joined looked up from their books or conversations and smiled. One man seemed to raise his eyes curiously and lean forward a little. Looking closer, Simon noticed he had a badge which said *Organiser* on his lapel.

'Marjorie.'

He nudged her, intending to point out the man's status, but she was looking over to the other side of the circle, was reddening. Was giving her uncertain smile.

'Hello,' she said to a well-built, fair-haired man, who was looking back at her, 'How's the isolation tank?'

'Fine.' The man's voice was low and flat. His skin seemed to have reddened to match hers, 'I have a Moor in it now.'

Simon had to strain his voice to hear. So, obviously, did Marjorie.

'Hang on.'

Simon watched, amazed, as she vacated her place, and went to sit next to the stranger. With her heavy thighs she walked slowly, awkwardly: it seemed to take an age. Still, the man seemed pleased to see her, bent his head closer. Must be the fish shop owner, Simon thought, with relief.

But it wasn't. Later, after a woman had spoken about the history of Koi, they trooped over to the area near the serving hatch.

'This is my flatmate, Simon,' Marjorie said. She turned to the other man. 'Sorry, you're...?'

'Douglas. Douglas Tate.'

Slightly embarrassed, the two men smiled at each other and half-raised their hands in greeting. The three of them walked on.

The tables, which had seats for four people, were rapidly being occupied.

'I'll get us that one,' Simon promised, hurrying ahead and putting his jacket over one of the chairs. He turned back to the others. 'Tea?'

Two nods.

Marjorie, he noticed, was flushed and vivid. Douglas had a much less expressive face. Still, you couldn't blame the man for his countenance. He seemed... pleasant enough.

When he came back with the three cups, Douglas was explaining something.

'... then you get a new kit and check for nitrates,' he said.

'Michael told me that at the shop,' Marjorie murmured.

'There he is over there,' added Douglas, nodding towards a table at the other side of the room.

All three of them looked over, and, as if sensing this, the fish shop owner looked back and smiled.

'There's John!' Marjorie added excitedly, starting to wave.

The two men hesitated, then the older one said something to the teenager and they both started walking towards Marjorie's table.

'Simon—this is Michael and John, the people I bought the aquarium from,' Marjorie said, looking a bit overwhelmed.

'Ah, so you're the ones who landed me with all that wiring,' Simon grinned, glancing up at the two newcomers hovering beside his chair.

'Guilty!' said Michael, smiling. He paused, 'Enjoy the lecture on Koi?'

Marjorie smiled back and nodded, then clasped her hands together.

'Their dorsal fins seem to clamp when they're confined,' Douglas said.

'We've found that,' John agreed, nodding, 'But there's such a demand...'

Michael was looking at Simon sympathetically.

'Did you just get roped in?'

'Yep, I'm the moral support.'

If he left now, he could phone Sue and meet her somewhere for a drink or several. A nightcap back at her place was looking more likely all the time. On the four dates they'd had so far her body language had been positive. He just didn't want to rush things, given that they worked in the same place.

'Do you come here every week?' Marjorie was asking.

John nodded but Michael shook his head: 'Only if they're covering something I'm especially interested in—like tonight.'

'Do you keep Koi at home, then?'

'No. But they're popular in the trade.'

There was a slight silence. In the pause, he noticed Douglas staring at Marjorie's breasts, his mouth opening slightly. Definitely not gay, then, and he didn't look married or even divorced. He had the slight air of detachment about him that signifies someone who's spent much time alone.

As he did with people he helped interview, he clocked

the guy's shoes and clothes, his hairstyle. Black polished leather slip-ons, with grey socks and grey trousers in a cotton mix. A plain white shirt, a black tie, hair which was trimmed regularly but which had probably been in the same style since secondary school. His face looked slightly heavy, pale: vaguely self indulgent. He'd hung what looked like a car coat, an unattractive brown thing, over the back of his chair.

There was a feeling of intellect—or at least of knowledge. Probably the capacity to be a first rate bore. After Michael and John moved on, Simon looked, listened, drifted in and out of the conversation. Douglas talked of photographic equipment, computer software, the house decorating he'd done.

Aquarium filters and aqua life seemed to be his current obsession. He gave detail after detail, as if in a formal talk. He knew a lot about machinery, Simon acknowledged, his thoughts turning to Sue again. Marjorie, who couldn't even put a plug on the toaster, was obviously impressed.

But which area of the city did Douglas live in? What was his occupation? Was his family based in Edinburgh? What did he do for fun apart from keeping fish? In the course of the evening, the others had divulged such things, offered personal details. Douglas had not. Was he just a private person, or did he have something to hide? Simon felt inexplicably uneasy as he listened to the man.

CHAPTER FOURTEEN

Moaning, Douglas pushed forward, and his body spasmed. The woman moved slightly: her breasts seemed to swell. Pleased, probably, to be appreciated. Pleased to know she was still desirable, still adored.

Marjorie had seemed to like him last night: she'd agreed with all his comments. At one stage, she'd undone the top button of her dress. He'd never had a woman undo a button for him before. Never had a woman who'd...

Feeling vapid, dazed, he slid from the Prep Room table. What had he been doing? He must have come in here to dress this corpse. Finding her gown on the floor, he pulled her into a sitting position and pushed her cold stiff arms through the sleeves. Button-through shifts like this were easier than the ones you slipped over the corpse's head.

Presumably he'd already washed her. The memory was hazy—he was so unused to having a drink, having several drinks. But Reevon had turned fifty, and insisted on taking them all for what Terry called 'a few jars at the local hostelry.' Jars was the operative word! He'd done his best to drink pints like the others, but his bladder had balked at the volume of the beer.

So he'd switched to vodka instead: vodka and orange. It was only slightly bitter, hardly seemed like alcohol at all. Reevon had bought him two and then Adrian had said they should start a kitty. That meant putting a fiver in the middle of the table, then another five.

At some stage, the girls had come along: they'd started off sitting across from them. Adrian knew the red haired one slightly: Terry had said he'd like to know the rest. He'd shouted some comment to one of them and she'd answered. Much laughter on all sides. Missing the joke, he'd grinned and grinned. Somehow they'd all ended up together, round the one table. Male thigh against female thigh. Brush of breast against upper arm, scent of perfume, of soft fair skin.

This place was closer to home than his bedsitting room was. Douglas sat back on his heels in the middle of the Prep Room, and put a cooling hand to his head. That must be why he'd returned at this hour of the night, and woken up feeling dislocated, hungry. He'd just put this body away and clean up a bit, then make himself a strong cup of tea and splash cold water on his face.

He'd had tea with Marjorie last night: two cups of it at the *Fish Are Fun* club. He'd bought her the second one after her friend, Simon left. She'd given the impression they were just flatmates as he walked her to the bus stop. He wondered if they'd...

No. Stop. That awful moaning. Pain and pain and pain and pain and pain. He couldn't imagine what it would be like, sharing a flat with another person. At home, he'd always stayed in his room.

Blinking, Douglas stared at the corpse on the Prep Table. She seemed to have shifted: pressure of gases again. Quickly he plugged her, combed her hair, lowered her into her coffin and returned it to its position in the metal frame. He breathed in, out, in, out, with effort: every muscle strained.

Even using the trolley on wheels, it was hard for one man to lift a coffin. He really must stop doing late night unauthorised overtime like this.

As he left the funeral parlour, a group of girls ran past him, heels clicking. One of them dropped her head to stare at his body, then laughed: following her gaze, he noticed his fly was undone. Funny. Mum had taught him a little rhyme about that. She'd made him repeat it from the age of four till... when?

He flushed, remembering the embarrassment of her watching him, staring at his... *Forget. Forget.* Looking around to make sure no one was watching, he pulled up his zipper, self consciously straightened the rest of his clothes. Strange: he was sure he could remember fastening it after he left the Gents in the pub tonight. Maybe the zip was loose.

CHAPTER FIFTEEN

Tonight—she would see him again tonight. Trekking downhill to the hairdressers, Marjorie hugged the knowledge to herself. They'd talked of fish and photographs and... almost everything. He'd admired her curves when he thought she wasn't looking. Had bought her tea and offered biscuits. He'd made her feel good.

As if it was okay to be buxom and womanly. There'd been a couple of teenage girls there in clingy white T-shirts and jeans.

'These are the ones the club was originally for,' the organiser had explained, coming over to each table for a brief chat, 'You know—kids under sixteen.'

She'd thought *Fish Are Fun* sounded young initially, but the posters said all ages were welcome. Marjorie followed Douglas's line of vision, which led to the girls. They were putting all the chairs away, trainers slapping the wooden floor as they hurried from corner to corner, large lipsticked mouths laughing out loud. She couldn't compete with their slimness, far less their agility. Douglas must be assessing, comparing, finding her dull. She sucked in her breath, preparing to see his features animate. But no, he was turning quickly away.

At last, someone who liked the fuller figure. Someone who got embarrassed and could be shy, and who also kept fish. They were soul mates, they were meant to be together. By the time she reached the salon, Marjorie was so elated she felt she could fly.

'Hello, I've a cut and blow dry booked for midday with Anne-Marie.'

She'd originally asked for Gordon, but he was already reserved.

'Take a seat. She'll not be long,' said the receptionist, smiling more broadly than usual.

Everyone seemed to like her today.

As she waited, she read the problem page of a women's magazine. *Why Don't I Orgasm? How Can I Please Him?* A whole new world of worries and thrilling words. *New men tend to prefer women who are confident*, confided the agony aunt, *whilst older men may want a women who takes a gentler, more modest approach.*

Douglas was older, so presumably he'd like modest. That suited her: it was hard pretending to be sure of yourself all the time. Always there was that feeling that strangers would find out in the long term, find out that you were the quiet type, a bit unadventurous, a bit shy.

'Come on through, Miss Milton.'

Hating the sound of the Miss, Marjorie put the magazine down, followed Anne-Marie to a chair that faced backwards onto a sink with a spray attachment. She hated backwashes, always felt her head was in danger of being chopped off.

'Will you want conditioner?'

Most places charged extra. Usually she said no: it was cheaper to condition it next day yourself.

'Great, thanks.'

She must have sounded happy.

'Going someplace special?' the hairdresser asked.

'To my fishkeeping club.' That didn't sound very exciting. 'But we'll be going on for coffee or drinks afterwards,' she said.

'Is there a few of you go?' Anne-Marie asked, rubbing hard at her curls.

'Oh, my flatmate Simon—and Douglas, my friend.'

Douglas, my friend: that sounded wonderful. It had been years since she'd even had a date. There'd been two boys at school, who she'd had a burger with. They hadn't as much as held hands and she'd heard later that one of them had gone out with her for a dare...

Then she'd left school, got a job as a typist. A sales rep in his forties had asked her out. She'd gone, not really fancying him, but flattered. He'd looked so pensive, with his slightly balding head and uncertain ginger moustache.

She'd been too young to drink but she'd sipped a coke in the pub whilst he talked of how his ex-wife had treated him. Talked of finding her in bed with another man. Marjorie hadn't known what to say, had gripped her bag till the strap left an imprint. *I worked hard*, he'd said over and over, *what did I do wrong?* Finally, his voice bordering on tears, he'd walked her to her bus stop. She'd boarded the bus and he'd walked away without another word.

Other than that... she thought of a series of cringe-worthy flirtations, fantasies. Like the TV repair man, whom she'd called out a second time on some feeble excuse. Or the market researcher who she'd invited to a neighbours party. Or...

Other people seemed to meet their mates at work but she'd been stationed in an all-girl office. When she had met men they were sales reps who were just passing through on an overnight stop. Which meant she'd had to rush things, get to know them too quickly or spend another night without hope by not getting to know them at all. She realised now she'd wanted too much, too soon. Tried too hard, too often, for too long.

God, she'd even done her best to ingratiate herself with the hospital staff when they were treating her for the fainting spells! She hadn't flirted, exactly: she didn't know how to do that well. But smiling, asking slightly probing questions, thinking about them in her spare time: her pulse had raced so much when the male nurse took it that he'd kept telling her to relax. With her mother encouraging her to marry a doctor, she'd even sent one of them a Valentine...

She swallowed hard, remembering, and the hairdresser asked if the water was too hot. Marjorie reassured her, then returned to her thoughts. Other than her ongoing asthma, the hospital had found nothing wrong. Still the faints had continued at two a month or so, until her boss had hinted he'd be prepared to let her go.

'You're not strong enough for that job,' Mrs Milton had said, meeting her from work each evening. So she'd applied for a cleaning job on the late shift instead. The money had been less than she'd thought, but the agency had said she could do an early morning shift too at a different office block. So she'd handed in her notice and said goodbye to her computer and to the girls.

Madness. She shuddered now, remembering. She'd been feeling ill, stressed out, not thinking straight. Had had some vague notion that the hours between shifts would give her masses of freedom, that she could walk for miles, get really fit. Join a day class to learn to swim, perhaps, another in watercolour painting or photography. Meet some new people, get more out of life.

Instead... She closed her eyes against the barrage of warm water. She could only bear to think about this today because at last things were going well. The nightly cleaning job had meant she left the house at 5pm to take the bus into the city centre—all those people coming home from work, all those staring eyes and stamping feet!

At least in her office job she'd been able to hang back a little, avoid the worst of the crowds. There'd been a kind of unspoken agreement between her and her boss that she came in an hour later and stayed for an extra hour at night.

Anyway, taking deep breaths, she'd stood on the bus each night all the way to the block where she was now a cleaner. Had gone round office after office with two older women for three hours. Got home for 10pm, and went to bed, exhausted. Got up again at five in the morning to be at her other cleaning job for half past six.

There were few buses at that time so she'd walked, taking a shortcut over waste ground. That's when the man... Her stomach tightened at the memory. She'd been on Invalidity Benefit, meeting no one, ever since.

But this time it would be different—special. There was no reason why she shouldn't meet Douglas at the fish club every week. Get to know each other: that was what the woman's magazines said. Find shared interests. Let things develop naturally.

'Alright. Let's get you over to the mirror.'

Holding her stomach in, Marjorie shuffled over to the allotted seat.

'How much do you want off it?' Anne-Marie asked, holding out a lock of Marjorie's hair as if it were poisonous.

'Oh, just thinned out, and trimmed.' She paused, 'Better leave the curls over my ears now that it's November. I don't want to get the cold.'

She looked at her lap to avoid her too-large reflection. God, she looked awful when her hair was wet. Still, her breasts were big: even the svelte stylist Gordon had given them the once over. He'd cut her hair last time she was here. They'd chatted about TV and films, about the books she was reading. Maybe she should buy a blouse that would cling to her bust? She'd put money into the building society every week when she was working: she'd hardly ever gotten the chance to spend any as they had so few nights out.

She wondered what it would be like to have a man stroke your breasts, to kiss them. Nipples sweet twenty seven, and never been kissed. She wondered what it would be like to... *do it*. People thought that if you reached a certain age and were still a virgin it was because you'd chosen to be.

Which wasn't true, at least not in her case. It was like going to a disco and not being asked to dance. She half smiled, remembering. Three months after she'd left the cleaning job mum had mentioned that they needed volunteers at the old folks home. She'd gone along: it helped fill in a few hours. Pity the hothouse atmosphere had made her asthma worse...

There'd been a woman there: seventy something. And a teenage care assistant who'd gotten pregnant whilst her parents were away for the weekend. The three of them had sat outside in the garden whilst the girl had her tea-break.

The older resident had seemed amazed that her parents had been so lax.

'My own mother watched over me from morn till night, you know,' she'd volunteered, as the three of them sat on a wooden bench. 'Hardly ever met anyone,' she added sadly, 'Never had the chance.'

She'd sat back in her chair, her eyes thoughtful. She still had traces of an Irish brogue.

'We lived in a small place—wasn't even a school there. There wasn't work for many men.'

I know the feeling, Marjorie had thought wearily. Trying to think of something to say, she'd patted the old woman's hand.

'And now I'm in here.' The resident had looked round the deserted garden, 'And it's mainly women. The men just come in to die!'

The care assistant had raised her eyes at Marjorie. Both had still thought she was joking, but then her voice had dropped slightly, become more intense.

'I'm still hoping. I'm curious, girls, you know? I'd like to try...'

Looking at the dry pale skin, Marjorie had felt both repulsed and moved by the statement. It was a brave thing for someone of that age group to say.

'Go for it,' she'd said awkwardly, patting the thin membrane over the equally thin bones, 'It's never too late.'

'It's slightly dry,' Anne-Marie said, starting on her fringe, and snipping the top layer away.

'I have to cut down on sweets,' Marjorie said. The way she was feeling, this wouldn't be difficult. She'd buy clothes instead.

That night, she looked at herself in the mirror before

going out. The rich gold of her new blouse clung to her breasts and her green wrap-around skirt looked fine providing she held in her stomach. She'd bought some dark grey 10-denier tights...

Her neater hair made her eyes look bigger, brighter. Maybe Douglas would offer to walk her home tonight? Then in his own time, he would ask her out, kiss her. Months from now she might even spend the night at his flat.

Stay calm, stay cool. She was going to play it his way. Let him make all the moves—or not. He was a self-contained man, a reserved man. He might not have done it with anyone yet. Might want to take things slowly, carefully, explore her one sensuous step at a time...

Marjorie shivered with hope as she prepared to leave the flat en route for the fish club.

'Go for it,' she whispered, 'It's never too late.'

CHAPTER SIXTEEN

Breathe in, out, in, out, smile brightly. The doorman at the fish club seemed to remember her: he said hello. She sucked in her breath and entered the main hall slowly. Wished she didn't find going to new places such a terrible ordeal. What was the worst that could happen to her, Simon had asked, meaning well. Marjorie felt cold: she didn't want to know. Please let Douglas, or at the very least Michael, be there. Please don't let her sit all night on her own.

In through the door, holding her breath... She focused. *There was Douglas.* He was sitting in one of the circles of chairs, studying a book.

The chair nearest to him was taken by a small man in his sixties. The one on his far away side was free.

'How are you?' She walked to his chair, spoke quietly, calmly.

He looked up, nodded quickly: 'Fine, fine.'

Marjorie hesitated, unsure whether to take the seat next to or across from him. He held up his book, 'Just reading this.'

'Any good?'

The title was *The Complete Tropical*.

'Easy to understand.'

Maybe she should borrow it? She considered asking, decided it would be too pushy. Stepping over his feet, she sat down on the chair to the far side of him and took a notepad from her bag. She'd bought it earlier in the week for the sole purpose of taking notes during the lecture. Maybe they'd give some tips on looking after a new tank of tropical fish.

Douglas set the book on his lap, and looked at her. 'I'm considering moving on into tropical. Keeping my coldwater aquarium too, of course.'

'Of course.' She nodded encouragingly, 'Do you have lots of space, then, a big house?'

'I rent a large room.'

It was obviously a nice room, an attractive room. Leastways, he'd announced it with some pride.

'I rent a flat, but there's not too much space. And I sublet a room to Simon...'

'He's not with you this week?' Douglas said.

'No. He just came along the first time, cause I was nervous.'

'The title doesn't help,' said Douglas, 'Sounds like a club for kids.'

She knew now he didn't have any: she'd hoped as much that first time in the fish shop, watching him buy the isolation tank. They already had a brief history together, were beginning to connect.

Silence. She panicked. 'Do you work with fish?'

That was unsubtle, pushing for information. She should have just talked about his book.

'No. I'm an undertaker.'

126

She stilled, stared at him: she'd never met an undertaker before.

'Oh.' Her mind raced, came up empty. She mustn't say anything silly: he was a thoughtful, learned man. 'Have you been one long?'

'Most of my working life.' He paused, 'It's quiet, peaceful work.'

She'd been right: he wanted quietude. 'I had to give up clerical work because it was too demanding,' she said.

'You worked in an office?' He turned more towards her, 'Which computer did you use?'

She gave him brief details, wanted to mention the fainting fits, the asthma, the tests.

'Shelley at work used to have one of those,' Douglas said.

'You work with female undertakers?' It had always seemed such a man's job, somehow.

'She's the receptionist.'

He didn't say *our* receptionist, which was good. When she'd been at school, Marjorie had wanted to be a receptionist. It had seemed like glamour without responsibility, sounded good. But by the time she was sixteen her weight was well above the average and mother had said that she wasn't very strong.

'I suppose if people are upset, they want a woman to comfort them.'

'Not all women are comforting, though.'

His voice had gone lower, flatter, more distant. Marjorie considered the women she knew. She certainly couldn't talk to her mother if she was having problems. And Simon's girlfriends always seemed to look down on her, not want to be left alone with her in the lounge. The women at work had been superficially nice, but as for supportive...? He was insightful, was Douglas: he was right.

When she said so out loud he seemed gratified. He smiled almost shyly. Something expanded in her chest. Oh, to have a man smile at you like this every day or so, to have a man as confidant, lover, friend.

Someone dimmed the lights. The club leader appeared briefly on stage.

'Ladies and gentleman, tonight's film will be about understanding Oscars. We'll have a question and answer session at the end.'

Ladies and Gentleman. *That meant herself and Douglas: she was part of something*. For the first few seconds after the speaker had left the stage, she forgot to focus on the film. When she did, she saw that Oscars were big and unusual fish which stirred up the gravel and plants and ornaments in their tank. They ate greedily, then spat out half their food again, attacked their own reflections: some even made warring dives at their owner's hands.

Head facing the screen, Marjorie squinted at Douglas with peripheral vision. He sat upright in his wooden seat, staring straight ahead. When the film contained a joke, there seemed a delay between the general crowd's laughter and his laugh. She wondered if this was too simple, too basic for him. After all, just weeks after setting up his coldwater tank he was ready to move on to tropical. He was obviously reading up on the subject all the time.

'Find a reputable dealer,' said the film voice over.

Marjorie touched Douglas's arm and whispered 'They mean the likes of Michael Meer.'

Douglas flinched slightly, stared at her without expression. Then he smiled.

Later, she must tell him about the shop she'd bought

the eight fish from. She needn't admit to the purchases: just say they'd tried to pressurise her into buying more than she thought was safe. If Douglas felt he was learning something new about fishkeeping he'd keep coming here every fortnight. And she wanted to keep seeing him so very much.

The lights went on. There was a scramble towards the refreshments hatch and tables at the back of the room.

'Tea?' Marjorie asked hopefully. There'd be no Simon to play gooseberry this time.

Douglas was frowning at the giggling girls as they raced each other towards the furthest table.

'No,' he said, 'This place isn't civilised enough for us quiet types. Let's go to the pub.'

CHAPTER SEVENTEEN

Five vodka and oranges: he'd almost kissed her. They'd been laughing their way along the road after the pub. She'd stumbled slightly and bumped into his side, and he'd put out an arm to steady her. She'd sort of nestled in to him: warm flesh against flesh.

So he'd kept his arm around her waist: he felt capable. Strong yet weak, happy yet able to think. He had to keep things going, keep things... stable. Oscars dirtied their water: you had to work hard at keeping their surroundings clean.

Marjorie was clean, Marjorie was... Simon's. Simon could hurt him. Simon wore a belt.

'Got to go.'

He twisted round, and took her shoulders, prising her away from him.

'My bus stop,' she muttered, 'Just here.'

He followed her along the road, feeling safe now it would soon be over. She was going away, away.

'I've had a brill night.'

She leaned back against the wall facing the bus stop. He did the same: a brill was a fish.

'Oscar night,' he said. Detail was important.

'Great,' she giggled.

She had a nice gentle laugh.

Whine of motor. She stepped forward. Looked back at him uncertainly. He flapped his palm up and down. He wanted to bring his mouth down on her, wanted to feel her tits and grab and knead at her ass.

'See you in two weeks?'

She said it as she boarded the bus and the bus driver looked at him.

'Two weeks,' he echoed.

It seemed very far away.

Anything could happen in two weeks—*anything*. Strange and bad things happened all the time. Not the crimes of the dead, but the crimes of the living. So many people got the situation wrong. Feared death in the home, believing that family ghosts returned to await the reunion. He snorted: he'd have a lonely end if that were true. Feared possession and poltergeists and haunting, the huge question mark of the unknown.

The Ancient Greeks had believed that dead souls traversed to Hades via a labyrinth of caves. Had seen it as a shadowy place, but not one of judgement. Paul, on the other hand, believed in an active Hell, though he said little of Heaven, whereas the Christadelphians thought...

Forget the various creeds. He started to walk along the street away from the bus stop. Had learned much about belief systems yet still didn't feel any happier in his day to day life. Uncertainty was spreading its chaotic tentacles everywhere, half the world pushing for change whilst the rest laboured to hold on to what they already knew.

He, Douglas, was... well, he'd like to do both, really. Go out like this but still feel anchored to something, still feel secure.

Mad people sometimes stole their relatives from the mortuary and tried to bring them back to life with home made potions. One man had wired his mother's corpse up to the mains and tried to revive her with electric shocks. Another had tried to warm his wife's cold hard limbs with the help of his electric blanket. Occultists might try incantations which ostensibly caused the dead to walk again.

He'd check Reevon's was secure now: better safe than sorry. His mother had used that expression all the time. He'd had a letter from her today, exclamation marks and imperatives jangling over the paper. Trying to pretend he was her little chum.

Would he like anything from Oz, she'd asked, with three more exclamations. Like what, he wondered, like a quiet life? Like love, and respect, and tenderness? Had she ever, once, thought of their relationship honestly?

She was there, lying quietly, when he reached the funeral parlour. There was, he thought, lifting her, a certain majesty in death. Though her eyes were closed, her lips were slightly parted, inviting. Her skin was already tinged with the faint blueness of neglect. Sweetly suspended, she was so wonderfully receptively waiting for him. *I'm here*, he whispered, lowering her to the table, *I'm here*.

CHAPTER EIGHTEEN

Rubbing, rubbing... Marjorie winced as the fish flipped its body against the gravel so that its side rubbed against the small, rough stones, causing a clanking sound. Could the poor creature have fish lice? She stared through the glass but could see nothing foreign against its flanks. Did fish even have flanks, come to that? At this rate she'd need a *Fish Are Fun* meeting every day.

She sighed, turning away from the aquarium, and going over to her armchair to reclaim her library book. Would it really be two whole weeks until she saw Douglas again? He'd rushed off very suddenly when her bus came. Still, she knew where he worked, the area in which he lived.

With an effort, she stopped her thoughts, redirected them. She was doing it again—rushing the pace.

'Let's find out what's wrong with you,' she said, addressing the fish tank, 'Let's hear what Michael has to say.'

Michael, as usual, said little but what he did say was helpful.

'This book on common fish ailments should help you identify most things,' he said, going over to the paperback stand and pulling it out. Marjorie tried to keep her smile friendly but platonic. If only there was a way of letting Michael know that she wasn't going to pursue him any more.

She flicked through the index, started to look up the sections dealing with irritants.

'Could they have whitespot?'

'Or leeches,' said Michael, 'They might even just be irritated by your water quality.'

He offered her a little bottle of medication, which claimed to treat a number of tropical problems.

'Reckon I should buy it in bulk?' Marjorie asked with a nervous laugh.

Then winced inwardly: maybe that sounded heartless. It wasn't that she didn't care about her fish: she did! Had gone to the Central Library, only to find that most of the fish books were out on loan.

'They're incredibly popular,' the girl at Enquiries had said. So she'd filled in postcards for three separate titles and given the woman the stamp money for them. They'd notify her when the books came in.

Meanwhile she'd use up some of her Invalidity Benefit to buy this one. 'See you at the club?' she asked lightly, handing over the money for the book plus the fish medicine.

'Hope so,' said Michael. It was great being so casual. She no longer cared if he went or not. The main thing was, she'd see Douglas there. They'd probably go on to the pub again and then...

Taking the long route home, Marjorie smiled to herself, and hummed a song from the radio. If her fish got well and Douglas asked her out, her happiness would be complete.

CHAPTER NINETEEN

By the time a person had been dead for three days, a greenish colour often spread from the area above their groin to their stomach button. By the fourth day this could spread up to the chest and down to the tops of the thighs.

'We should start calling this the Green Room,' said Terry, as Douglas began to prepare a slightly jaded man in his eighties. In Ancient China, the corpses of the rich had been encased in costumes made of jade...

This, though, was modern Scotland. Coffins and body bags were stacked on the floor of the Chesting Area, their inhabitants the victims of the flu epidemic now reaching its height. The phone rarely stopped ringing with the promise of further carcasses. They were all working overtime most nights. 60% of Britain's dead died in hospital, 40% of the deceased were buried, the rest went to the flames.

This one had died from some sort of infection, Douglas realised, studying the torso. The old man's veins were bluish brown, standing out in relief against the papery skin. Odorous pus encrusted his orifices. Watery blood seeped through his nostrils and coloured his lips.

Still, he'd seen worse—much worse. A week from now the belly would be distended, gases moving about. The eyes would start to bulge, the tongue swell and harden. By week three the entire cadaver would be bloated, decomposing within. Yet, to the last, a trace of sexuality lingered in the females, for though the breast tissues separated, the uterus remained recognisable for a year or more.

'Needs a bath in disinfectant, this one does,' said Terry, breaking into his thoughts again.

Separate to the cadaver, Douglas could smell his own and the other undertaker's fresh sweat scent. He breathed in again, noting the scent of brandy from either his own or the other man's breath, shrugged his shoulders, and grimaced: 'Don't we all!'

Terry looked at him sharply, and Douglas willed himself to stare back at the older man. After a few seconds, Terry turned away: 'Hope this flu's finished by Christmas. I don't want to stuff anything more than a turkey on the 25th.'

Christmas. Turkey. Douglas made a mental note to buy himself one of those frozen chicken dinners and a frozen trifle or something. He'd have to put them in the back of the freezer where Eleanor Denning couldn't see. Otherwise she'd insist he join her for some home cooking. Crackers and carols and cavorting round the tree.

Nice, this year, not to go through the make-believe hell of a happy family Christmas. Nice to read and eat and sleep when he wanted with the companionship of his fish. Maybe he'd buy himself a special bottle of brandy: he'd recently acquired a taste for it. Well, his working day at the moment was exceptionally long and the nights were cold.

'Next,' said Terry, grinning as they placed the old man

into his veneered hardwood dwelling. A lady in her sixties took his place. There'd been two children this week, a boy of four and a girl of six and a half who'd succumbed to the virus. Better, perhaps, that they were spared the pains of adolescence and adulthood.

Douglas hummed the latest Christmas song as he washed off the ravages of illness and perspiration. In days of yore they'd done this to cleanse the departing soul. The Old Testament dictated that the corpse and all who approached it were unclean. Paul had just hated Douglas's job.

Still, it was an important job, a necessary job. Without people like him, bodies would rot where they fell or be abandoned in the streets. Once paupers had been thrown into mass graves which weren't properly covered. Disease had spread and spread.

Anyway, even less sophisticated creatures sometimes buried their nearest and dearest. Elephants had been known to cover their dead with branches and use their feet to scrape soil towards the corpse. Some even laid fruit next to the departed, or, like humans, brought gifts of flowers to their dead.

Next in line to be prepared was a lady in her seventies. She looked comfortable on the Prep Table, her features steady, serene. Hard to see spirits as malignant when you looked at her in her timeless slumber. In all his years of dealing with the dead, he'd never felt chilled, far less been possessed or haunted. He'd never been afraid.

Afraid of the living, perhaps: of Terry's humour. Of Adrian's advanced vocabulary, of Reevon's success in life. Afraid, too, of the cloyingness of Eleanor Denning. Of Val's vivacity, of Michael's extensive knowledge of fish.

Douglas sighed as he helped Terry slot the latest coffin into the coffin frame. Demands came at you from all sides in this life. The days were as uncertain as ever, but recently he'd begun to look forward to the nights.

That was the great thing about drinking in your room or with someone like Marjorie. It made late night overtime such a hazy pleasure and afterwards you felt incredibly relaxed. Too relaxed, perhaps, he chided himself. Afterwards it was sometimes difficult to remember which bodies he'd been working on.

CHAPTER TWENTY

The Calico Fantail was chasing the Red and White one around the tank again. As it was December, this signalled mild aggression or was just for fun. In Summer their activities might take a more erotic, or at least biological turn, for the male fish chased the females into the plants in the hope that they would spawn.

Douglas shook his head, turning away from his aquarium. He'd decided not to encourage the fish to breed. That is, he'd let them produce eggs and scatter them over the plants and surfaces as nature intended. But he wouldn't buy a breeding tank in which to rear the potential fry. Trapped within the artificial confines of the aquarium, the parent fish would soon eat their own eggs or even the embryonic babies. Life would return to normal again.

He sighed and reached for his vodka and orange. The alternative was to change the status quo, set up a fry tank either on its own or within the larger tank. But then you had to feed the fry carefully, measured drop by drop.

If you put in too much food—known as infusoria—you polluted the water and killed the babies. If you didn't put in enough, they starved. And you were supposed to go through a selection process, culling the weak and poorly-shaped ones by feeding them to your adult stock. Much more interesting, instead, to set up a tropical tank and buy bright new occupants. Already his second aquarium was maturing, getting ready for such warm-water fish.

Still, the weekend stretched before him, hollow, hateful. In the past few months he'd done everything he needed to do to make this room look good. Plus he'd read copious amounts about coldwater and tropical fish, and visited Michael's shop so often that they were on first name terms. He'd keyed reams of notes onto his computer disks about matters piscine. And now...?

Douglas wandered round the room examining its contours. It was only Saturday teatime: the DIY shops didn't close till 8pm. Plenty of time to go out for materials to build something. He looked critically around, assessing what he might need.

Nothing. The answer was nothing. He could go outside anyway, but he always felt aimless just going for a walk. He wanted the satisfaction of feeling he was doing something. He wanted...

... to go to the launderette. He stared over at the curtains: Val's curtains. They'd been on the window when he moved in, their light blue fullness complimenting the large, airy room. But by now they'd been up at least four months, which meant they needed washing. He'd get them done straight away.

Feeling positive again, Douglas strolled over to the wooden chair that sat behind his computer desk. Carrying it over to the window, he stood on its seat. Inhaling softly, he edged the material away from the curtain frame. Looked down, and gasped.

Breasts in a cream or white bra appeared sideways to his line of vision, set atop a slim, unseasonably tanned waist. For a second he stepped back, almost lost his footing. *Look, look* he chided himself, *she doesn't know that you're there*. From his usual position standing on the floor, he couldn't see into this particular window. Now, standing on his chair like this, he had a bird's eye view.

Of nipples with heavy, rouged-looking aerolae. As he stared she unhooked the bra and he saw them both, imagined their softness. She sat down at her dressing table, still clearly within his view. Pity she was wearing that knee-length skirt. He wondered what shape and size the panties beneath it were. He decided they'd be white and transparent, moulded to her ass.

Some girls wore briefs that were cut high in the leg, showing the length of their thighs up to their hipbones. He'd seen underwear of all descriptions in Reevon's over the years. Silky French knickers were favoured by some of the classier women. He never failed to enjoy edging them down.

As he watched, scarcely breathing, she reached for something on the back of her chair and put it on, a fawn or ivory-coloured bra with straps as thin as ribbons. This one seemed to be lower-cut, to show more of her cleavage, pushing it pertly up. Swallowing, he pressed his nose against the fast-misting glass. Felt his groin jerk.

Disappointment weighed his stomach as she covered herself with a lemon blouse, buttoned it up to the neckline. Leaning towards what was presumably a mirror, she started to put some form of makeup on.

Show over. Though he watched for long, long minutes, nothing more happened. She was presumably changing to go out for the night. He could go out, too—maybe sit in the same pub for a while, close by her. Exciting to study a woman, knowing what she wore beneath her blouse.

Occasionally unhooking part of the curtain in case anyone was watching, he continued to stare into the woman's window as she perfected her make up. About ten minutes later she disappeared. Had she just stepped from his sight to the other side of the room, or vacated it altogether? It was more likely that she'd left the actual flat.

Letting go of the material, Douglas hurried to unhook his jacket from the wardrobe door. He wouldn't introduce himself or anything: just follow at a distance watching the way she walked. Then, maybe when he came home, the gods would be kind to him, and he'd have that special dream. The dream from which he woke, feeling breathless, the one which brought him tension-ebbing release.

Hair neat, clothes pressed, teeth cleaned. He didn't need to look in the mirror again: he'd been staring at it on and off all day. He'd been trying to see what Marjorie saw in him. She really seemed to like him, she did. She'd touched his arm in the fish club in the intimate darkness. She'd smiled at him a lot in the pub.

The pub! He hurried down the stairs towards the street, towards adventure. Men could go alone into pubs: Terry did it all the time. He wished now that he hadn't been so dismissive of Alice for drinking alcohol. Now he'd really tasted it, he understood how she felt. That hot, wild energy, followed by that sure, strong calmingness. Just remembering its mad rush made his thirst grow and grow.

A bachelor, out for a drink at the end of a long week heavy with overtime. He looked up and down for the girl but she was gone. Maybe she'd hurried along the road, to the place which ought to be his local? It was about time he gave that pub a try.

As he pushed the door inwards, he tensed up, ready for the pulse of the jukebox. He'd hated the pop songs, shouts and overlapping laughter when in the pub with Reevon or Marjorie for the night. But after the second or third vodka the background backed away even further. Even the laughter and loud voices didn't seem so bad.

No noise. Not many people. A long vacant seat against the further wall. As he reached the bar, the barmaid smiled, smoothing back her shoulder-length hair.

'Nice time for a peaceful pint, eh?'

'Is it always this quiet?'

She obviously misunderstood, thought he wanted action.

'It'll get better! The afternoon drinkers have gone, and it'll be an hour or two before the evening crowd comes in.'

Nodding, he ordered his vodka and orange. When she gave him his change, she smiled again: she seemed nice. *Say something, anything*. His mind was blank, but for those earlier breasts and unseen buttocks. Turning towards the seat he'd seen earlier, he crossed to it and sat down.

The barmaid had nice breasts also—firm, pert ones. When she reached up for another glass they moved with her arms. Her waist wasn't as slim as his neighbours had been: but then this girl looked older. Her buttocks were hidden by the height of the bar.

White buttocks. It would be nice to stare at white buttocks. Buttocks in which the cold blood hadn't pooled and congealed. He gripped his glass, surprised to find that he had finished it. There was a hot, raw feeling in his throat.

'Same again.'

He felt good saying that. Adrian said it. Terry said it too. *Show me your breasts lifting again, show me your buttocks.* The barmaid looked at him as she handed over his drink, and he blushed.

Sat down quickly, drank it just as rapidly. Felt braver when he went back for a third.

'Rough week?' she asked, accepting his fiver.

'They all are.'

She seemed to be looking at him more intently now, more seriously. Standing by the bar, he gulped down his third drink. He'd go someplace else, somewhere he wasn't being spied upon. He'd look for that girl who'd showed him her tits.

He walked for a while: the streets were surprisingly quiet. Ignored two pubs with signs saying Merry Christmas: it was only about the 5th. The third bar he came to said: *Try our question machine.* He would, had a good grasp of general knowledge. Loved reels whirling, pressing buttons, the controlled clatter of coins.

'Can you give me ten pences in my change, please?'

The words came out confidently. He paid for his vodka then took it over to the machine.

When did Rock Hudson Die? Who wrote Hollyoaks? It was all trivia, just TV and film stuff. Nothing about psychology, inventions, nature—academic things. Alice should be here he thought sourly. He'd go elsewhere for another drink.

There were a lot of pubs in Edinburgh, once you started walking. He lurched down to the city centre, found a take-away in Rose Street that sold chips. Ambling along, eating them, he eyed the girls in their mini-skirts and elfin leggings. Thought of high-cut knickers and low-cut ivory bras.

The bars were getting busy, now: men shoulder to shoulder. Women clutching tiny shoulder bags, staying close to their friends.

'I'll have a pint, love.'

'Fill her up, again, darlin'.'

He listened to the other men ordering. When it came to his turn he said 'A vodka and orange, please.'

Next time he'd say 'love', just the way Terry said it to Shelley. Next time...

A different pub at the other end of Princes Street. This one wasn't crowded out to the door, so he went in.

'Bacardi and coke,' said the woman in front: it looked tall and dark and refreshing. When the bar man nodded at him, he ordered the same. It was a hard word to say, was bacardi. Somehow the syllables didn't want to leave his lips.

A couple were dithering about in his way as he turned to search for a seat that was vacant. The woman backed into his stomach, then jumped away. Someone said 'Careful,' and glared at him. He wondered where the half-naked girl was now.

Totally naked, maybe. With some man in some bed being felt up. The half-cups of bra would be lying on the floor with her scanty briefs. She'd lie still and open her legs. She'd...

'Anyone sitting here, mate?'

He looked up at the two men pointing at the space beside him. They were big man. They were rough man. They could hurt.

'No.'

Finishing his drink in a gulp, he stood up, edged past them. He wanted to find the girl.

Going downhill, now, past the St James Centre, past

the concert-holding Playhouse. Past shops and restaurants and second hand shops till he realised he was in Leith. Alice had had a boyfriend here once, before Paul came along. With the drink flowing, Leith could get pretty wild. He looked into each bar as he passed: people were herded round, holding out fivers. There were lots more men than women.

Women, women. He had a drink in a pub, crossed the road and had a drink in another. He'd talk to that women if he could find her, tell her how beautiful she'd looked. The sight of her standing, arms behind her back as she undid her bra clip, was superimposed over his imagination. So quiet, so fleshy, so good.

'Can ye move up the bus a bit?'

The voice said the words twice before he realised they were addressed to him. He looked up. She was small, forty-something, with curly black hair, a lipsticked half-grin.

'Sorry.'

His voice sounded different, as if coming from the ceiling.

He edged himself closer to the window, wondering what she meant by a bus. He was in a pub somewhere, was having a drink like Terry did. He squinted into the room through the smoke.

'Hell in here on a Saturday,' she said, and sat down next to him. Her knee rubbing his, her hip against his hip. He looked down at her purple skirt, then up at her yellow V-necked T-shirt, her choker chain. Her make up was purple too, the lipstick plum coloured to almost match the eye shadow. Her tights were tan, shoes black with long thin heels.

'Yer not usually in here, are ye?'

He shook his head. What day was this? Saturday. On Saturdays he usually made improvements to his room. He looked up. She was staring at him, seemed to be expecting something.

'Fancied a change,' he said, gripping his glass.

He downed its contents: the burning rush wasn't happening any more. He felt kind of sleepy, kind of numb.

'I could use another as well,' said the woman, putting a hand on his inner thigh. And suddenly he was electrically, insistently awake.

'Want me to get them?'

He nodded, not sure if he could stand up any more. She stared as he took out his wallet, handed her a five pound note.

'What's your fancy, love?'

Fancy... she wanted to know about the stillness.

'What're you drinking?' she prompted.

'Bacardi and coke.'

'Mine's a gin,' she said, going off towards the counter. When she came back, he could smell it on her breath.

'Doing anything special at Christmas, then?'

She put some money in her pocket.

He shook his head.

'Same here. It's for the kiddies, really.' She gulped her gin, looked at the empty glass, looked at him. 'Fancy another?'

Fancy. Another. His bladder felt distended. When he looked at her queryingly she put her hand on his knee, painted fingernails splayed. 'Reckon you've had enough for the night!'

Night. Enough. A girl in a bra, girl without one. Now with her hand on his body, stroking up.

'Want a good time with me?' she asked quietly.

He nodded. He'd spent too much time alone in his room with a book.

When she stood up, he stared at her buttocks. You could see the swell of them beneath the tight skirt, but not the dividing crack. He liked trousers better: they clung to the hips more insistently. He'd seen so many buttocks and breasts and bellies over the years.

'I've no got all night, ye ken!' When his eyes travelled further upwards, he realised she was holding out her hand to him. She grasped his fingers in her own bonier ones, half pulled him to his feet. 'You'll think Christmas has come early,' she muttered as he hung back a little, unsure how to break through the crowds. She pushed forwards, still holding his nerveless hand.

CHAPTER TWENTY ONE

Outside. Darkness. Crisp clear air. He breathed in, glad that the smokiness had gone.

'Not long now,' said the woman, still leading him. 'Just down here,' she added after a few minutes, 'Mind yer step.'

You could step up the coffin frame to reach your desired one. You could...

Broken windows. A half-unhinged shop door. Stairs leading down to them.

'I remember when this wee store sold a'thing,' she said.

A'thing. What thing was she talking about? He blinked, almost stumbled, almost fell.

'Save yer dancin' till ye see what I've got for ye! We'll go through the back here,' she explained.

Feet feeling blindly, he shuffled through the near dark building behind her. Came out into another room, with old newspapers on the floor. Moonlight glowed its way in through glass smeared with windowlene.

'The bed's over here, love,' she said.

Bed. Sleep. She took hold of his jacket at the shoulders, but he shrugged her away from him. Other than as a little child, no one except himself had taken off his clothes. Alice had always been in too much of a hurry to button him up properly, so he'd learned early. She'd bought him slip-on shoes so she didn't have any laces to tie.

'Ye'll be comfier,' the woman wheedled, trying again.

'No... don't.'

'All the same tae me,' she said, shrugging, 'You're the boss.' He swayed a little and she turned him sideways, 'Lie down. We're awa' frae the street here. Ye'll be alright.'

He sunk back, stretched out on the mattress. She knelt, one knee to each side of him, smiled and smiled.

'What would ye like, pet?'

He'd never said it out loud before. Thought about it endlessly. Still and silent. Tranquil, tame.

'French or straight? It'll cost ye more without a condom, though.'

He couldn't think. Couldn't answer.

'How much dae ye want to spend?'

He blinked.

She sighed: 'Ten, twenty?'

'Twenty,' he mumbled, eyelids closing down.

'Ye can give me that now.'

Give her twenty... twenty. When he sat up to get his wallet, his groin moved against hers. *Softness. Warmth. Female Parts.* He jerked and swelled down below.

'Maybe ye'll gie me a tip after if I'm especially nice tae ye?' said the woman, putting a hand over the pulsatingness. With the other she tucked his twenty pound note into her shoe.

Nice. Nice. He was nice to all his women: thoughtful, caring. Yet none of the others had touched him like this. No hand had ever wrapped itself around his manhood and squeezed gently. Even the few times when the sensations had gotten too much for him, he hadn't touched himself down there. Just pushed against the mattress or his pillow. Just...

He felt his zip go down, bare flesh against his flesh. She wasn't just stroking him through the material. She was holding him close. Sliding something onto him, then spitting on her hand and rubbing it against her crotch. Raising her hips and looking down, and murmuring.

'No!' he said, 'No!'

Her head jerked up, and she stared at him: 'Just relax. Take it easy.'

'No... no.'

'It'll cost ye extra without it, ye ken.'

Without what? He didn't know what she was talking about.

'Don't talk,' he muttered, 'Lie still.'

'Ye'll need tae go on the top, then.'

She stared at him some more. All the heat and need were going. Then she climbed off him and went on to her back and parted her thighs.

Stay. Stay. He put his hands on her breasts through her T-shirt, and they remained immobile. *Stay. Stay.* Her skirt was already up around her waist, showing stocking tops and wonderfully naked thighs.

No panties. He hadn't known if his ivory-bra clad girl wore panties. His flesh swelled, and he nudged forward, and went in. Wetness. Warmth. She seemed to close around him. Her very being seemed to be spiralling arousal through his cock.

Yes. Yes. Thrust harder and harder and harder. Knead breasts, clutch waist, grab clumps of unresisting hair. She whimpered slightly: just escaping gas, he told himself. He reared back, then forward. Push and push and push.

And came, crying out, face buried in her shoulder.

'Ye needed that, love,' she said with a low snort.

Her voice shocked him, demanded a response—something. Erection shrinking, he pulled out of her, rolled over till he reached the floor.

Think. Think. What was her name? Who was she? Where was this street, this house, this room? Sitting on the dusty boards, he stared at the polish-smeared window, wished he could see out into the area beyond. He sensed her moving, felt her touch his jacket-clad shoulder, nails scraping down.

'Ye enjoyed yersel. Ye said ye'd gie me something extra,' she said.

Extra. Something. He turned round and looked at her: she was pulling her T-shirt down. They'd had sex, had sex. He would give her anything. Fingers clumsy, he took out his wallet, went into the note section. He had just five pounds left.

'I'll need to get to a Cashline machine,' he muttered, unwilling to leave himself penniless.

She raised her eyes. 'That's dead handy.'

Her mouth twisted up at one corner. She was upset, enraged. Where was the nearest machine? Where was he? He realised he couldn't remember his number, felt afraid.

'Got to go!' He stood up. The ground seemed to shift almost imperceptibly. He wondered if he should ask to see her again. He'd never had a girlfriend before.

'That makes two o' us, mate,' the woman said, walking smartly towards the door.

Wait, wait. He followed: she was a moving blur ahead of him. Through another room and out onto some steps, leading up. By the time he set his foot on the first step she had disappeared from his vision. He could hear her heels tapping swiftly along the street.

That same tapping made him falter, hang back a little. Heels could hurt as they came crashing down. And that noise, too: on and on like a rock beat. He'd had to plead with her not to speak.

Let her go, let her go: she'd been noisy, jerky. A man shouted somewhere in the distance, a dog barked. The street was full of shadows, of recent urine. What time was it? He looked at his watch, found a bare wrist with faint strap marks on. He'd worn it till recently, then. It could have fallen off back there...

He looked back, at decay, at dampness. The building smelt: why hadn't he noticed it before? Five pounds: was five pounds enough for a taxi? He wanted to be alone, in his room, with the door locked tight.

His nose started to run and he put his hand in his trouser pocket and brought out his handkerchief. Found two pound coins and some silver: now he had more than enough for a cab. Slowly he started to move up the street, keeping to the outside of the pavement. Within a few minutes he saw the familiar hulk of blackness, waved it down.

'Where to, sir?'

He thought hard, almost gave Alice's address, then remembered. No Paul now, no Alice. He gave his new area, followed by the name of the street.

'Just missed the pub's comin' out,' said the driver cheerfully. That put the hour at 11pm or so. Funny, it felt like 2 or 3am.

Home, home. It was all he could think about. He wanted a cup of coffee to clear his head, a long soapy bath.

'That'll be six pounds,' said the driver, drawing up outside the rooming house.

The note and coins were damp and hot in his hand.

Relax, relax. He let himself into the quiet house, wishing all the lights weren't on. He wanted soothing darkness, he wanted to hide away. He tensed on each stair, waiting for Eleanor Denning to appear and ask him about his evening. She'd probably heard his cab drawing up outside.

Almost, almost. He reached the near-sanctity of his threshold. Slid his key into the lock, slipped quickly into familiar surroundings, shut and locked the door. His body was crying out for attention, wanted to do everything at once: eat, drink, bathe, think, sleep.

Quickly he refilled and plugged in his electric kettle. Settled for a quick sponge-wash at the sink in his room whilst it came to the boil. Then he struggled into his familiar, beloved dressing gown. As soon as he'd had some coffee, he'd get a clean towel and sneak to the bathroom next door. He hoped there was lots of hot water: he wanted to stay there for a long, long time.

Heartbeat beginning to slow, he made and sipped the hot, sweet mixture. Lay on his bed, and gazed at his mostly-sleeping fish. Soothing the way they stayed, immobile, in the water. Reassuring the way they rested at the same place on the gravel every night.

He made a second coffee: his head felt less hazy now, his vision clearer. He could vaguely remember buying chips, but felt ravenous all the same. Reaching out to the biscuit tin, Douglas picked out an almond thin and nibbled it delicately. Starting to feel better, he gnawed at a second and a third.

Now, at last, he could face the landing bathroom—could even face Miss Denning. Nicer, though, if he didn't have to, could be alone. Humming quietly, he picked up his key, his towel, his shower gel. Went next door and ran a full hot bath.

And lay in the bubbles, occasionally adding to them. Feeling his mind settle, feeling the dirt and tension leave each limb. He was thirsty now, wanted a long clear glass of water. Going back to his room, he poured himself one from the tap.

Sipped it, had another then made himself a tomato sandwich. He'd have liked cheese, but kept it downstairs in the kitchen fridge. He didn't want to venture out again to uncharted territory. He was feeling so much better now, here in his room. He wondered if every night would be like tonight from now on. He wondered if all women would prove to be so accommodating as his new friend.

CHAPTER TWENTY TWO

'Slow down a little—you hardly know this man!'

'I know all I need to,' Marjorie said.

Simon looked again at the scrap of paper forming her bookmark. She'd scribbled *Marjorie & Douglas* and *Mrs Douglas Tate* all down one side.

He sighed, wishing he hadn't picked up her reading matter. The mag he worked on was running a series of emotional features, so he was reading a text on women who loved too much. If he left it lying around, Marj might just get round to flicking through it. She wasn't big on self analysis, though, let alone analysing anyone else.

Like Douglas. The man had taken her to the pub one night after the fish club. She'd come home drunk, let slip he hadn't seen her home. Since then, he didn't seem to have asked her to go for another drink, let alone for a premeditated date somewhere. Yet she was just as keen.

And probably heading for a let down. He, Simon, would have to rebuild her confidence if this man backed away. He loved her as a sister, as a pal—even a surrogate mother. Sometimes, between relationships, he wondered if she could ever mean something more.

But no, he was basically too honest to start something sexual. He'd be using her, or pitying her: he could never marry a Marjorie, live a domestic life. But lots of men would want to, would welcome it. She needed someone uncomplicated and sincere.

Someone who wanted children quickly, and liked to watch TV of an evening. Someone who didn't mind if the gravy was burnt. She'd cook and clean and talk, and not expect much in the way of presents and compliments. Just his being there would be enough.

She'd never had anyone special in her life, and she was twenty seven. He sighed. It was so much harder for women when they were shy. They couldn't just walk into pubs to make friends and influence people. Well, they could—but the recipients tended to get the wrong idea, to pounce. He sighed, studying Marjorie surreptitiously. He suspected she was still a virgin, or pretty close.

One of life's unclaimed treasures, as his mother had said—as her own mother would say, come to that. But surely human beings didn't have a *best before* date like supermarket goods? He suspected she'd be one of life's late developers. From the little she'd said, she'd already come a long way since school.

At least she tried to start up conversations, no matter how awkward she found them. Offered people coffee, always spoke to her neighbours on the stair. There'd been a girl worked on *Stella* once who never said a word to anybody. It had grown exhausting, felt pushy always having to make the first move.

If only he dared get Marjorie a job in one of his firm's offices. She'd been a good secretary before... before she'd cracked up. Just a touch of nervousness, but her mother had worked and worked on it. Convinced her she couldn't cope, a form of learned helplessness.

It was hard to piece together everything, with Marjorie being loyal to her mother. But it seemed that Mrs Milton had fussed over her daughter's ongoing asthma, made Marj's timidity worse and worse. So she'd fainted a few times, and Mrs Milton had convinced her she couldn't cope with secretarial work, had got her doing cleaning jobs instead.

Marjorie as a cleaner: it didn't bear thinking about. Marjorie had been good at word processing, at filing things neatly, at answering the phone. Suddenly she was getting up at odd hours and trekking about pushing industrial vacuum cleaners, had swapped her navy blue skirts and white blouses for an overall and a scarf to keep the dust from her head.

Then there'd been some kind of incident. She'd given up the cleaning, gone for what she called 'a board'. It seemed to have been some kind of assessment panel which agreed she couldn't hold down a job due to the asthma attacks. Now, every so often, she had to go back for a check up and got into such a state that she couldn't breathe properly, was allowed to stay on Invalidity for another year.

Another year of putting on weight, of becoming increasingly afraid of the world. Another year in which Mrs Milton could wreak havoc with her life.

Simon stared at his flatmate thoughtfully. Funny how it was always the small people that did the damage, the Mrs Miltons who'd lived a cramped, restricted existence. The young, who hadn't been searching long but thought they knew all the answers. The religious, who lived by the book instead of embracing life. Yes, the people with the most limited vision made the most noise, however empty-sounding. And the Marjories were confused and deafened by the din.

On television, a crop-headed woman was talking about femininity, about relationships. Simon leaned forward, ready to mention the self-analysing book.

'Douglas said that not all women are comforting,' said Marjorie, responding to the speaker. And there was such hope in her eyes that he had to look away.

CHAPTER TWENTY THREE

Splayed thighs and kneadable breasts: he couldn't stop thinking about them. Usually he enjoyed the Monday return to work but now the nine to five routine seemed pedestrian. All his mind could focus on was what had happened on Saturday night.

I met a woman, he thought, *I lost my virginity... fucked her*. He shivered, bit the top of his pen till his teeth met through the plastic cap. He was allowed to take his pleasure with a girlfriend: *Paul had gone, Paul had gone, Paul had gone*.

'Eviction pending, is it?' asked Adrian, resting a buttock on the corner of the table.

Douglas looked up from his form-filling. 'What makes you say that?'

'You were looking worried—nervous.'

'Things on my mind.'

Like brownish nipples that hardened when you put your fingers over them. Like a flat belly that you squashed against your own. He could do it, do it—if only they stayed still enough. He could knead and thrust and push and pull and spurt.

'Stationer hasn't delivered those forms,' said Shelley as the postman handed her several letters. His blood quickened. Damn! He should have mentioned them before.

'They came by van earlier. I put them under the desk.'

'Lucky I didn't phone and complain,' said Shelley, staring. He willed himself to stare back, and failed.

Still, tonight he'd relax, spend some time in quiet contemplation. He'd come back here after tea to see his girls. Recently he'd felt better after a visit to Reevon's. Just to sit there silently digesting a double brandy, holding someone's hand. It made the evenings more companiable, more rounded. He'd spent too many nights alone in his room whilst Alice and Paul watched TV downstairs. Now he could go out for the evening without them asking questions. Could stay out all night if he so desired.

That teatime he was so excited he couldn't concentrate on the book he was reading. Abandoned his onion pizza after eating the third slice. No bad thing: he'd put on weight since Paul and Alice left: his shirts felt tighter. He wasn't eating more, so maybe the drink was to blame. Either that or his metabolism had slowed because he was calmer and more assured.

Smiling to himself, he hurried down the stairs of the rooming house, noting that the hall clock was chiming 7pm. Eleanor Denning appeared behind him, and shouted something. Quickening his pace even further, he called back a quick hello. Dashed out of the front door, and down the path, listening to make sure she didn't follow suit.

Loathsome woman. No one would ever want to cup

her buttocks, pull her legs apart. No eager eye or hand would trace her body from waist to hip and back again, would willingly remove the buttons from her cavernous garments, would want to buck and thrust.

The December streets were in darkness, people hurrying to do their late night Christmas shopping. None of them looked twice at him in his long black coat as he let himself into work. If anyone *was* there he'd explain he'd come back for his *Tropical Answers* book. He'd left it in the Prep Room's wall-mounted cabinet just in case.

Not that he was doing anything wrong: never, never. He was a good man, a thoughtful man, a man who kept himself to himself. He just needed to... see his girls, to check on them. Make them feel less alone—well, whatever of them that remained.

Shivering lightly, he walked to the coolness of the Chesting Area. Hunkered down towards the coffin at the foot of the frame. The youngest here today, she was, a well-preserved fifty. A strong face with a Roman nose and a chignon of iron grey hair. Very middle class: the kind of woman who wore well-cut fawn trousers and a tailored brown cord jacket, the kind of woman who owned gardening gloves and a terrier and a car.

Stomach trembling, he edged her coffin out, put it on the trolley and wheeled it to the Prep Room table. Lifted her up, out, laid her gently down. Looked at her cold sad waxiness and felt a curious disappointment. Felt an emptiness, felt horribly bereft. For long moments he stared at her, seeking something he couldn't put a name to. He wouldn't find it here. *Go. Go.*

He packaged her up and let himself into the street again, the tightening feeling increasing in his forehead. Usually he felt peaceful by the time he left here, even dazed. Two women walked past, clingy suits padding them out in all the right places. He could imagine the glowing, warming, living flesh beneath.

He wanted a second woman, or the one he'd met in Leith again. Craved creamy skin, eyes that had lustre and depth. Wanted wetness without wordiness—pliability. Wanted someone that wouldn't fidget but was fresh.

Mind roaming, Douglas began to play 'what if?' games. Imagine being able to preserve a female at the moment of death! Her limbs would stay tender, life-like, movable. Yet she wouldn't laugh and shout and move her torso around. They'd have fun, but there'd be no fear attached. No fear.

He walked on, musing fancifully. Preservation in alcohol caused shrinkage and loss of colour in the flesh but formaldehyde would stop putrefaction for two months or more, which was a step in the right direction. An exciting step.

He smiled to himself, imagining the ever-ready body. *If only there was a way to keep a warm woman at home.* He'd read that arsenic could preserve the limbs and vital organs even within the dampness of the graveyard. He wondered if there were other methods waiting to be explored.

CHAPTER TWENTY FOUR

'Guess what I'm going as?'

A whore. A tramp. A geisha. A good time girl. He stared at Val, at the pushed-up wantonness of her cleavage above the white mesh top. The red skirt of her dress stuck out around her as if it had been starched, betraying her slim thighs. Her shoes were matchingly sparkly and small. Red stiletto heels pressing furiously into the carpet, strange leaf-like shapes stuck over each toe.

'Surprise me,' he said.

She did indeed look surprised: he must sound different. Blame it on night after night in a smoky pub. But there was little else to do during the stretching Christmas holidays, least not when you lived alone in a single room. He'd finished work numerous hours ago on the 20th. This, amazingly, was only the 23rd.

'I'm a fairy, of course!' If Terry had been here he'd have risen to the situation. 'It's a fancy dress party,' she added with a grin. She opened her eyes wide, inviting comment.

He smiled: 'Enjoy.'

Enjoy flaunting your tits, enjoy wriggling your ass, enjoy showing your legs to thigh-level. Mouth tasting of copper, he turned away.

He'd try the hair of the dog: just go back to his room and get his coat and wallet. He'd only come down to the hall table tonight to see if there was any mail. He'd forgotten earlier: had spent the day in his room decorating the tropical tank. He'd ordered four Indian Glassfish from Michael, was expecting the shop to get them in stock any day. They liked lots of plants and rocks and dark-coloured gravel, did Glass fish. He'd provided all three.

'Hang on—I'll show you something,' said Val, and giggled foolishly. He stepped backed a little, came up against the banister of the stair. He could smell sweet sherry on her breath: he half-hoped she'd offer him a glass or two. Amber heat.

Dashing through the doorway that led to her quarters, she came back a second later waving a silver stick with a lop-sided star on top.

'I'll give you three wishes,' she fluttered, 'Eleanor made this for me.'

Leave me alone. Drop dead. Make it January 3rd right now. He was shocked at the sudden rage inside himself.

'I wish I was in the pub,' he said, twisting his mouth into what he hoped was a smile. Vodka or bacardi slipping down, down, down.

'Spoil-sport!' laughed Val, and her earrings swung against her cheeks, and away again. She tossed her head and smirked at him and tapped his shoulder with her wand. He wanted to hit her across the face, knock her sideways. He wanted to grind her into the ground.

'Got to go,' he said, turning on his heel, beginning

to mount the stairs. Heard Eleanor Denning's door click shut.

The bitch had been watching him again—they were all watching him! Watching and flaunting, and giving him nothing at all. Tension: they gave him head-gripping tension. Made him look away, made him shudder, made him sweat.

He went to the pub and sweated some more, surrounded by mixed groupings. Most looked like office parties, celebrating Christmas with mistletoe and wine. Office juniors clicked on pointed heels, older women jangled charm bracelets and beads made of plastic. Stay still, still, urged the voice in his head: he fed it bacardi and vodka but it refused to quieten down.

'Cheer up. It might never happen, mate,' someone said lightly. He wasn't their mate, that was an Alice word! She'd written again this week: she was always writing. She said more to him on blue paper than she'd said in a lifetime spent living in the same house.

Paul sends his love, she wrote. *Liar, liar*. Paul had never once shown him any love. Nor had Alice, for that matter: not I'm-interested-in-you kind of love. She'd patted his head when the neighbours were watching, had been briefly mumsy when some new boyfriend expressed an interest in kids. Had liked the idea of having a son, perhaps, but not the reality. Had given him a football or boxing gloves for Christmas and birthdays every year. When he was older he'd saved up his paper round money to buy himself a Lego set, cheap camera; the things he really wanted. He wouldn't have cared if she couldn't afford them: if she'd only asked.

Screw her. He went up to the bar and got another drink. We haven't seen a koala bear yet, she'd added, in her big, sloping hand. Had she even been looking for one? She was so hopelessly vague.

A teenage girl across the room whispered something to her pal and they both looked over and giggled. He wanted to outstare them. He wanted to make them afraid. Drained his glass instead, using it to hide the flush starting up from his collar. The wrong word could get you attacked, get you killed.

Hauling himself out of his seat, he walked heavily to the door, stepped into the icy darkness. Walked on through the expectant streets till he found another pub. This one had a video screen: drum beats, guitar sounds, red and blue images. Still, most people stared at it instead of staring at him. He got another vodka, found a big torn armchair, perched warily on the edge of it. Held his hands closer to the fire they had roaring in the grate.

'It's hot in here,' said a voice. He tensed, looked up, trying to formulate an answer. But its owner wasn't speaking to him, was talking to her friend. As he watched, she pulled her cowl-necked jumper off, which briefly forced her vest top up her midriff. She smoothed it down again, revealing spirited young breasts.

He wanted someone, wanted, wanted, wanted. His body felt transfixed with unused energy, with the strain of holding himself in check. Slowly he walked up to the bar, pushed over his empty glass. 'Fill 'er up, please,' he said.

He might as well stay for a while: he had few decent options. He could go to Reevon's, but nowadays it wasn't the same. He'd gone back to Leith three times, scoured its streets, searching, searching. She'd lain still for him, hadn't spoken a word.

But she was gone, gone: just like Alice had gone. He'd had a Christmas card with a kangaroo from her, the only one apart from Marjorie's that he'd received. She must have got his full address when they'd all signed a petition to stop big business polluting the waters. He'd filled in his details then handed the form to her. Nice that she cared enough to commit his details to memory. Nice that someone cared at all. There'd been little written on her card, but it had been affectionate. The walls of the pub felt like they were closing in.

Same with his room these days: he couldn't settle. Wanted more, more—sighed and thought and paced. Amazed that he'd spent all those years in his childhood cell, whilst the world beckoned. Drink and women and sex and women and drink. He looked over at the girl, sucked in his breath, wondering. Then she laughed loudly at something her friend said and he looked wincingly away.

Laughing, wiggling, jangling. They always spoilt it. Heels flailing, coming down on you in agonised spikes. From magic wands and wishes to the blackest betrayal. They'd take your skin, your watch, your hope, your soul, your heart...

Go. Go. He drained his glass, new scorching added to the internal fire. Stood up and lurched out into the unrelenting cold. Just walk, walk: get away from so-called civilisation. The pubs were busy, but the streets were getting quiet.

He'd been wandering for a while when he first saw her. Grey-stockinged legs disappearing into a coat the colour of grass. Of summer grass, that was: the kind bikinied girls stretched out on. The coat swung loosely above the knee, was held at the waist by a buckleless tie belt.

He stared at her legs as he began to follow her. She kept stopping, looking up at the street names, crossing back and forth. Finally she pulled something out of her clutch-bag and came to an abrupt stop. Twelve feet behind, he slowed right down.

Now what? He didn't want to walk past her. Trailing her had given him a purpose, helped the emptiness inside. He wouldn't do anything of course: just imagine. Just look at her legs and ankles, and pretend. Unless she took his hand and led him to a mattress and splayed her thighs apart like in his waking dreams. They'd been real for a night, though—they'd been solid. Like the... *girlfriend* he had foolishly let slip away.

'Excuse me.' He stopped at her words, tried to smile, look friendly. His mouth burned with the vodka, his eyelids felt dry and tight. 'I'm looking for this street,' she continued, pushing a piece of paper towards him, 'I can't find it on the map anywhere.'

'I think they renamed some of those roads.' His voice sounded fine, considering.

'That explains it.' She laughed. He hoped she'd take his hand.

Take the tension, take the neediness, take the energy. He needed someone amenable: he needed her.

'So do you know where...?'

He blinked: his mind drifted on ahead. She was frowning slightly.

'Sorry. Late night last night!' he explained.

'Oh, I see.' People forgave you quickly when you were a pub person. That's probably why Terry could chat up Shelley, why Adrian got away with going home late to his wife.

'Just keep going along this way,' he said, pointing straight ahead of her, 'It's at the other end of the park.'

'Oh. You mean I've to cut through it?' She hesitated slightly, 'Isn't there another way?'

'Only if you take the long route round and that'll add at least half an hour to your journey. But the park's always busy, well lit.'

It wasn't: it was a shifting mass of branches and leaves and shadows. He crossed one leg behind the other to avoid swaying, admired her face. When they got there maybe she'd step closer to him for protection. She might touch his arm. They'd lie down...

The girl pursed her lips: full, pink attractive lips. Strands of her fair straight hair were periodically lifted and spread out by the wind. A spatter of rain fell on both their upturned faces, seemed to settle it.

'Straight ahead, you say?' she repeated, turning to move on.

'I'm going that way myself.'

Again the slight pause then she started walking. He increased his step to keep up with her. His throat felt clogged.

'Party, is it?'

Alice used to come home from her shopping trips with men's addresses scribbled on her shopping lists. She always said it was details of a party. A party a deux...

'Mmm. Girl at the office.'

They went in through the park gates: she moved her clutch bag to the other side of her.

'We've had ours,' he said.

For the first time he'd gone to Reevon's Christmas bash: he'd always claimed illness or conflicting agendas before. He, Reevon, Adrian, Terry, Shelley and the cleaning woman had taken two taxis to a restaurant straight from work. They'd eaten beef madras and hadn't done the Hokey Cokey or anything stupid. It hadn't been as bad as he'd feared.

Terry told lots of jokes and the others groaned loudly. Reevon had given them all an envelope containing a fifty pound note. Stumbling along, Douglas wished he was back there after the New Year. At work he knew how to act, what to do, what to say...

'Your party—was it fun?'

She had a nice voice, did the girl, though she spoke much too quickly. She seemed to gulp air at the end of her sentences: he knew what that was like. Was his party fun? He sucked in the chill air, tried to think clearly. It was the only party he'd been to: he had nothing to compare it with. Fun was what Alice sought: something high-pitched and artificial. He shrugged awkwardly. The girl increased her step and they hurried on.

Her breasts were bouncing beneath the coat now: he could see them. She probably wanted him to look, like Val had earlier tonight.

'Watch you don't trip,' he said, as she went over on an ankle. He put his hand on her arm. She pushed him away.

She must want steps to a basement or something equally secluded. Go through the back here, his lover had said, no one will see.

'We've got the place to ourselves,' he said confidingly, scanning what little he could see of the shady driveway. The girl broke into a run.

He followed, glad that she was so eager to accommodate him. Between them they'd find privacy, a space of their own. His limbs felt weighted, like they had in his dreams throughout childhood. Entering her body would soothe all his tension away.

Thick hedges three feet from the main walkway of the park, forming a triangle. For a few seconds, he only vaguely registered them, their shade. His new friend hadn't noticed at all, for she was running past them. They mustn't let this mad yearning ebb away.

'In here,' he urged, lurching forward to grab her by the shoulders. She seemed to collapse back into him with a squeaky sigh.

Buttocks against his stomach, thighs pressing against his thighs. He reached round to cup her breasts, pulled her back into the thickets where they'd be safe. Lowered her to the ground and put his arms on either side of her, waited for her to pull up her T-shirt, scissor her legs.

For a second she just lay there, eyes screwed tight, mouth a grimace. Then she opened her eyes and mouth and screamed and screamed.

'Christ, don't!'

He put his hand over her lips, pressed the screaming inwards. Paul would kill him for saying *Christ*.

'I need quiet... quiet,' he muttered, shivering, trembling, 'Please—stay still. Please.'

He could feel her lips moving against his palm with difficulty. Maybe she wanted to apologise—he could understand that. If she said sorry he'd forgive her. Then she'd lie back and he'd push forward and the tension would go away.

He rocked back on his knees, letting go of her.

'Aaaaaaaaaaaaaaaaah!'

The shriek went on and on, Even when he gagged her with his hand again, he could hear it reverberating round the park, through the darkness. *God, don't, don't.* He pressed down, and she arched her body up, and her button at the throat burst open. It was then he saw the cross.

A crucifix, on a silver chain, just like Paul used to wear. *Paul could hurt, Paul could hurt, Paul could hurt.* Paul believed in Jesus and Paul was mad and often angry.

Staring at the symbol, he pushed down, down, down. He watched, fascinated as the pale flesh bulged slightly. Must be all that hypocrisy and half-understood dogma coming out.

Calm and controlled and compliant and caring and comforting. After a while she went that way, let him edge up the material over her knees. Her eyes stared unmoving at a point beyond his head by the hedgerows. He'd seen eyes like that before...

But this body was warm and pink-tinged, the limbs pliant. He edged down cotton briefs over warm, pulsing limbs. Hiccupped a few times, bringing vodka and orange to his throat and mouth: liquid sourness. But the apprehension in his gut was fast fading away.

To be replaced by a tension downstairs, that manly needing.

'Stay still,' he warned, moving his flesh inside her flesh. His new girlfriend didn't move: she was being good now. He wouldn't let this one get away.

Thrust and thrust and thrust—this was perfect. She was so helpful, keeping her arms by her sides. Hateful to have arms round your neck, trapping you. Hateful if she'd wrapped her thighs round his back like they did in some of the girlie magazines.

A girl could do anything whilst she had you in such a vulnerable position. Worse if she had a boyfriend, a violent man... But this girl had given up a party to be with him. This girl had agreed to become his in the park.

He moved and moved, torso taking over. Forget Val's tits, the girl in the pub's midriff—this was it. If she would just see him once a week or so, and they could do it like this, cause silent sensations. He'd had such a pleasureless life...

This, though, was Nirvana—the ultimate! A second session after years of looking at photos and wondering what it would be like. He looked at her breasts, spread out through gravity, and rubbed them. Came with a whimper, then looked guiltily around.

No one. They were alone in the park, hidden under bushes. Slipping out of her, he lay down by her side. Rest, rest... too much drink and walking and aquarium decorating. Too much thinking and throbbing about the female form.

Eyes closing, he put his head on her breast, feeling safer. She'd done what he wanted. She'd wanted to please. Now they'd just curl here for a while, a silent thank you. For a few more moments he could be at peace.

He awoke to hear sparrows chirping, a flurry of larger wings. He must be a little child at the zoo. Alice had taken him there once, with one of her boyfriends. Alice and the man had kissed and held hands all day. She'd told Douglas to go on his own to the *Touch A Terrapin* talk. She'd told him not to poke his head through the bars.

He opened his eyes. Saw orange-blue sky, leaves and branches. Turned his head, saw... He scrambled away. God, she was dead, dead—he'd know that colouring anywhere, had seen so many mouths loll open that way.

She must have frozen to death: hypothermia was very common. Belatedly he realised that his own arms and legs felt stiff and chilled. Pain twinged through his back: his right hand was swollen. The girl's face was bruised around the mouth.

He had to get out of here, get home to his room, to safety. He got to his knees, reached for some branches, pulled himself half-erect. Pins and needles worried at his ankle like an army of ants. Some species tidied their dead away into the deserted chambers of their nests. *Home, home: have a bath, have a coffee, have breakfast.* His thick black trousers felt chilly and patchily damp.

He staggered out into the grassy section of the park before it occurred to him that someone might see him, get the wrong idea. Thankfully there was no one around. But in day-time the place was usually full of mothers with children. People of all ages walked their dogs...

Vaguely wondering if there'd been some huge disaster, Douglas began to hobble towards home, towards the rooming house. After a few minutes his circulation came back. *Home. Home.* He walked faster, concentrating on the movement. Soon he broke into a run.

He turned the corner and almost catapulted into a small man carrying a dirty green satchel. The man nodded: he wore a cloth cap on his head. He must be going to work... but no, this was Christmas Eve day. Did people work then at... at 5.30am?

Checking his watch for the first time, he realised why it was so quiet. People were sleeping off the rigours of yesterday's late night shopping trips. Adrian had said his wife always shopped till she dropped. Maybe the girl had also been overdoing it at the shops? Some teenagers over-exercised as well, forgot to eat or decided not to: he'd washed and dressed their emaciated forms.

Slowing down to a trot, he went on, on, on till he reached the rooming house, let himself in quietly, slipped equally noiselessly to his room. Closing the curtains, he tore off his clothes and replaced them with his dressing gown. Grabbed his toiletries and towel, slipped next door to the bathroom and had a bath.

At 7am he went down to the kitchen and boiled himself two eggs. Everything was getting back to normal.

He sliced the top off the first egg, put it aside to cool so he could feed it to his coldwater fish. Soon he'd go out to Michael's shop and pick up some tropical granules. After all, the place would be closed from tonight till around January 3rd.

As he left his room at a quarter to nine, Eleanor Denning emerged from her quarters.

'Not long now,' she said and added 'I've got a chicken in.'

'That's nice.' He felt so calm and safe he almost loved her, 'I'm just going out for some more biscuits,' he said.

Biscuits and fish food and intelligent conversation with Michael, then maybe a light lunch, and a much needed sleep on his bed. God knows how much rest he'd gotten last night, lying on the grass like that. As Alice would have said: 'You're lucky you didn't catch your death...'

Death. The girl was dead. His girl. Yet she hadn't really been right for him: it had been a momentary fling. She'd picked him up in the street, the way Alice used to attract total strangers. She'd just gone to sleep in his arms, the ultimate rest.

He walked down the path, remembering. She'd worn a crucifix: shades of mind-control, shades of Paul. She'd lost her way, was noisy and complaining. She'd breathed funny and shouted and pushed and yelled. By the time he reached Michael's shop he realised she'd been lucky, really. With so much lingering disease about, a natural death in the park was the kindest way.

CHAPTER TWENTY FIVE

'... And then dad insisted on playing his old Louis Armstrong records,' said Simon. He'd come back an hour before, to find Marjorie finishing off a chocolate Santa Claus in front of the TV.

'Douglas said that people use music as an escape from thinking about things,' she murmured, turning round and grinning at him.

Douglas would. Though tempted to make the comment, Simon fought it.

'So, how was Christmas lunch at your mothers?' he asked.

'Uh, same as usual.'

Marjorie slowly unpeeled the foil from the chocolate hat. Which meant bland, boring: she'd obviously had a highlight-was-the-Queen's-speech kind of a day.

Not that his own had been much better.

'God, it's great to get back to normal,' he said, yawning exaggeratedly and stretching out on the settee.

For the first time since he'd moved in, Marjorie

didn't stare at the way his ribs moved beneath his shirt and make him feel uncomfortable. She didn't look at him wistfully. She didn't sigh. The tension had gone from their relationship, he admitted, since she turned her attentions towards Douglas. She totally accepted he, Simon, as platonic for the first time.

'Anything exciting happen while I was away?'

He expected an answer in the negative. Marjorie shifted her position slightly. Something she considered news was obviously coming down the line.

'Well, after you left for your Mums, I went to Michael's.'

He hoped Michael had asked her out—the man seemed honest, hard-working, sincere.

'Oh?' He propped himself up on one elbow, looking interested.

'Douglas was there. He asked me to go on with him to the pub.'

'And did you?' It was a rhetorical question.

'Thought I might as well. I wouldn't get the chance to talk to anyone else until going to mum's the next day.'

Ouch. She was still capable of the occasional guilt-making one liner. That was a none-too-subtle hint that he could've taken her to Newcastle with him for the Christmas break. She'd gone on well with his parents both times they'd visited him here at the flat. But then his mother got on well with most young women. Except...

'Nice pub?'

He wondered if she was still too nervous to notice. When they'd gone in a group to restaurants she could never recollect the decor or paintings if he mentioned them the next day.

'Big. It was noisy.'

'I didn't think fishkeepers liked noise?'

'We don't. Douglas hated it.' She ran her fingers through her heavy curls, 'We walked for ages to find this quiet place instead.'

'Where was that, then?'

She named a downmarket area. He winced inwardly.

'Did he see you home this time?'

Again the hesitation. 'I caught a bus. We were too tired to walk.'

'And are you seeing him again?'

'Of course!'

He opened his eyes wider, more expectantly. When she didn't offer further details, he knew that Douglas hadn't arranged a proper date.

Still, he'd taken her to the pub—that was something. Though women like Marjorie preferred a little cafe instead. Or even one of those restaurants that sold pizza and fried haddock. He hoped Douglas hadn't been trying to get her drunk.

It was easy to get Marjorie drunk: she drank so seldom. No nights out with cocktails before the theatre, no friends houses to go to for regular glasses of wine. Sometimes he took her to the cinema or to The King's Theatre. Two cointreau's in the bar beforehand and she'd start giggling away.

'Have a hangover on Christmas Day, then?'

'No, I was sensible.'

That meant they hadn't stayed long. Had Douglas something better to do?

He looked down at the carpet, wondering what to ask next. Hard not to sound like a disapproving father worrying about his little girl. But then Marjorie hadn't had a real dad in her life for long—he'd died years and years ago.

From what little she'd said, he'd gathered the man had been a shadowy presence at the best of times, a figurehead sleeping in his chair. Mum was always the organised one, Marjorie had said on more that one occasion. Yes, Mrs Milton had definitely ruled that roost long before widowhood came round.

'Douglas doesn't really celebrate Christmas.'

That was the great think about Marjorie: she told you most things, unasked, if you stayed silent for long enough.

'Was he going to his parents, or...?'

'No, they emigrated to Australia a few months back. His rooming house is having a party, though, in their communal lounge.'

It was difficult to imagine Douglas at a party. Not that the image of his features was still sharp. But that voice, dispassionately measuring, analysing, stayed in Simon's head like a bad record. So little humour, so little humanity there. The man was liable to know the calorific energy needed to pull a cracker, the industrial cost of making a paper hat.

People like that gave so little to life, to relationships. Better to be emotional, to he warm. Not too sensitive, though, or the world could overwhelm you. Not easily hurt like...

... like Jo, he acknowledged with a sigh. He thought of her more than ever when he'd been home to Newcastle for a holiday. The memories jangled in, piece by discordant piece. The tiny scratch mark where her photo had sat for years atop the seldom-played piano, the space next to his on the Welsh Dresser where her graduation pictures would ultimately have been. Only she'd never gotten beyond second term of first year, had dropped out in the most spectacular way.

Just another new University student taking a while to settle down to things—that's what his parents had told themselves when she'd turned up unannounced a month into her first term. Lots of students probably made the four hour train journey home to mother at this stage, driven by a sudden burst of homesickness. Lots of students took a while to adjust.

After a few weeks, though, his mum had phoned him. He'd been living in London at the time, an editorial trainee on a twenty-something's mag.

'We see more of her than when she lived at home, Simon. She should be making friends down there. It's not good.'

So he'd driven through to Newcastle, as if for an impulse visit. Acted surprised to find her there, instead of in her University Hall. Her face had grown rounder, blotchier in the eight weeks since he'd last seen her. Still, collegiate food wasn't ideal.

'No parties this weekend, then?'

She'd shrugged, looked awkward.

'Studies alright?'

She'd gazed down at him sadly, perched, as she was, on the edge of his chair.

'Well... the lecturers talk too fast sometimes. It's not at all like school.'

'It's not supposed to be. Don't aim to copy the entire lecture—just write the key words down.'

He'd been there, adjusted, he'd told himself. Everything felt strange at first.

'And my room's like a cupboard.'

'What did you expect—the Ritz?'

Not meaning to be cruel, of course: he loved her. She was the baby of the family, taking a little longer than was usual to fully grow up. But he had to help her enter the wider world, integrate with it. They call it tough love, his dad had said that Sunday afternoon, taking him aside for a moment. So Simon had waved as their father drove a glassy-eyed Jo back to the station. Thought 'one day she'll thank us for sending her away'.

Only she hadn't grown up—had grown away from them. Fewer letters, fewer calls: they congratulated themselves on their success. She's obviously made friends, dad had said on the phone, she's liking the work better. Maybe she's joined a few clubs or met a young man. So mum got her weekends alone with dad, just as she wanted. And they went for drives and replanted the garden and...

... and then the phone call came. *Don't think about it. Don't think.* That hellish phone call. His parents had received two visitors then dad had dialled him at his rented London flat. 'Simon. It's dad. Your sister's... the police came round.' He hadn't been able to finish, had cried and cried. His uncle had phoned back to explain that Jo had hung herself, self-strangulation in a corner of that hated student hall. She'd planned it all in horrible DIY detail: bought the rope from a hardware store, tied it to the outside door handle, fed it through the gap at the top of the door into her room.

He shuddered and Marjorie glanced curiously at him then returned to her TV movie. He almost wished he'd seen the body: the reality couldn't be worse than the snapshots in his head. Horror-movie images of blackened faces, lolling tongues, eyeballs bursting out of sockets. Not his little sister, not his Jo. Suicide happened to other families: dysfunctional families. Jo and dad and he had always been so close.

Okay, so mum hadn't coped so well with teenage

moods and clothes and contraceptives. She'd clung to her ideal of flowery dresses and nice boyfriends who just held hands. Jo had preferred jeans and had gone on the pill when all her friends had. 'Just in case,' she'd said, which to their mother's rigid generation was a promiscuous lie. So there'd been tears and tantrums on both sides, a bit of door-slamming. But nothing had been bad enough to make them think she'd take her own life.

If only. If only he'd been there for her. If only he'd taken a month off work, taken her to the Students Union, made sure she got in with a suitable crowd. He was good at talking to strangers: a journalist had to be. He could have chatted away her shyness, brought out the best in her, made them love her too.

Or just listened more, realised her terror was growing. Supported her, made her understand that she wasn't alone. If he'd told mum and dad she'd be best dropping out they'd have believed him. He'd always been the mature one, the one who didn't take chances, who buckled down. They'd have realised he had a younger persons view of the situation. They'd have known if he recommended she quit that she was doing the right thing.

Instead he did what they all did: made light of it. Sent her jokey cards and teased her when she came back for weekends.

Weekends were terrible when you were in a place you didn't want to be. Later, when Amy joined the staff at *Stella*, he'd seen that. She'd been an editorial trainee, one of several his employers took on at the same time. The others had been put on various middle market and retirement titles. Amy had wanted to work on an older women's magazine but as she was only seventeen they'd put her on *Stella* instead.

In retrospect, that had been a mistake. She was an old fashioned person, a girl who'd grown up in a small Fifeshire village. A girl who knew more about making jam and exploring the countryside than she did about fashion and makeup and boys. But the other editorial staff knew lots about boys—about men, really. Knew lots about most things, even if they weren't always the things that should matter most.

He could still remember overhearing a conversation between Amy and two of the others on her second day at work.

'Coming to the bistro, Amy, for lunch?'

She'd looked up, seemed slightly startled. His back to them, standing at the filing cabinets, Simon had listened to her response.

'I... yes, I'd like that. Mum made me up a packed lunch, but I can have it at night for my tea. She won't mind.'

'Unhygienic things, anyway.' This from Gwenda—a big girl, a brash girl.

'Why...?'

'Think about it! Cheese or chicken wrapped in clingfilm all day in a plastic box. In the heat of an office, too... a germ trap. We always eat out.'

He'd stared at the metal cabinet, feeling angry. Looking for a natural opening where he could make some remark to Gwenda, make her realise how cruel she could be.

'What do you drink anyway, Amy?' Gwenda's voice again.

'Oh, just tea.'

Laughter. Quite a few of them were laughing. The editorial assistants were all grouped round in a big oblong:

sound tended to carry across the room. People worked, half listening to others conversations. Laughed when a joke which appealed to all came along.

'I meant cocktails, actually.' Gwenda was half-laughing, half-sneering.

'Oh. I don't... I'm only seventeen.'

'I used to have hangovers at twelve.'

Someone else's voice—it sounded like Trisha's.

He turned round, looked at them all till they looked back at him and looked away.

He'd gone back to his desk, then, beginning to understand more and more what it must have been like for Jo. Had cornered Amy before she went home that night, saying he'd show her how to bring house-style guide-lines to a freelances work.

'Settling in alright?'

She'd nodded, pale blue eyes somehow blank beneath unstyled fair hair. Already this wasn't the girl he'd interviewed, the excited teenager whose vocabulary and ability to make plays on words had impressed both his employers and himself.

'I know it's difficult,' he'd added, thinking *I didn't realise till now just how difficult*. He'd tried to keep the intensity from his voice, knowing he mustn't frighten her further, make her feel singled out. 'Some of the older girls—they, well, they can get a bit full of themselves. It's just bravado, really. It's only a couple of years since most of them left home.'

She'd looked surprised. 'They seem so much older. And they know all about which belts and necklaces to wear and everything.'

'You can pick it up from the magazine—from other magazines—if you're really interested.' He'd sucked in his breath, 'But don't let them worry you, change you. Be yourself.'

He'd known even as he spoke that the words were hollow, that she'd have to become like them or remain in a corner alone for however many years it took the others to fully grow up. You could only be different in a place like this if you had masses of self esteem—and Amy didn't have the kind of panache that would carry it off. She was a wren in an eyrie of eagles. They'd crush her for breakfast and move on to larger prey for lunch.

The next three weeks had played out like a slow horror film. *Don't let her do what Jo did.* He'd watched out for signs, unsure exactly what he was looking for, day after day. Watched her shoulders grow more rounded, watched her take a deep breath that caused her upper body to tense up as she walked in the door. Watched her flinch every time someone addressed her. Watched errors begin to appear in her work.

He'd smiled whenever she looked his way until he thought his face would break. That brittle smile. Those almost nightly friendly chats. He'd had a word with the editor about transferring her to their retirement title. The fifty year olds on the staff would mother her, she'd be safe.

'No vacancies there,' the editor had said after making a phone call. So she'd stayed and eaten her packed lunch alone, holding her plastic lunch box on her lap under the desk. Had sipped tea and read a magazine whilst the others drove into town to have their lunchtime cocktails. Had worn a white jumper and black skirt when low slung jeans and hooded tops were in.

And oh, the misery, the misery. Downcast eyes, a patchy complexion, a voice that hesitated on the simplest reply. And his own inadequacy, his terror. What could he do? Say? How could he make this situation turn out right?

It had been a relief when she left—walked out in tears one lunchtime. She'd been there six weeks: he felt he'd aged six years. Hadn't handled it well, hadn't handled it at all, really. But at least she'd had the sense to quit the job rather than quit Earth.

'Sleepy?'

He opened his eyes to see Marjorie looking at him.

'Unrested. It's an antique, my old bed.'

Once after he'd said something like this there would be an awkward silence, an awareness of Marjorie in her small corner and him in his, but thankfully, these days seemed over. Even if nothing ever came of it, Douglas was the love object for now.

He sighed. Marjorie's fixations always left him free to bring home girlfriends. She'd be chatty and friendly to them providing she had her own dream man to bring into the conversation as often as she possibly could. She was happy as long as she had some doctor or handyman to lavish her affections on. She certainly seemed hell bent on lavishing lots of them on Douglas now. Wondering if he should ask Sue to dinner at the flat, introduce her to Marj at last, Simon again closed his eyes.

For a moment he mused, then he pushed his girlfriend from his racing thoughts. Much as he liked Sue, he'd not bring her here for a while. Unfounded though it might be, Douglas as Marjorie's would-be lover made him feel uneasy. He still wasn't convinced things were quite right.

CHAPTER TWENTY SIX

Mouths and fins and scales and skin and fingers. The blonde girl was going to touch the octopus: it grinned and grinned. Douglas tried to tell her no, that it was toxic. Found he couldn't concentrate, couldn't move, couldn't speak.

So fair of flesh, of hair, of limbs, of everything. She leaned forward, denim tightening against high, curved buttocks, emphasising a concave stomach, long, lean thighs.

'Cute little thing,' she murmured. Douglas whimpered as she stretched out twenty or thirty fingers to tickle it. Paul appeared above Douglas's head with a Bible. Douglas shrieked. The girl laughed at him, and continued laughing. The tentacles glowed blue, seemed to form teeth.

'Bad.' He tried to back away, but Paul could come from any direction.

'It's only a little pet,' said the girl, 'You're a big boy now.'

Big, big... he was growing bigger. She'd be sorry she

hadn't been his friend. She was holding the little creature in her palm now, half-lifting it out of the water. Were they at the seaside? Or the zoo? He couldn't think.

Heard the shout, though: outrage, not fear: 'The damn thing's bitten me.'

Paul should hurt her for swearing like that. Paul should pull her pants down and touch her private parts and... He imagined her secret, velvet places. Big, bigger, biggest at the thought.

A bead-like blot of blood: he watched it ooze from her. She opened her mouth again: 'It doesn't hurt.'

Her voice sounded metallic now, as if played through a machine specialising in sound effects. Slowed, like an ancient gramophone winding down.

He stared as her arms stopped flailing, as her fingers stopped wriggling, wrists static. She let her hands trail at her sides, legs immobile and openly inviting. He thrust in. *He was safe, safe. She couldn't hurt him. The octopus had stopped her tongue: she couldn't tell Paul or anyone about what they'd done.*

He opened his eyes to find the pillow flattened beneath him. Damp with his secrets—the type of thing Paul might find. He whimpered, closed his eyes again: think nice thoughts, clean thoughts, good thoughts. Paul was miles away. It was only a dream.

But what a dream! Could a—what was it again?—an octopus really paralyse a woman? He'd heard jellyfish could and sting rays and the like.

Still shaky, he levered himself carefully into a sitting position. Stood up equally slowly and gathered the undersheet in his hands. He'd put it in his laundry bag now, take it there tonight after work. He'd put a clean sheet on right away.

By the time he was finished changing the bed it was 8am. Shrugging on his dressing gown, he hurried to the bathroom hoping Eleanor Denning hadn't gotten there first. Whatever kind of work the woman did seemed to have flexi hours. Some days he'd try the bathroom handle at 7am and she'd twitter 'Only me!' from behind the steam-leaking locked door. Other times he'd go in as late as eight thirty and the lack of warmth and dearth of spilled talcum powder showed she'd still not been in.

Forget her. Check out the dream. Stepping into the bath whilst the taps were still running, Douglas soaped himself thoroughly, returned to his room. As his electric kettle boiled, he made up a quick cheese spread sandwich. He wouldn't bother making toast: it would give him more time to read his book.

Adaptivity. Bull frogs. Captivity. He ran his hands down the index of his *Oceanic Overview*, wondering what category his creature would be in. Ah, there it was—a tiny paragraph on toxic types. The blue-ringed octopus was mentioned: he must have seen it as he was browsing through the pages yesterday. Yes, it could paralyse—as could various other creatures of the sea.

Or the aquarium. He paused, and closed the book noiselessly. Not that anyone would want to keep such a thing. Still, he could find out more: knowledge for knowledge's sake. It would be something new to key into his data base.

As he passed through the hallway, he saw Eleanor Denning rummaging through the newly arrived letters. 'Nice morning,' he said brightly, and walked on before she could start a lengthy reply. Walking to work he whistled quietly. Though the morning was cold, his daydreams kept him warm.

CHAPTER TWENTY SEVEN

'This one's mega!'

Sometimes Terry used the language of the school playground. Sometimes he used the language of the gutter, too.

'Oh?'

Douglas cringed at the sound of his own voice. It sounded thin and disapproving. He wished he had a vodka rather than a pen in his hand right now.

He turned back to the cremation form he was filling in and ringed another two boxes. No, the deceased did not have a cardiac pace-maker. No she didn't have an implant, radioactive or otherwise.

'Made my Christmas, meeting her,' added Terry, who'd been talking to anyone who'd listen about his new conquest. Douglas nodded. He'd met some women over the holidays himself...

He forced back the thoughts, thoughts that were blurred and shadowy. Women in pubs or leaving them had... given themselves to him: it was the natural way. He was a man, and men slept with women when opportunity knocked. He winced inwardly again: that was the kind of expression Alice used.

The airmail that had arrived from her today still lay unopened in his pocket. He'd skim through it after he'd had lunch—a pub lunch. Staying in his room all day these past two holiday weeks had become boring so he'd gotten used to pub lunches and teas. He'd varied the venue, walking miles across town sometimes. People weren't surprised to find a man having a quiet meal out after the Christmas rush.

'Divorcee, works in a bakery,' Terry continued. For once he'd lost weight over one of the vacations, his black waistcoat no longer bulging out at the front. He winked as Douglas looked up at him, 'Only part time, though. Loads of energy left, if you know what I mean.'

He wouldn't blush—he wouldn't. Women weren't unknown to him any more. Terry wasn't the only one who could have sex, even if he did have the benefit of an easy chat up line.

'Have fun,' he said, picking up the Registration of Death form.

'I'm bankin' on it,' Terry said, and grinned.

'Banking on what?'

Shelley propelled herself through the glass door, high heels efficient, eyebrows arched menacingly.

'A good time,' said Terry, staring at her hips as she clip-clopped past. She was always so brisk, so horribly brittle thought Douglas, watching too. When she came by Terry again, now clutching a cardboard folder, he put his arms round her waist and pulled her against him, 'Although if you were free I'd never look at another woman, of course.'

'Nutter!' She hit his head very lightly with the cardboard file. The thin pink cotton of her blouse lifted with her bosom. She opened her eyes wider: 'Did you enjoy your hols?'

She'd finished the sentence before Douglas realised it was directed at him.

'Em, fine.'

'What did you do?'

Do? When? Oh God, she was staring again in that 'you're pathetic' tight-lipped sort of a way. Blood was rushing to his face, his neck, pounding through his airways. People expected you to say that you went to your parents or had a friend round. You couldn't say you were entirely alone on Christmas Day. *Think quickly. Say anything. Just get the pressure turned off.* He cleared his throat quickly then coughed into his handkerchief.

'We had a party in our communal lounge.'

To his relief, she looked away from him, flicked at Terry's bald spot. Eleanor Denning's wishful thinking had come in useful once more. He'd mentioned that mythical lounge to Marjorie, to Terry, to barmaids in public houses. They smiled then and talked of other things.

'Not too much kissing under the mistletoe, I hope.'

He started to say 'Just a little', mixed the words all together like he did when he was drunk. Remembered Val's legs, the deep shadow of her cleavage in its fairy dress moving just under his nose...

'In a world of his own, that one,' said Shelley, in a loud whisper, making eye contact with Terry. Wasn't he, Douglas, supposed to see or hear her? A pulse began to beat drily at one side of his head.

Forget women for now: concentrate on the deads calm despatch. He bent his head to the forms again, looked up as Adrian came hurrying in.

'Told you I could do it in an hour!' Adrian said, holding out his hand to Terry. Grinning, the older man gave him a fifty pence piece. The others had little bets and inside jokes like that all the time, Douglas thought wearily. Something in his stomach dropped downwards, like it did in a lift.

'I come bearing gifts,' Adrian added, starting to open the larger of his two carrier bags.

Terry grabbed the smaller one, hauled out a nightie, whirled it around.

'For Marie's birthday,' Adrian said patiently, trying to snatch it back from him.

'*Your* birthday, more like,' Terry whooped, holding it against his chest.

Thin ribbon straps led on to a baby-doll style body which looked short enough to skim the top of a woman's thigh. The neckline had tiny red satin hearts clustered round a deep V. The rest of the garment was black.

'I've booked her a set of driving lessons as well,' Adrian said, taking the nightie back and shoving it into the bag again, 'And ordered flowers.' He'd gone slightly pink, was no longer looking at them. 'This is for you lot,' he continued, bringing a small board with some wooden blocks and triangles from the bottom of the bag.

'I'd rather have Marie in that nightdress,' grinned Terry, examining the wooden puzzle.

'This was in the sales,' said Adrian, 'I thought it'd keep you amused during quiet times.'

What quiet times? Douglas picked up another form and began to transfer information to it from the telephone message pad. Still, it was good to keep busy. As Paul said, the devil made work for idle hands...

'So, you taking Marie out or what?'

'Not till the weekend.' Adrian's voice held a smile in it, 'I've got in prawns and Chinese vegetables and wild rice. I'm cooking for us both tonight.'

'Aha, a quiet night in—just you, she and the nightdress.'

'And wine and chocolates,' said Adrian, obviously fighting to hold back a laugh.

The pain in Douglas's temple spread over to encompass the centre. He'd be doing his laundry tonight, whilst they...

'Did you have a nice holiday?'

Other than a hurried hello as they passed in the corridor, this was the first time Adrian had spoken to him all morning.

'Yes, fine, thanks.'

Lonely. Dull. Afraid.

'And you?'

He tried to smile at his friend, but his jaw felt stiff and grim-looking.

'Quiet,' Adrian said, putting the nightdress bag away in his locker and pocketing the key.

Quiet for Adrian meant just his wife, his parents, an aunt and uncle. Quiet for Terry meant the football team not getting into a fight in the pub.

Two hours to go until lunchtime, until relaxation. He thought about asking the others to join him, but ultimately slipped off on his own to the bar across the road. It was too hard to request their company after years of eating his sandwiches alone in a corner of the office, or on the paint-chipped wooden seat two streets away that always caught the sun.

'A tuna bap and a G & T, please,' he said to the woman behind the bar, trying to keep his voice manly, even. She seemed to look at him strangely. Could she tell he was a fishkeeper? He wondered if fishkeepers usually ate fish.

It would be alright, alright. Carrying his cling-filmed meal and glass over to the seat furthest away from the jukebox, he tried to think happy thoughts. So what if Terry would be making it tonight with some exciting new conquest? So what if Adrian's wife would parade before him in that amazing little gown? He, Douglas, could get a woman if he really wanted one. Val seemed to like him. Maybe one day they'd go out together for a drink.

He downed his gin, thought about ordering a second. Better not: he might be asked to drive the hearse this afternoon. Even holding a conversation got harder after a couple of drinks, especially the generous measures he poured for himself in the rooming house. He felt more carefree, but found it hard to think.

Think of your responsibilities... For the first time since he'd started at Reevon's, he had to force himself to go back to work, to preparing bodies that were fated never to see the January sales. The obese ones tended to predominate at this festive time. *Eat your heart out*. Most of them had literally eaten and drank themselves to death.

Still, you could find beauty in a large white breast, the luscious weight of full, round buttocks. He stared at first one then the other as, after lunch, he helped Reevon to chest another corpse. His fingers dug into his palms as he stared at the flesh before him. Soon Adrian and Terry would enjoy all this and more.

His head throbbed as he cleaned and cosmeticised his clients. His thoughts returned to the bag containing the sheet throughout the day. It was in his locker and was staying there till everyone else had gone home for the night. Otherwise Terry might whoop and grab it, show everyone proof of Douglas's damply boyish dreams. Not that he didn't enjoy the sensations, the limb-relaxing aftermath. But he still felt such guilt.

'Great to have the papers again.' Terry came in from his lunch holding a broadsheet and a tabloid. He sat down on the corner of the desk Douglas was reading at and began to flick through to the sporting page.

'I see they haven't caught that maniac yet,' said Shelley, peering at the headline. Douglas looked up. *Help Us Find Karen's Killer* the tabloid read.

'Poor bitch,' said Terry.

'Imagine what Christmas that poor family had,' Shelley added, sighing so that her shoulders slumped. Douglas nodded, wondering why his skin felt itchy. Was he becoming allergic to gin?

'Police say she was a cautious girl, who was unlikely to have gone into the park with her killer unless she knew him,' Terry continued reading.

Shelley nodded: 'I heard most assaults and rapes are carried out by someone the victim knows.'

'The ex-husband, probably!' Terry half-laughed, without his usual bitterness. He looked back at the page, 'But this lassie was only nineteen.'

Nineteen and dead. It was a waste, thought Douglas. Unless she was unhappy, in which case it was for the best. He couldn't imagine killing someone he knew—killing anyone. You'd have to find so much energy, such rage. Once, maybe when he was small, he'd said he wished Alice was dead, that he hated her. Now, though, that passion had gone underground. She irritated him or made him feel sad more often than she made him feel enraged.

Change the subject. Keep occupied. He watched the others leave one by one, kept working. Walked alone afterwards to the launderette, sat in a corner watching his solitary sheet go round and round. He'd brought in some of his usual hand wash too, to bulk out the load a little. Those Y-fronts that no one else had seen—would ever see?—made him feel even more alone.

He was also hungry, thirsty. The first day back at work after the holidays had never seemed so long before. Shivering, spun-dry laundry now hurting his arm, he stood with his carrier bag in the shufflingly slow take-away queue. Bought an onion pizza, carried it back to his room. Opened the carton and tore off a chunk.

Boom! Boom! The sound ricocheted through the room: a fist against his door, forceful, insistent. The fish in both aquariums flinched as the vibrations went through the tanks.

Who...? The police? Paul? He dropped the cheese and onion slice, unbitten. *Get a grip, a grip.* It'll be a tradesman or someone from work... Inhaling strongly, he opened the door a few inches, fingers gripping the wood.

'Hi. It's me.'

She sounded girlishly breathlessly. Looked like what she was: an overweight woman who'd let herself go.

'Oh, hello.'

He was relieved it wasn't trouble. Raised his right hand in a half wave, let it fall to his side. That looked silly. He mustn't encourage her. He took a step back.

'Not interrupting you, am I? I heard you come in, thought I'd have a chat before you cooked your tea.'

'I brought in a take-away.'

'Oh, I see.' Her mouth levelled into a narrow sympathetic line.

'It's a thought, sometimes, cooking for yourself, isn't it? Now I know how my gran used to feel.'

A gran: he'd never had a gran. Alice had been brought up by the local authorities. His real dad hadn't stuck around long enough for there to be in-laws and Paul's folks had died and been sanctified in his extremely selective mind.

'Mmm.'

He nodded, noticed a stain on her collar. It was a scallop-edged white lacy thing, the type a child of eight or so would choose to wear. Sometimes little girls from Reevon's were buried in such blouses, with a little green tartan or black velvet skirt covering their lower limbs.

'It was her favourite,' the mothers would say, quivering, 'It's what she'd have wanted to wear.'

'Anyway, talking of food...'

He'd thought they were talking about grans: his headache was increasing.

'... I've got this voucher.' She waggled it about in the vicinity of his chest.

'A voucher?' His pizza would be getting cold, he hadn't unpacked his laundry.

'Two meals for the price of one. So I thought...'

Oh no—she wanted him to go out with her. Eat in a restaurant, talk for hours and hours.

'Just companionship, you know,' she added, passing the piece of paper from one hand to the other.

'I'm not sure what I'm doing yet,' he said, staring to the right of her head.

'Well... no problem.' To his relief she backed away, 'You've got until the 20th of the month to decide.'

'My diary's at work. I'll have to check it,' he added, watching her bulky retreat.

There, that was quick thinking. He forced himself to close the door slowly. They were neighbours, like it or not: it was simpler if they didn't fall out. Still, he'd had a close shave, could easily have blurted yes, out of panic. Once women like that got hold of you, they never let go.

Forget her. Forget everything. He'd been giving himself calming talks all week, but especially today. Eat, he told himself, but the pizza had gone lukewarm, and oil or butter had risen up, causing it to sag in the centre, curl at the sides. He could put it in the oven, of course, but that meant going downstairs and Eleanor might follow him there.

He sighed, pushing the dough away: suddenly he no longer felt hungry. Pain was drawing his brows together in the centre of his forehead as if pulled by invisible strings.

Lie down, lie down. He lay down on his back on the bed, and his jacket fell open, revealing a thin blue envelope: Alice's airmail. He was destined not to escape. Unsticking the seal, he skimmed the few sentences scrawled over every page. Doing hairdressing for the neighbours... Paul found a new Church... telling them about my son. Making out like they were one big happy family, yet she'd had no interest in the courses he'd passed during his early years at Reevon's, had never once asked to see how his computer worked.

Pulling the duvet over his fully clothed body, he closed his eyes, tried not to think about the past, the future. He hoped sleep would come to soothe away his headache. He hoped he wouldn't have any more days like this.

CHAPTER TWENTY EIGHT

'Good night last night?'

Terry looked at Adrian as he spoke, and they both burst out laughing.

'Same as yours, I imagine,' Adrian grinned, taking off his coat.

They'd sunk into womanly wet velvet whilst he'd lain alone, fully dressed, waiting for his head to stop hurting. They didn't ask him how he'd spent his night: they probably knew.

Without waiting to be asked, he went through to the Chesting Area, and unzipped the waiting corpse from its body bag. This man had died suddenly: the eyes were open, staring somewhere beyond Douglas's sight. When people slid gradually into death, the eyes tended to close of their own volition. With violent and accidental deaths, the gaze remained.

'You're keen.'

He knew by the voice that it was Terry who'd entered the room, full of flippancy. Damn, he preferred working with Adrian or Reevon, or, better still, alone.

'Finished late last night. Want to get on with things today,' he said to explain his impatience.

The older man raised his eyebrows and still failed to make them reach his receding hairline: 'Hot date?'

He'd lost count of the number of times Terry had said that to him, mouth twisted cynically.

'Uh uh.' That sounded so typical, boring, as if he was a failure, alone. He sucked in his breath, 'But the promise of it—if I'm interested. A woman asked me out last night.'

'The looker?'

For a second his mind raced round, baffled.

'Landlady,' Terry clarified, 'Small, you said. Not your type, but quite cute.'

'Oh—no.' No such luck. He could get through an evening with Val if he had to. Would rather have a night, though, just mutely touching these pushed-up breasts...

'Put us out of our misery, then.'

Terry leaned across the Prep Table towards him.

'What? Oh, the woman in the room next door. She's... a bit too forward if you know what I mean.'

He'd almost said ugly and huge but he wanted Terry to be impressed, to envy him.

'Who exactly is your type, Duggie?' asked Terry, and laughed, looking around at the furnishings as if expecting them to approve.

His type, his type... His type was the still, mute women of the photographs. The women he'd... made love to had also been his type.

'Varies,' he said, moving up to the corpse's eyelids to close them.

'You'll have to bring one of them here to meet us,' Terry said. 'There's nothing like a good woman,' he added in an upbeat voice, fetching the hydraulic trolley. He hadn't said that after his divorce, Douglas thought sullenly. There had been no such thing as a good woman then.

Six good men and true lay in their coffins waiting for him to prepare them. One by one he and Terry got their shadowy pallor ready for the dark, dank earth. Sometimes he envied them their calm, still state: all the worrying was over. Yet none of his fellow directors seemed to feel that way.

Different. He was different. He'd always been different. Funny how doing some conventional things had made his alienation seem worse. Now he had pets—but no one to share them with. Except Michael, of course: but he couldn't exactly call in at the shop every day.

And Marjorie had only chosen an aquarium because it fitted easily into her upstairs flat. She didn't really love fish for fishes sake. He hadn't spoken to anyone else at the *Fish Are Fun* club. They all seemed to sit in stranger-excluding cliques.

He sighed and Terry said 'Cheer up, mate. It's not that bad.'

Rage rushed to his fists—he wanted to kick, bite, knock out the man's shallowness. He'd gone to the pub last night after lying awake for an hour under the duvet. A double brandy had soothed his headache but the vodka had made him mad.

And again that made him different: it relaxed most people. It relaxed him, too, at the time, but now without it he felt more and more hate. He'd wanted to hit Val and Terry and Eleanor Denning. He'd ripped Alice's last airmail until the pieces got too small to tear. How dare she pretend they were a trio of love when for years she'd ignored him? Even before Paul came along he'd been a nuisance for whom she had to provide.

'Ready?' asked Terry, and he realised he'd been scrubbing the same patch of work surface over and over. He nodded, throat feeling closed in and glutinous, not trusting himself to speak.

He'd go to the aquarists tonight, buy some more tropical and coldwater plants. The fish in both tanks had already nibbled substantial areas away. Maybe the walk there would ease his headache. If not, he could call into the late night chemist for aspirin on his way back.

Backs, fronts, legs, arms, waistlines. Touching body after body, he listened to Terry whistle tunes. Songs about touching, telling, teasing... The man was actually smiling to himself, remembering a night of ecstasy and release.

Release, release. He wanted release from this latest headache. Release from this internal emptiness, this increasing void.

'Night in front of the box, tonight?' said Terry, who always forgot Douglas didn't have a television.

'No. I'm going to the aquarists for plants.'

'Right.' Terry jerked his head back in a kind of snorting acknowledgement. Nothing new there.

Forget him. Forget this place. Have an intelligent talk with Michael. He looked at his watch at least hourly as the afternoon dragged on.

'Got a bus to catch?' Reevon grinned as he hurried out of the door at exactly five-thirty. Douglas faltered, looked back open mouthed, couldn't think of a reply.

'Off you go, Doug—only joking.' Reevon looked at him more closely, 'The hours you put in, I wish they were all like you.'

There, the boss had paid him a compliment. He was a useful employee, even if he was slightly overweight and didn't have much to say for himself. At least he treated his fish well, gave them the best food and surroundings that money could buy.

****

'... And I'll buy two more cabomba plants.' He practiced saying it inside his head as he walked along the road towards Michael's shop. He'd rehearsed things like this since he was... oh, seven or eight at the most. Had basic conversations over and over again in his mind, varying their speed and delivery. Many of them had never finally taken place.

He could ask Michael what his feelings were about plants and undergravel filters. Some authorities suggested that the constant water these filters flushed around their roots made it difficult for the plants to grow. So far, his seemed to be thriving, pushing new growth above the water line. But he'd mention it, none the less.

Men in raincoats, kids in anoraks, adolescents in long parkas. He walked in the door to find them all milling around. Some had pieces of driftwood and hunks of granite in their hands and were queuing in front of the counter. Michael was netting a flock of White Cloud Mountain Minnows for an excited boy of about five whilst his smiling mother looked on.

Sadness weighing down his stomach, he turned away from their happiness. If only Alice had been like that. If only she'd loved his goldfish, or even... even what? His memory faltered, clouded over. The knot in his temple closed in upon itself even more.

'Alright?'

John had rushed past him before he could form an

answer. He said 'Fine, thanks' to the assistant's retreating back, and a little girl stared.

'Julia!' Her guardian tugged at her sleeve, raised her eyes to Douglas and smiled. He watched as the girl placed her small hand in the woman's larger one.

Relax. Relax. Buy what you've come for. Talk to Michael. Some intelligent conversation would make him feel better, help his head. He practiced breathing in, out, in as he stood in the queue that occasionally shuffled forward. He got out his wallet and checked it again: lots of cash.

Clear throat, straighten tie. He did so before he reached the counter, again as he came up to it.

'Hello, what can we do for you?' asked Michael, smiling his familiar smile.

'I'd like another two cabomba plants.'

He paused for a second, about to add that the fish were eating them as fast as he could plant them.

'John. Cabomba—two,' Michael said.

'And two more elodea,' Douglas added quickly. The boy began to move towards the little waterfall that contained the foliage.

'Anything else?' Michael asked.

Already, he was looking over his head at the next customer. For a second Douglas's mind stalled.

'Different dried food for the tropicals,' he lied, seeing some on the shelf behind the counter.

'Flake?' Michael said, already reaching for a medium sized drum.

'I read it keeps their colours vibrant,' Douglas added quickly. He hesitated. 'I wondered... one of my Ryukins seems to be fading on one side. Do you have a colour-boosting food for coldwater fish or should...?'

'You want to deal with the cause,' Michael cut in,

going beneath the counter and bringing up a bottle of goldfish medicine, 'This is great for the diseases that cause erratic swimming and colour loss.'

'One of my Moors seems to swim a bit sideways sometimes.' There—he was keeping the conversation moving.

Michael nodded, and once again looked over his head.

And suddenly Douglas realised that the man was interested in fish—but not particularly in *his* fish. They were a fascinating species, a lucrative business with a wide product range.

'Go ahead,' he said, standing aside and indicating the next customer. John came back with his plants in two polythene bags, and he paid him for them plus the unwanted tropical food and coldwater medication.

'Bye,' he said, and John echoed the word though Michael didn't. Clutching his little brown paper bag, Douglas headed for the door.

Maybe he could get something exciting for tea— something filling. He hadn't had a prawn biryani for an age. Eating that much rice always made him feel calm, almost sated. He'd have one, plus a side dish of bombay potato, some garlic nan.

He reached the restaurant to find half of Edinburgh had had the same idea. Colouring slightly, he stepped over slender ladies shoes and thick black male ones to reach a vacant seat in the take-away room. Awkward minutes ticked by as he stared over heads, down at shoes, pretended to reread the menu. Eventually a waiter came over and took his order, frowned. 'It'll be twenty minutes.'

'Fine. That's fine.' Douglas felt himself nodding, grinning: he'd been trying to make up for Paul and Alice's racism most of his life. He sat flicking through the menu, deciding what he'd have next time, as the door opened and closed, opened and closed.

After a few minutes, he felt the top of his head start to prickle. Someone was staring at him: *Don't, don't, don't.* He kept his head down till his neck muscles ached at the back, till his eyes blurred the italicised script before him. Then he looked up, tried to glance round casually, eyes barely focusing on the circle of strangers closing round.

'Thought it was you,' said a rich, assured voice.

He turned his head to the side, saw the man smiling at him. So was the woman whose hand he was holding. What was his name? Simon. Simon and some bint.

'Miles away,' Douglas said, 'Hungry. Been to the fish shop.' He paused. The woman looked sophisticated: he didn't want her thinking he'd been to the fishmongers for a piece of lemon sole. 'The aquarists, that is,' he added tightly.

He held up his brown paper bag before realising no one could see through it. The other people in the room stared. Douglas dropped his hand to his lap again. Simon nodded. The girl smiled.

'So. What have you been buying?'

Simon's voice sounded forcedly jovial, as though he were making an effort.

'Plants. Food. Medication.' He shrugged, refusing to elaborate. He could tell the journalist didn't really want to know.

'Marjorie could do with some of the latter,' laughed Simon. He stopped, looked awkward, 'Not that she doesn't look after them well, but there's so much that can go wrong.'

The female sat next to Simon, smiling, nodding.

'You know a lot about fish, then?' Douglas asked her, and her smile disappeared.

'No. I... I'm just interested.'

Simon frowned at Douglas. His partner looked at the floor. Douglas's gaze followed hers, down to small feet in little russet-coloured ankle boots. She had placed one of them against Simon's, and was rubbing it up and down. If she did this to a man in public, God knows what she'd do in private. Uncertainty cartwheeling through his empty stomach, Douglas looked up and concentrated on the wall ahead.

A stretching silence. This was terrible. They might be here together for another fifteen minutes. *Speak. Speak. Speak.*

'So, been doing anything special?' His voice sounded low and slowed down.

He turned to see her lips brush Simon's neck, and fancied he knew.

'Oh, just working away,' Simon said evenly. He seemed embarrassed at being caught in the act. 'You?' he added, turning to Douglas.

'It's our busiest time of year.'

'We're quiet at this time—January and August,' put in the girl, leaning forward.

'Oh?'

Her brown calf jacket and skirt looked strokable and soft.

'People are broke after Christmas, then by August they're on holiday.'

He nodded, feeling stupid. He'd left it too late to ask what she actually did.

'Sue's in magazine publishing with me,' Simon added belatedly.

I'm in death, he thought savagely. 'I tend to buy books,' he said, and though he hadn't meant it to, it came out sounding censorious and stiff.

Sue lifted and crossed one stockinged leg over the other. Half an inch of lace-trimmed coral underskirt appeared beneath her rising hem.

'One prawn biryani, one nan, one...'

He'd heard enough to claim his order.

'Mine!' he said, jumping up, ready to escape. He turned back, said goodbye to Simon and his girlfriend. Handed the waiter twenty pounds, kept his hand out for his change, heart beating overtime, wetness pooling beneath the arms of his shirt.

'I have to get money,' said the waiter, pointing towards the lounge bar. Feeling foolish, Douglas sat down again to wait.

Make up an impressive exit line. His skin felt taut and juiceless, his temples had little sparks of pain shooting through them. Say something clever, witty. He wanted to go home. Maybe after his meal he could ask Val to come out for a drink with him. He could explain he had a headache then perhaps she wouldn't jangle and giggle too much.

The waiter returned, handed him a leather-bound book, stood back, expressionless. It took him a second to realise his change was inside.

'Oh... thanks.' He stood up again, praying he hadn't forgotten anything, 'Well, bye,' he said to the smiling, hand-holding pair.

'Bye!'

They managed to chorus it together, a disarming duo. Their happiness floated out after him into the cold dark street.

Home, home: all his instincts cried out for the safety of his room in the rooming house. *Police Closing In On Parkland Killer* read three consecutive newsstands that he passed. Head down, carrier bag of food bumping against his leg, he hurried along streets that were becoming deserted. Rehearsed putting on the kettle, looking out his largest plate.

He'd find a side plate for the accompaniments, a cup for the sauce. Eat, drink, unwind a little. By the time he got home he was so hungry he started to eat the food direct from the cartons with a spoon.

The kettle boiled as he tore off his second piece of nan and dipped it in the gravy, and he hastily poured water onto a tea-bag he'd placed in his biggest mug. It'll be alright, he told himself but even as his urge for food was sated, his need for alcohol grew and grew.

What a day—a night! The world was still against him. Getting your independence didn't make you safe. Terry had still mocked and Michael had yawned and Simon had humoured him. And that Sue had showed off her legs, and smiled her condescending smile.

Rice, dough, prawns: he put aside a cardamom pod. Suddenly remembered setting down his little bag of aqua plants and fish food as he searched for his wallet to pay for his meal. Damn Simon and Sue—their small talk had distracted him. He usually had ample time to get out his money in advance.

Now, thanks to them, he'd left his purchases at the take-away. He'd go back tomorrow: he couldn't face it now. He sighed, reflecting further. Deprived of water the aqua plants would go brown, and die...

Right, he'd have to go back after he'd finished eating. He could call in at the off licence on his return.

He didn't feel up to the pub tonight, much as he wanted some undemanding company. Maybe he could bring back a bottle of wine, and see if Val...

Three quarters of an hour later he walked down the stairs, still rehearsing.

'Just going out to replenish my stock after the New Year,' he could say, casual as you like. She'd been away over Hogmanay so wouldn't know he hadn't had guests to help him polish off his drink. 'Thought I'd see if you wanted anything,' he could add, 'Bottles being heavy for a woman to carry, and all that.'

When he came back she might ask him in for a sherry as a thank you. If not, he'd ask her to help him sample his new purchases now. He could get a peach wine, or something equally light and drinkable. If the conversation went too badly, he could down his drink, hurry back to his room. If it went well, they might have a second and a third drink. After that, who could tell?

Reaching the foot of the stairs, his stomach felt shaky. This was the difficult bit, approaching her door. As he hesitated, deep male laughter spread out from her living quarters. *A man. She had a man in her room.*

Douglas stopped, gripped the banister, stared ahead at the foyer light. Adrian had his wife, Terry his girlfriend, Simon had Sue. Shelley had her husband and child. And now Val...

He let himself out into a night that had become even colder. He needed new interests, excitement: putting in his new plants tonight would no longer be enough.

Head down, Douglas walked along trying to find a plan to fill his lonely evening. Of course—he could call in at the reference library on his way home. He'd just find out which aquarium-kept fish could paralyse. After all, it couldn't hurt to look.

CHAPTER TWENTY NINE

Something about that man was distinctly unhealthy. Handing out work to each editorial assistant to sub, Simon thought back to his meeting with Douglas the previous night.

'Give me three or four alternative titles,' he said absentmindedly, handing over a feature to the nearest editorial assistant, a recent graduate, 'Something short.'

'Simon?'

It took him a second to realise she was talking to him.

'D'you want a colour in the title or is the by-line covering it?'

'Sorry. Colour's fine. Something dramatic.'

Stella magazine was running a cut-price Rainbow T-shirt offer in the issue they were planning now.

'Show a rainbow fashion spread, rainbow make up tips... you know a kind of colour co-ordination backlash type of thing,' the editor had said, before disappearing off for another luncheon with the management. *A kind of colour co-ordination backlash type of thing.*

Simon sighed, remembering, and the editorial assistant he was standing beside echoed him. But the editor wanted rainbows, so rainbows he would get.

He walked past the row of bent heads to his desk as his phone started ringing. It was Sue, finalising their concert plans for the following night. After a few words he sent a smile down the phone line, and ended the conversation. He'd planned to go back to her house yesterday, and spend the night. Until...

Until he'd met Douglas in the take-away. Something about those lost yet all-seeing eyes had troubled him and he'd decided not to leave Marjorie alone in the flat overnight. Probably nothing, he chided himself, the man was just lonely. But even lonely men didn't usually stare at a woman the way that Douglas had stared at Sue.

Not a frankly admiring glance, but a cold, appraising one. As if he was checking her out, muscle by muscle, measuring each sound and movement that she made.

'Hard to talk to,' she'd said in a high-pitched voice when he finally exited the restaurant. In fairness, Simon thought, they hadn't had much to say to him in return.

Still, fair or not, he didn't like the man, wished that Marjorie wasn't looking forward so eagerly to the new years meetings of *Fish Are Fun*.

As he mused, one of the assistants came over and put a dummy copy of *Stella* in front of him. This was the swotting survival issue, geared to come out when the schoolgirls were preparing for their exams. Forcing his mind back into work mode, he began to peruse it, checking the blend of graphics and adverts and text on each page.

'Great!' he said eventually, stretching out so that he

could reach the editor's desk and deposit the copy. The editor rarely changed anything, but he had to be seen to be considering altering the mag.

'We've an illustration with black hair and a text with red hair.'

Simon looked up impatiently at the assistant before him.

'Well, change the text to read *black hair*,' he said, with an edge.

The girl raised her eyes.

'Ordinarily I would, but her red hair's the whole point of the story. She gets called carrot-head and ginger nut, and thinks she'll never find a boy to love.'

She would, of course: they all found a boy to love within the pages of *Stella*. The early teens wanted a prince and a prince they would have.

'Okay, I'll have a word with the artists.'

He stood up and walked over to what was known as Picture Corner, three artists' desks and easels in one part of the enormous room.

Bill, who was in his fifties, and Ross, their twenty-four year newcomer were painting busily away.

'We've a continuity error,' said Simon, hating how often the men had to change their work to help iron out editorial confusions, 'Change black hair to red or find another pic?'

'What kind of pose d'you want?'

Simon had rarely seen Bill smile in the time they'd worked together on *Stella*. Seemingly the man had worked in this corner of the office for years and years.

'Dramatic. Kids laughing at her, or pointing, or something. Though we'd get away with her looking dreamily at a boy she can't have.'

'I'll go.' Ross took off for the pile of canvases stored behind the sectioned-off area facing him. 'This do? We were going to use it for the football fans issue but that's months away,' he said, returning with a pastel print. The girl was looking into the middle distance, her red hair flowing out behind her. A little thought bubble enclosed a football-playing boy.

'Perfect.' Simon smiled at Ross, who smiled back then blushed a little. Did he have a girlfriend? Did he want one? He'd never seen him with anyone yet.

Thoughtfully, Simon walked back to his desk, hands in his pockets. He'd ask the Head Secretary, an older woman who doled out aspirins and Kleenex and strong Assam tea. She'd met Marjorie, probably sensed her loneliness, could be relied upon to be discreet.

Beginning to relax, Simon turned to the pile of freelance manuscripts before him which had been vetted by his editorial assistants so wouldn't be total dross. He looked at the first title, winced, moved on to the second. *Are You His Astro-Dream?* They got a lot of those. This one had a long list of pop stars birth signs, which separated it slightly from all the usual astrological quizzes. He wrote the author's name and address into the Acceptance Book.

Boys, blokes, fellas... His thoughts returned to Marjorie. He'd tried to fix her up with a colleague once before. Colin had been the chosen one, a small nervy guy from the printing department. It had been his last day before he left for a mature students course at the local Tech. Ten of them, all couples except Colin and Marjorie, had gone for a celebratory meal in the city centre. They'd ordered chopsticks with their Chinese meal.

Simon sighed, remembering. Colin had been pissed and told the most awful misogynistic jokes. Marjorie had laughed loudly, encouragingly. Simon doubted if she was even taking in the words: she just wanted to please. But the other women had glared at her and she'd noticed. Gotten quieter and sadder and drunk more and more of the house white wine.

Then she'd gone on to the blush red and gone an equally funny colour. Had told Colin he could come round any time for a cup of tea. He'd said he'd be too busy, and her cheeks had become hectic. Simon had taken her home then, said they had friends coming early the next day.

Sighing, he wrote 'cut by one hundred words' over the envelope of a safety first feature, and left it on the relevant assistant's desk. Ross was an artist, which hopefully ruled out the rude jokes and world weary cynicism which Colin had displayed. More importantly, he was new to town, hadn't had an opportunity to meet many people yet.

Simon looked over at the boy's slim back, imagining him talking enthusiastically to Marjorie about something safe like oil painting or photography. At the very best he'd become a long term partner. At the very worst he'd help get Douglas out of her head.

CHAPTER THIRTY

She was a black girl and he had to be nice to black girls. Had to make up for Paul calling them niggers, for Alice saying she wasn't convinced all the 'Paki' shops in the area were clean. He'd had a few drinks here in Leith, and now he was feeling friendly. Last time he'd been in Leith the women had been friendly too...

Denim shorts, frayed at the bottoms. Reaching to her thighs, which were clad in prussian blue nylon. A white top that clung to her waistline, made the most of her small bosom. A walk in which she swung her hips provocatively from side to side. Only the mass of black hair and her black arms told him she was African. His first African. *His*.

He followed, wondering where she would lead him. He'd spotted her a few minutes after leaving his third pub of the night. Which night was it—a Wednesday? Thursday? Either way, he had work tomorrow, wanted to walk off the tension in his head before then.

Fascinating the contrast of strong black arms swinging from a skimpy white T-shirt. 'Descended from the apes,'

Paul would have said, yet Paul was the one who repeated the priest's phrases like a brain-dead parrot would. Now she was turning into a side street, disappearing. He rushed across the road, round the corner, hoping she hadn't disappeared.

'Looking for business, love?'

He ran into the side street and almost bumped into her. She had her back against the wall, was lighting a cigarette.

'What? Oh. I don't have a match.' His thoughts felt laden.

'Got a twenty?' she asked.

'Uh... yes.'

'That's for straight, that is. You want extra?'

'I... no.' Lying straight on her back, arms by her sides.

'Just along here. I've got a place.' Her voice sounded deep for a woman. He staggered along beside her, glad that it had gotten dark.

Dark skin, dark eyes, dark hair, dark everything. He looked at her more closely as they climbed a narrow stair to the scarred door of a first floor flat. Mail for... said a piece of paper. There were two names on it. He realised he didn't care what she was called.

A receptacle. She was going to be his receptacle. She'd lie down and spread her legs and he'd pump back and forth till the pleasure came.

'This way.'

That deep voice again. He wished she wouldn't speak or push him about so. It killed the pretty pictures in his head.

But her hands were on his shoulders, moving him towards a half open unpainted door. He could see part of a bed, a pale pink underskirt and what looked like a large T-shirt on the floor.

'Lie down.'

He lay on his back. His calves had started to itch fiercely.

'Let's see what you've got for me,' she said in a monotone, reaching for his zip.

He felt himself shrivel, shrink back against his inner thigh. The hardness that had been growing as he followed her up the stair went away.

'Needs a little kiss, does he?' she said: it didn't sound like a question. He felt soft warmth on his delicate parts, felt them flicker back into life.

'Stay still,' he muttered. She took her mouth away, and opened it.

'It'll cost you extra for full French.'

'I want...'

Language was inadequate. His word centre felt broken. Trembling, he sat up and rolled to one side of her, pulled her down.

Got on top and straddled her, feeling better. She had a bemused look. *Stay that way. Stay.*

'Hang on.' She sat up and went into her shorts pocket, brought out a small package. Tore it open with her teeth.

Be quiet. Lie down. He was losing the momentum again. Paul might come in. Paul might be mad. He felt her fingers on his manhood, felt her pushing something slick down over it. Hardened further. Pushed her down, drew back.

'Costs extra without it.' He was just about ready for action when she said the words.

'Don't talk,' he begged, 'Don't move.'

He wanted to close her eyes, keep them closed. They

kept staring at him. She shrugged, and he felt himself partially deflate.

Her breasts looked smaller now, doubtless flattened back against her body. He tugged clumsily at the edge of her top and she lifted it over her head. Her bra was translucent white, her nipples darker than the flesh around them. As he stared, he heard her unzip her shorts, ease them down.

The tights, the tights. He wanted them off, wanted in before she said something else to spoil things. He looked down, saw they were specially cut away at the crotch. She wasn't wearing any panties, either. All barriers had gone.

He pushed forward, encountered no resistance. She felt hot, moist. He pulled back a little, drove himself into her again.

'Like being fucked?' she asked in her deep male voice.

He shuddered. He wasn't supposed to like being touched down there...

Don't think. He concentrated on her tiny earrings. They looked like silver pandas—or were they bears? He impaled himself more fully, shifted slightly to ease the burden on his elbows. No matter how many coffins he lifted, his arms still sometimes showed the strain.

'God, you want this sweetheart, like being up my love hole.'

He screwed his eyes up, wishing he could screw up his ears. Could block her out, could reduce her to the size of her pleasure dome. *Stupid words, stupid actions, stupid bitch.*

'That's it, honey, push.'

He put the palm of his hand hard over her mouth: just enough to silence her.

'Fucker! What are you trying to...?' She shot up, all huge black hands and tiger-like teeth. One of her nails scratched between his legs for agonising seconds. He came out, waves of sickness washing through him, like that night when Paul had...

Afterwards, just himself and Lucky. He and Lucky for... several days. He lay back in the blackness, vaguely aware that he hadn't noted the dates before. Hadn't realised there'd been so little time between Paul doing something terrible to him and Lucky's... demise. Here today, gone tomorrow, as he said at the funeral parlour. Yet he didn't appear to have buried the fish, or fully acknowledged by some other ritual the part it had played in his life.

Just a fish, as Shelley would have said—but it wasn't just a fish if it was the only thing that loved you. The only thing that never hit you or abandoned you. The one creature in your life who didn't shout or call you names.

'Get out, you bastard!' a deep voice was saying in the background, 'Get the fuck out of my flat before I call the police!'

Police—the police were searching for a killer. Most people were assaulted by someone they knew. Paul had beaten him. Alice had... Alice had thrown out his fish. Down the loo—to follow years and years of stinking waste matter. His beloved Lucky. His golden friend.

He'd come home and gone to his bedroom as usual, only to find both bowl and contents gone.

'Paul's sick of that thing needing to be cleaned out,' she'd said, scouring the plate she was washing as if she wanted to scrub it out of existence, 'So I flushed it down the loo.'

That thing. Down the loo. These were mere words. They were always using stupid words. Most of them didn't mean much, filled up the space.

'I would have cleaned him out myself,' he'd stammered, 'You said I wasn't to be trusted, that I wouldn't do it right.'

It still wasn't a reality. Not real. Not happening.

'Anyway, you said yourself it wasnae fair, keeping the thing in a wee bowl like that.'

'What I meant was... I wanted to get him a tank.'

He'd still thought that she must be joking—that she couldn't be that bad to him. Had found the empty bowl in the bathroom cupboard under the sink. Had looked—well, everywhere, for that little trusting orange body. Looked behind the wardrobe, down the side of his bed.

'Get out, I mean it.' Something tugging at his ankles, jabbing at his consciousness, 'Little bastard.' Someone who sounded really mad. He blinked, focused, saw a woman's face—an angry face, with pressure marks round her nose and mouth. She wore pandas in her ears, yet she'd killed his fish.

'Cunt! Cunt!' He'd never used the word before—it wasn't like him. His voice sounded different. His hands felt like metal grips. He saw himself come off the bed in what seemed like a single movement, saw him grab at the bad woman's throat, saw her fall back onto the carpet, himself on top.

He had to keep her down. Had to. Had to. She could kill more fish... hurt him... tell what they'd almost done. She'd hurt his private parts whilst he was lying there helpless. Now she was thrusting her lower body up, trying to shake him off.

No. He kept his knees clamped to her sides, kept her flat on her back on the carpet. He was holding both her wrists in one hand but that hand was starting to tire. He had to keep her in place, keep her immobile. She had to be still, mustn't make a sound.

He looked round the room, saw the red and black scarf a few inches from her. Reached out and dragged it towards him, rolled it with one-handed awkwardness into a makeshift gag.

'Bas...'

She'd been quiet up till now, staring at him with her slightly puffy face which looked as if someone had hit her. Now she was getting rude and noisy. *Paul would hear.*

'Don't.' He got the gag in place, tied it behind her head. Her arms came up, grabbed at his nipples through his shirt. He screamed like a girl. Had to make her lie there, not moving, pretty as a picture. He reached for her flailing arms, got them free of his chest. Held them in front of her, looked for another scarf—something with which to bind her wrists together. Failed to find one, took off his belt.

Her eyes widened when she saw it. He could see the look of fear in the way her lips went slack. She'd been bad, then, been disobedient. She knew he had to do this. It was the only way.

To make her motionless, keep her quiet, get her ready for him. He wound black leather over slick black wrists. Licked the perspiration away from her breasts to show it wasn't racism. He liked the idea of her, if she'd only lie still.

Her feet were drumming on the floor now. Uncalled for. He thought of tying them together but that seemed such a waste. Went behind her instead, and got his hands beneath her armpits, dragging her into a sitting position, still bound and gagged.

'Walk to the bed, or it'll be worse for you,' he said, like he'd heard others say, keeping his grip on her.

'Uuh... aaah.' She was trying to say something, trying to twist her head round to look at him. He tightened his grip and started to pull her towards the bed. Felt rage spurt up at her stupid, splay-legged resistance. Put his hands around her throat, stupefied when she almost knocked him over in her haste to run backwards to the bed.

Better. She was looking better, acting better. He felt better. The sick pain in his balls had mellowed to a dull twinge. He put a hand down his trousers, surprised to find them unzipped and unbuttoned. Massaged himself through his underpants as she stared.

Did she want him? She must be trying to tempt him. Trying to get him into trouble. Trying to hurt him some more. He hiccupped and tasted brandy or whisky in his mouth: something warm and sour. The girl was watching. As he stared down at her, she spread her legs. Looked up at him, moved her eyeballs down to look at herself as if offering. It was probably a trick: he must outmanoeuvre her, must be a man.

Think. Think. His head felt laden, as if he had to think through an opaque mass of heavy duty putty. He blinked several times. Brown eyeballs in white surroundings continued to stare. Bad to look at him like that. He didn't like her staring. Thought of covering her eyes, looked around for a blindfold to...

But no! A better idea. He moved his legs so he was no longer squatting on her belly. Started to roll her over, slapping her across the face when she used her heels to try to keep her body in situ. She let out a sigh through the gag, eyes half-closing. He flipped her over fast, stared down at her buttocks. Paul beat wicked buttocks. Paul got his belt and beat down and down and down. But his belt was already holding her wrists. He needed another one. He got off the bed, then saw that she was trying to roll onto her side, to sit up.

Such disobedience. Such wickedness. He picked up her bra, used it to bind her left foot to the bed leg. Tore off her crotchless tights, and tied the right foot to the opposite side of the bed. Now her legs were scissored apart, her hands tied in front of her. She'd been so very, very bad...

He got off the bed again, went over to her dressing table, a cigarette-burnt unpainted thing. The top drawer held bras and briefs and stockings. A few lipsticks and eye-shadows. A magazine about black makeup and hair.

He looked at her in the mirror: her face was buried in the pillow. She was making little noises through the gag, as if spitting into the material. Dirty to spit. He'd never been allowed to. Not even when one of his frequent childhood colds caused the back of his throat to fill with catarrh.

The second drawer held fingerless gloves, a red beret, a leotard-like garment in a soft white material. He sifted through several more scarves before he found the belt. Thick, brown, with one hole more used than the others. One hole more used...

He walked back to the bed, flexing the leather. She turned her face to the side, watched his approach. Started to raise her upper body, shaking her head in a convulsive movement. He had to make her lie still, like she'd been told.

He struck down hard across her ass and she moaned into the gag and buried her head in the pillow. Then tried to get up as far as her tied apart legs would allow. He hit her again and again. Paul had a black heart. Paul deserved this. Alice deserved this. She'd flushed away his Lucky, his fish.

Purple weals on black skin. He traced one with his

middle finger, watching the flesh writhe underneath it. Traced round her arsehole. The hole least used...

When he pulled back she seemed to tense, but at least she was being quiet. He pushed forward, encountered resistance, slid his hands round to the front to grasp her tits. Pushed in again, felt the muscles give a little, got in half an inch or so. She made a sound, and he lost some of his erectness. Pushed her head down hard into the pillow, pushed in up to the hilt.

And rocked slowly, feeling his balls brush against her body. Feeling the front of his thighs slide against the back of her thighs, white flesh on black. Stared down at the contrast, wondering what Paul would think. Paul had caught him and Alice before...

Tight. She was tight and ungiving. He'd give her what for. He'd teach her not to look. He started bucking faster, going as hard as the tight confines of her sphincter would allow. Kept his hand on the back of her head, holding her into the pillow so that she wouldn't say the wrong thing.

Wouldn't say *anything*. Not even ask for her money. He came with a half-scream, collapsed over her, waited for the next stage of the transaction to begin. Now she'd demand some outlandish sum because he'd had the more private part of her.

He wouldn't argue, would pay up. Anything for a quiet life, that was his motto. If only the girl had been as quiet throughout as she was now.

'How much?' He tried to roll her over to face him, realised her legs were tied apart to the bed, holding her in place. Edged himself down to the bed legs and slowly untied her knots.

He'd remove the gag now, too: he hoped she wouldn't get obstreperous. After all, she hadn't said he *couldn't* have her arsehole, only that everything had its price. Holding his breath, he rolled her over, quickly turning his gaze to the wall above him rather than confront her accusing eyes.

'How much?' he said, still not looking at her, as the gag came away in his hand.

No answer. She was in the huff with him. Sometimes Paul had had huffs that lasted for days and days. If he'd tried to keep talking, the man had hit him. He looked warily at the girl now, surprised to find her hands tied before her in silent prayer. What was she repenting? He undid the knots, rubbed at the red lines imprinted in her flesh. A pulse had begun to beat drily in his head.

'Coffee?' he asked. He'd probably have to pay for it as well. You paid for most things. Alice used to say that nothing was free.

No answer. He'd try to stare her out, hoped she wasn't another Shelley. Focused on not cold eyes, but blank eyes, eyes that stayed unfocused and fixed. Slightly parted lips that would forever remain slightly parted. Until someone closed them, at least, or they rotted away.

Dead. A dead prostitute. He looked at her dead limbs, her dead face, her dead calm. Still warm blooded, pretty as a picture. Pretty in pink weals that braceletted her wrists.

She was nice like this—approachable. He reached for her nearest nipple and rubbed its soft warmth between forefinger and thumb. Slid his hand between her breasts and stroked down to the hard ribs, the flat belly. Slid his palm down further to the rough triangle of hair that felt as if it had been recently trimmed.

Silky. Sultry. With female parts that still merited exploring. She was willing—eager. She'd invited him back to her flat. He leaned forward to kiss her, aware that he'd rarely kissed a woman before. If only all women would stay this still.

CHAPTER THIRTY ONE

'... So I was just reading about the fish that paralyse.'

There. He'd said it. He waited for Michael to stare at him, to back away.

'You'll not catch me stocking anything like that,' the shop owner said, smiling, 'Bad enough the nip you get from some of those sharks.'

'Oh, I know. It's—just academic interest. I'm doing a dissertation...'

Oh God, he hadn't meant to say that. Don't let him ask.

'At the Institute?'

'Mmm?' He picked up a dolphin key ring from the box on the counter and pretended to study it, 'Just... Open University actually.'

Saved! Some racing self-served part of his brain had come up with that one. Michael presumably knew about local courses, but not the vast subject range of the OU.

Douglas took a deep breath. 'I've done the introductory modules on different types. Wondered... do some people keep the species which paralyse? What kind of aquarium would you need?'

Michael paused, and despite his earlier offhandedness, Douglas was impressed by the way the shopkeeper stopped to consider each technicality. He was a calm, methodical man.

'Well, for most creatures you'd need a tropical marine set-up.'

Douglas forced a smile: 'Given some time and money, anyone could put that together, though, couldn't they?'

Michael nodded, gesturing towards the marine section of their book stand, 'And then you'd need to import the creature or bring it into the country yourself.'

He shrugged as if to say 'who cares?' and let his gaze drift round the shop.

'I suppose there are laws?' Douglas added.

The aquarist shook his head, paused to answer a quick phone query, put the receiver down.

'A licensed importer can legally import them,' he continued, looking at Douglas evenly, 'But they're not generally brought in as they're too dangerous, of course.' He paused to direct a customer to a Pufferfish tank, 'Anyway half of them are pretty dull to own, hiding under the sand for much of the time.'

Not illegal. Douglas felt his heart lurch a little, and his blood start to race. A marine set-up sounded educational and challenging. After all, the coldwater and tropical tanks were going well. Not that he'd paralyse anyone, of course: he was just curious. According to the book he'd been reading some of those fifty gram creatures could immobilise a man...

'Great to get back to normal, isn't it?'

Michael was the third person to say that to him this

month. Douglas nodded his agreement: February was going to be kinder to him than January, the so-called new year, had been.

'Milder,' he said, pointing out the bags of live food he wanted and the iron tonic for his aquatic plants.

The next night, he went back to the reference library. The librarian nodded at him as he walked up to the nearest microfiche. The last time he'd been here he hadn't known exactly what he was looking for. Now he did...

Marine shells, marine tests, marine toxicology. He came to the right-sounding listing and noted down the reference guide. When he found the place on the shelf, it turned out to be a thick, dusty volume. Breathing quickly, he carried it to a table, sat down. Began to skim through its copious index, looked at the pages which had especial appeal. Octopus and urchins and spiny fish and aqua snakes and frogs which could render a person near-lifeless. Dangerous sea life from exotic climes like South East Asia and Japan. He read on, on, noting the lethal water babies than inhabited Southern California. New Zealand also had its share. His gaze focused on the various listings for Australia and he sucked in his breath, feeling a strange excitement begin.

CHAPTER THIRTY TWO

Low-heeled shoes moved almost soundlessly along the pavement. Douglas shrank further into the doorway of the pub he was about to vacate. Leaned back against the side wall, watching her carefully. Watching her retreating back in its heavy brown car coat, the shapeless fabric in contrast to her long, slim legs.

Was she walking to the car park? He might as well trail along for a while. It was of sociological interest, knowing the make and year of car that women in their thirties drove today. Anyway, the pub was about to close and he had nothing to rush home for. Even the aquarium lights went off at 10pm, thanks to the automatic timer he'd fixed up.

Legs in tan-coloured nylon: he wondered if they were tights or stockings. You could also get hold-ups which clung, courtesy of strong elastic tops, to the thigh. Two of the corpses he'd seen in the past few days had been wearing them, bare expanse of flesh awaiting his knowing touch. So cold, though, so cold, and unyielding. A mature man—a real man—wanted more.

The woman crossed the road and her hot breath misted the air before her. She pulled her shoulder bag closer and the car coat lifted and clung to the vague outline of her breasts. Exciting, this, just imagining the rounded contours below the material. Her buttocks would be silky, creamy, her sex lips hot and wet.

No one around. No one. He increased his pace slightly. Hiccupped and tasted the aromatic aftermath of gin. His left eye began to water, a thin line of warmth snaking from one corner. His feet felt numbed and strange. She was obviously alone, probably lusting for male companionship. He'd never... done it in a car, far less over one before. Don't worry. His manhood jerked and partially hardened. In adult magazines men took women over car bonnets all the time.

Women who spread their legs out, pushed their asses up, peeked over their shoulders and smiled lovingly. They didn't look as if they'd speak or shout or jump about. You just slid in and up and thrust hard once you'd found your rhythm. Kept their heads against the windscreen, glassy eyes on ungiving glass.

They walked down a main road, along a street where a Chinese Take-away spilled its unwelcome light over the pavement. Then up an avenue, along another major road, past a disco with a doorman who stared. When the woman turned into a side street, Douglas felt his heartbeat speed: this would be a good place to... talk to her, make her acquaintance. He forced his feet to move faster, tilting his body forward to avoid slipping on the frosty slabs.

A gate. She was going into a gate. He could get to her just before she got her keys out... He had his hand on the iron of the gateway even as she was halfway up the path. Saw her fumble for her key, start forward again and...

... And saw the door open, saw the tall dark figure framed there, hand flapping in a silly wave.

'Saved you the trouble,' said a male voice, sounding pleased with itself.

'Hope you've put the kettle on as well,' the woman replied, with a laugh.

Douglas shrank back against the bushes beside the gate, ready to run if they saw him. Seconds later the door closed, blotting out the domesticity of their little world.

And the sex, the sex! Tonight her husband would peel her stockings and her panties off, revealing her creaminess. He'd unclip her bra, and let her heavy white bosom hang free. He'd... Heat expanded Douglas's testes as he lumbered on, picturing their excitement. *Want, want, want* cried his balls. He turned towards the rooming house, wishing he'd paid more attention to the route he'd been following. It was going to take him ages to get back.

Pulling his black winter coat more closely around his body, he half shut his eyes against the increasing sharpness of the February wind, put his head down as if he were in mourning. Walked past house after house of warm, companiable folk.

He needed something new in his life—or at least the promise of it. Something to look forward to, something to plan for that was more satisfying than a night at the pub.

His existing fish weren't enough any more, much as he liked them. The coldwater and tropical tanks only needed a partial water change every three weeks. Even allowing for trimming the plants and removing small traces of algae, he could clean them both in an hour and a half. Anyway, it would be exciting to have marine creatures like crabs and starfish and sea apples, the electrifying enigmas in the world's waters, just waiting to be fished...

When he got home, he opened one of the miniature vodkas he'd bought, poured it into a glass and added a little orange juice. Dutch courage to phone mummy dearest, something he thought he'd never do. It was midnight in Edinburgh. It would be day-time there.

Taking a print-out of her phone number from the computer, he went to the pay phone on the stairway. As a teenager he'd once been given an address book by a neighbour: she'd received a spare one as a gift. He'd written his own address in the owners section, then, after some hesitation, inked in the address of his school and his doctor. That was it. The blank pages had mocked him, a memorial to his isolation. Now he kept the few workmates names and details he needed on disk.

'Hello?'

She seemed to pick up the phone seconds after he finished dialling. She sounded just as hyped up as she'd ever been.

'Alice—it's Douglas.'

If he said 'It's me' she invariably asked 'Who?' and angered and upset him, got the conversation off to a bad start.

'Douglas! Is something wrong! Are you...?'

'Everything's fine, Alice. I... you said I could have a present from Australia. There's this Cone...'

'A what?' In the background he heard her say 'No' and 'It's Douglas.'

'A Geography Cone. It's a kind of water snail.'

'And I can post it to you?'

He closed his eyes. Had she really ever given birth to him?

'No, you'd have to... I don't suppose you know anyone who's coming to Britain soon?'

He half listened as she muttered on about still finding their feet, and the Aussies being different. If she could have bought a Cone direct from a dealer and given it to someone to carry in their hand luggage, that would have been ideal. According to the books he'd been reading if you wrapped the creature in something damp and kept it moist, it probably wouldn't come to any harm. Instinct would take over. It would retreat into its shell until conditions were conducive to coming out.

But no friends equalled no hand luggage. He took a deep breath. He'd have to do things the riskier way. Risky, because he couldn't let Alice know that his purchase was suspect, could kill a man. If he did she'd tell Paul who would abort the whole project. Or worse...

He stared at the wallpaper, trying to focus on the pattern, wishing he'd forgone that last gin and tonic.

'Well...' He'd almost called her 'mum', which would make her go all remote on him, 'Well, Alice, could you visit one of the big aquarists that promise to get you anything? Tell them your son's an aquarist in Scotland. Say that he wants a collection of cone shells. I'll spell out the names.'

He went through the list, starting with Conus Textile, the Textile Cone. It would cause severe symptoms in those that were stung. 'Tulip Cone,' he added, 'As in the flower, Alice.' He took a deep breath before mentioning the one he really wanted—the Geography Cone. This, Conus Geographicus, had the venom to end all venoms. He swallowed hard then added his final request, the Striated Cone. All he really cared about was the Geography Cone, but it looked best to buy a collection of the snails.

'And do I get them in a bag, or...?'

'No, just give them my address and details, ask for them to be delivered to me. Pay whatever they ask when you place the order and add enough for a generous tip.'

He spent a moment or two working out the exchange rate before telling her exactly how much of a gratuity to give them, 'There are planes coming over all the time with specimens for the aquarium trade.' He listened impatiently for a moment, 'Yes, they'll notify me to collect them. I'll reimburse you within days.' He winced as he heard footsteps creaking behind Eleanor's door, 'It'd be a great help.'

'You always did like fish—remember that goldfish?'

He'd done it! Done it! Full of tiredness and gratitude, he fed coins into the slot and let her ramble on. It should be fine, now: importing the animals wasn't illegal. And the non-toxic cones looked so similar to the toxic ones that only a trained specialist could tell them apart.

He said 'Uh huh' to show he was still listening to her monologue. Felt his shoulders beginning to relax as she said she'd go to the aquarists in the city the next day. He had little to lose and much to gain... like a new creature. One with hidden powers—the power to paralyse.

He'd be safe if a burglar broke in and thrust his hand into the marine tank, safe if Eleanor Denning interfered. It was exciting to own something which could hold a woman... a *person* in limbo. Breathing quickly, Douglas brought the conversation to an end.

CHAPTER THIRTY THREE

Australia had masses of land that remained uncultivated. You could go to the beach at Christmas to sunbathe. You could...

Marjorie's thoughts faltered and her heart leapt as her casually flickering eyes took in the floating occupant at the top of the aquarium. Not another casualty, not again. Holding her breath, she walked over to the tank to find if the occupant was ill or actually dead.

Fins moved as she got closer, lidless eyes staring at her from a funny angle. So the creature was down but not out. She watched for a moment, feeling responsible, feeling helpless. The other fish looked at her, then swum up to the surface of the water, begging for food. Were they genuinely hungry or just being greedy? Maybe this fish was having problems because it had been overfed?

But poor water quality could also affect the inhabitants. So could the tank's temperature—the chill caused by a particularly cold night, the sudden heat of a fiercer than usual early morning sun. Then there were internal diseases which the fish might have been harbouring before she purchased it. Some of those could lie dormant for months before the illness showed itself. Even a simple water change could bring out latent diseases. It was hard to know if she was doing anything wrong or not.

Marjorie returned to her armchair, focused on the TV again with its jovial afternoon presenter. How did the woman manage to remain so slim when she did that cookery slot, tasted these rich cream sauces every day? And every time a camera man's wife or female producer had a baby they toasted it with champagne on the show and during Wimbledon they had strawberries with double cream. Moreover these celebrities were always appearing at three course luncheons and five course dinners, or shared a platter of croissants over a working brunch...

Averting her eyes from the tank, Marjorie tried to concentrate on the programme. Damn, the *Keep Fit With Karen* slot was about to start. Fixed grins and flailing arm movements, legs held at hip distance. Boring to watch and doubtless impossible to do unless you were thin. Marjorie made a face at the instructor and changed to another channel. A lion was bringing an antelope to the ground, determined teeth locked into its neck.

She flicked another switch: a black and white movie. The next channel was showing ballroom dancing: women with stiff smiles and even stiffer arms.

Sighing, Marjorie turned off the TV with the remote and walked into the kitchen. The clock on the microwave told her it was 3pm. Hurrying to the fridge, she got out the Red Leicester, a jar of pickles, butter and a tomato. Took a large crusty loaf from the bread bin and cut herself four thick, uneven slices. Time for an afternoon snack.

When she'd finished making up the sandwiches, she

tossed the knife into the sink where it joined the plate that had held her lunchtime lasagne. Tea was to be tuna salad and chips: she'd make them herself.

Well, it helped pass the time, peeling the potatoes and flaking the pink fish and chopping the lettuce and carrots. Though if you bought them, you had the interlude of a walk to the delicatessen and the chip shop and back...

Cheering up, Marjorie took her food and mug of tea over to the kitchen's breakfast bar where her confessions magazine lay. Pulling up a stool, she began to read about a woman who'd left her newborn baby on the steps of a hotel. Well, not a woman, really—a girl. Sweet sixteen and only been kissed etcetera the one time. Which was still more than she, Marjorie, had been!

She bit into her sandwich, the sharp taste of the cheese contrasting with the softness of the bread and moist crunchiness of the pickle. She could sit here and read all afternoon. Just relax, not worry about anything, not expect too much. Even people who worked full time had days off and holidays, and they didn't feel low and trapped, didn't pace the room or cry.

She finished her second sandwich, sipped her mug of tea until it was over. The story ended ambiguously with the baby going to a good home but the mother still wondering if she'd done the right thing. Marjorie went back to the TV: the same black and white film was on, plus more cookery. The fish in her aquarium was now turning increasingly belly up.

Do the dishes, wipe the surfaces down. She did so. Empty the waste paper baskets. She shook a few tissues and sweet wrappers into the bin liner and knotted it at the top. She should really go to Michael's and get something for this poor floating creature. But it was cold outside, and she couldn't bear to ask him for medication yet again.

Simon—she could phone Simon. Her pulse speeded up, and she looked uncertainly in the direction of the telephone. Some days he put on his cold 'what do you want now?' kind of voice. Other times he could be quite chatty, pleased to hear from her.

'Just stopping for a tea-break,' he'd say, 'You wouldn't believe...'

The editorial assistants all went down to the canteen together for their breaks, but Simon, as Chief Sub Editor stayed at his desk and had his tea and biscuits there. Which, unless he made or received a personal phone call, usually meant reading yet another copy of *Stella* to while away the time. He'd mentioned that if he read a rival publishers newspaper for entertainment rather than research, the editor disapproved.

He'll be glad I called. Glad. She dialled the company's number, put her professional voice on. Some of his ex-girlfriends had told her they got through by saying they were the mothers of *Stella* readers. Sometimes Reception tried to screen out personal calls.

'Just connecting you now,' said an efficient but pleasant voice: there was a momentary pause then a girl answered.

'Can I speak to Simon?' Marjorie asked.

She held her breath, but the girl didn't ask who was calling, merely summoned him.

'Simon Brent,' said a rich, familiar voice.

'Oh, hi. It's me.' Her voice sounded high and breathless even to her own ears, 'I was wondering if you could do me a favour. You see...'

'Make it quick, Marj. I'm about to go into a meeting.'

'My Flame Tetra is sick.'

A sigh. A very loud sigh. A sigh that said he was mad at her.

'If you could just go to Michael's on your way home...'

'You're the one with all the free time, Marj. I've said before—try not to phone during the day.'

'I'm sorry.' She felt the tears gather and her throat start to ache, 'I didn't think.'

'Right. I'll speak to you later.'

He put the phone down and she wept.

It was twenty to four: he might not get home until eight or so. He might go out with Sue and not come back till the early hours. Marjorie thought of phoning her mum, decided against it. She liked to call when she had some news to tell her, something good.

She started walking towards the lounge again, caught sight of her reflection in the hall mirror. God, her hair was looking awful. She could at least trim a few centimetres from her fringe. Going into the bathroom cabinet, she found some nail varnish, a pearly pink colour. Trimmed her hair, then took the varnish back to her armchair and painted her nails.

When they were dry, she took off her tights and coloured her toe nails. Would anyone ever see them? It wasn't true that people who wanted to have sex usually did. What did you do if people wouldn't even come in for tea, for a sandwich? You waited and dreamed, wanting it to be nice...

She shuddered, remembering the incident. That was how she always thought of it, when she could bear to think about it at all. Such a normal early morning, still half-grey, with a little sunlight threatening. A normal early morning cleaning stint. She'd walked slowly along the road.

Still missing her secretarial job, still feeling slightly dislocated. A bit tired from getting up so early, a bit bored at the thought of the polishing and vacuuming tasks that lay ahead.

She'd wandered on to the piece of waste ground without really seeing it. After the second day she'd found this shortcut, which cut her journey by a good twelve minutes or so. Could vaguely recall stepping over half of a bicycle. Then suddenly he was there.

In front of her, staring, mouth open in a grin surrounded by a beard that was patchy. She'd stopped, jerked back a little. He'd grinned and grinned. Rocking back and forward slightly, though his feet stayed in the same place. She'd looked up from scuffed brown suede shoes to a grey coat to grey trousers with...

With the zip undone, and his hand beside it, holding himself. She'd only half registered the flesh-coloured appendage sticking through his curled fingers, but the rubbing movements he was making made it clear. Moving his hand up and down, he'd moved towards her. His pubic hair looked dry and aged.

Running, then, not able to see, to breathe, to concentrate. He might be running after her. He could kill her here, or take her someplace else and do what he liked. She stumbled, fancied she felt his breath on her neck, kept going. Didn't see the clump of weeds and almost fell again. Going towards the cleaning job out of habit. Trying to draw the early morning air deep into her lungs.

Trying and failing. *Inhale, inhale, inhale*. She'd dropped her bag when he first appeared, had raced on without it. No medication. Gasp and wheeze and choke.

She'd reached the office block that she was supposed

to clean, collapsed outside it. A janitor had called an ambulance—they'd told her so afterwards. Well mum had, asking why she hadn't had her inhaler, her handbag. She'd lied, saying she'd left it in the house. Couldn't bear to...

Well, it would have meant telling the police about what she'd seen—his maleness. Mum would find out. Mum would think she'd brought it on herself. And if they caught him, she'd have to look at his horrible grinning face again. And she didn't want to testify in court.

The next day she'd slept through the alarm, and the next day. You're not up to this job, mum had said, and she'd agreed. Sank back gratefully against the pillows as the older woman phoned the doctor for an appointment. A few days later she'd heard she was eligible for invalidity benefit, and mum had cancelled both her cleaning jobs. Mum had wanted Marjorie to come home and live with her again but she'd held out on that score. Advertised for a lodger to help pay the rent instead and got Simon. And now she had the *Fish Are Fun* outings as well.

She must have known that one day she'd feel better, feel strong enough to take a lover. She could never have brought a man home if she lived with mum. She smiled: Douglas was courting her slowly, gently. It was as if he knew she'd been through an ordeal. After the pub one night he'd put his arm tentatively round her waist. Then, at the last *Fish Are Fun* meeting his hand had brushed hers.

After it did so, he'd trembled and reddened. He was shy and sweet, and quite handsome in a slightly chubby way. A subtle touch, a smile, a look of longing. Maybe he'd take things further tomorrow night.

CHAPTER THIRTY FOUR

Maybe he'd take things further tomorrow night. With a shrug, Douglas turned his thoughts away from Marjorie and back to the text spread out before him. *Setting Up The Marine Tank* was the book's title, and he was on chapter three.

He'd bought the book and the tank and various other marine accoutrements from Michael, telling the man that he was getting the actual fish in a few days from a friend. Had brought the coral home with him as it had to be soaked for seventy two hours. The next day Michael had delivered the tank and hood and the heavy bags of substrate, plus the various mechanical devices that would keep his water warm and clear.

Carefully he washed the empty aquarium with warm water. Dried it, and fitted in the undergravel filter, inserted the airlift tubes. As he put the air pump in place, March tossed one of her gale-force winds against the window pane. Douglas shivered and rubbed his hands against his arms.

He'd already turned up the radiator but suspected Val had some central control that kept the power low. Perhaps he could buy an extra-warm jumper or start wearing his jacket in the house? Really, he'd have preferred an additional external source of heating but the rules forbid him to bring in an electric fire.

Cold. He was cold all the time nowadays. He felt... empty. He'd complained about it earlier today and Terry had snorted and pointed at the cadaver they were working on.

'That's what the Big Chill feels like, Duggie!'

The woman's arms had felt icy to the touch.

If only you could keep a warm, live woman in a kind of limbo. Keep her kittenish beauty, prevent her turning into a nagging bitch. There were instances throughout history of people who'd removed their loved ones from the grave and tried to keep them tender. Anointed them with spices, wrapped them in bandages, rubbed them with creams.

Others, too, who'd tried to revive the corpses. Men who'd wired their women up to the electricity and tried to shock them back to life. Men and women who'd promised their very souls to Satan for a few more years on this Earth together. Women who'd tried to milk their limp dead husbands of their dead cold sperm in the hope of producing his image in a live, warm child.

None of which worked—within days the tissues would dry as water evaporated. The eyes became cloudy, eyeballs sinking into the sockets, going brown. Then the lips would go hard and perhaps blacken, become unkissable. The veins would begin to rise, and blisters would appear.

He'd seen it all in corpses that hadn't been found for three or four weeks. Both belly and breasts became bloated, the hair falling out as you supported the head. The nails would start to come loose, the teeth equally liberated. The stomach would rupture, gases rise...

No, what one wanted to achieve was a near-death state: the peacefulness without the putrefaction, the malleability without the movement, the warmth without the wordiness. Imagine the sensual spectacle of a body just yours for the taking: nipples you could lick and suck on, breasts you could tongue, a cleavage you could create by the varying pressures of your hands.

And a waist that would never grow any less toned, any bigger. Smaller if you so wished it, if you fed the body less and less. He wasn't sure how you'd do this exactly, if you'd have to set a drip up. Maybe if you kept the head tilted you could squeeze a little honeyed water or liquefied broth down the throat?

Think nice thoughts, positive thoughts. He was getting tense again. Think of pushing her on her tummy and sliding in between her receptive legs. Picture ramming forward, pulling back, doing what you wanted to. A life of non-stop release...

His cock nosed at his trousers and he rocked back on his heels to take the pressure off it. Concentrate. Concentrate. He stood up and stretched over for the buckets of substrate he'd washed earlier and his elbow banged against the desk. Sent his aquarium hood flying, thankfully not in the direction of the glass rectangle. He winced as the heavy black cover hit the ground. *Damn*. The sound ricocheted round the walls for a moment. As he cringed at the discord, there was a knock on his door.

Given the noise he'd just made, there was no way he couldn't answer. Whoever was outside knew he was in. Awkwardly he hobbled across the room, stopping to put on and button up his jacket before holding his marine book in front of his erection. Undid the lock and opened the door slowly, eyes meeting those of the person they least wanted to meet.

'Raffle ticket time!'

Eleanor Denning waved a little booklet of coloured strips before him.

'I'll take two,' he said evenly.

'And you haven't even asked what it's for.'

I don't care, he thought, pushing his book closer to his maleness.

'What are you reading?' she asked, glancing down.

Die. Die. He willed his hardness to deflate but tension seemed to have turned it to concrete. When he said nothing, she read the title for herself.

'And that's what you're doing now?'

He nodded, shifted his footing slightly.

'Can I come in and see...?'

'No—it's not ready yet.'

He didn't want her in his room—ever.

'But you've other tanks of fish, haven't you? I've seen... Val said that's the third aquarium you've had delivered to the house.'

'She said I could,' he muttered, feeling like a five year old.

'Oh, I'm not saying you shouldn't, not speaking out of turn.'

Jingling the change in his pocket, he brought out a fifty pence piece and held it out to her.

'I'll just give you your tickets,' she said, looking pleased.

'No rush.'

He wanted to be in his room, alone, dreaming of his ever-ready lover.

'Rules is rules,' said Eleanor, writing something on two stubs and handing him a red ticket and a blue. 'Don't you want to know what you could win?'

She was being coquettish again: it sickened him.

'Surprise me,' he said, aiming for coldness. He sounded tired and weak.

'A tea set or a ten year old malt or a weekend in Brighton.' She was relentless, 'The weekend's for two,' she added with a shy little smile.

'I could take my girlfriend, then.' As he said it, he thought of Marjorie. Well they were meeting fairly often at the *Fish Are Fun* club, so she was the nearest thing he had.

'I didn't know you had a girlfriend.' Eleanor's rounded cheeks pinkened slightly, 'I've never seen you with anyone,' she said.

He looked down at the floor as he put his tickets in his pocket. There was no answer to that. What did she think she was—the all-seeing eye?

'Was that who you were chatting to on the phone recently?'

'No.' He tried to leave it there but she kept staring at him, 'I phoned Alice, my... my mum.'

'In Australia? Oh my gosh, that would set you back a bit. And you just dialled direct?'

He nodded, looked over her head at the stairwell. Had a sudden image of himself as a little boy, rushing desperately up a stair.

'She must know that she's loved, your calling her all that distance.'

Loved—there was that stupid word again.

'She was surprised to hear from me.'

'They can tell if it's not a local call out there. I've seen it in *Home And Away*.'

'Mmm?' He blinked: she'd lost him.

'It's a programme set in Australia. A real treat!'

'Oh.'

He must find a way to close the door—this was getting ridiculous.

'I'll have to return to my tank.'

'Can I see?'

He had a feeling they'd covered this ground before, would return there.

'There's nothing to see, yet. I haven't set the tank up.'

'But your other tanks—they're ready.'

Oh God, think, think. 'I was just going out. The... em...' He cast his eyes round the room, saw the sink full of coral, 'The sink's blocked,' he lied, forcing himself to make eye contact, 'I've got to buy a plunger from the store.'

'Val should do that.'

He shrugged: 'She's probably entertaining. Anyway I'm more than capable of doing it myself.'

When she still didn't step back he crossed over the threshold and pulled the door closed behind him, locking it quickly.

'See you later,' he said, edging round her and setting off down the stairs for a thoughtful walk.

CHAPTER THIRTY FIVE

'Tonight's the night for *Fish Are Fun*, I take it?'

Simon walked into the lounge and smiled at Marjorie. Then he took a deep breath, 'As it happens, I'm free all evening. Mind if a bored flatmate tags along?'

The way Marjorie looked at him, you'd have thought he'd suggested visiting a brothel.

'What's brought this on?' she asked, putting down her handbag-sized perfume spray and shifting her gaze from the TV news.

'Well, I don't want to see Sue *every* night. Anyway, I share a flat with these beasties. If I'm to be sent for fish medication, I might as well find out what's making them ill.'

It was the best he could come up with at short notice. He'd just walked in and seen her all dressed up and had feared things wouldn't turn out right, that Douglas, or someone equally remote, would exploit her. That she'd end up pregnant or diseased or worse.

'So when do we leave?'

He was determined to keep the conversation upbeat, jovial. He knew he'd been too harsh when she phoned before. But to apologise to Marjorie was to bring on a full-scale attack of martyrdom. Being nice was a better way of making amends.

'This dress alright?'

He spent the next few minutes going through the usual reassurances. No, her hemline wasn't too long, yes her fringe was straight, no, it would be overkill to wear her one high-heeled pair of sparkly shoes.

'What's the topic tonight, anyway?'

'You can check the prospectus in the letter rack,' Marjorie said, with a smiling shrug.

'Interested in all things fishy, are we?' Knowing she went there for the men, it was hard not to jest.

'It's my social life!' Marjorie flopped back in her chair, but her eyes were laughing. Moments like this showed him she had more insight into her existence than he usually realised.

'Talking of social life—I saw Douglas a few weeks ago in an Indian Take-away.'

Her shoulders stiffened, and she looked over at him again: 'Alone?'

'Uh huh.' He hadn't mentioned it till now, didn't want to remind her more than necessary of the man. But they were seeing him tonight and he might make reference to that earlier time.

'Were you talking to him, then?'

'Oh, just a few words in passing. I was with Sue. He'd been to Michael's, I think.'

'Oh.' Marjorie looked back at the television then glanced at her watch again, 'Do you think we should leave now?'

He smiled at her, feeling the old familiar pain start up again.

'No, Marj. Not for at least half an hour.'

Even at that, they were still too early. Marjorie went to the Ladies and Simon paced the room. Looked at the walls, at children's drawings of heavenly choirs and not-so-heavenly donkeys. He'd liked Sunday School—an opportunity to win pencils and books for naming the saints or simply attending. Jo had hated it, though, felt trapped by the relentless gaze of the teachers, the little circles of seats.

He waited for Marjorie to come back, determined to support her. She wouldn't end up like his sister: no way. He walked round again, wondering what the readers of *Stella* would make of a *Fish Are Fun* club. Many of them loved dogs and horses, but boys and fashion were the order of the day...

'I'm back,' Simon smiled as Marjorie made the obvious statement, 'Hasn't got any busier,' she added. He reminded himself that the only person she regularly spoke to beside himself was her intellectually-challenged mum.

'They'll be here soon enough. Where do you want to sit?'

She chose the circle with the largest number of chairs, near the speaker. Lots of space for Douglas to make an appearance, Simon thought.

A moment later she started blushing and he looked up to see the man appear in the doorway. Marjorie waved to him and noisily scraped back her chair.

'Cold again,' called Douglas, when he was half way across the room. Moving awkwardly, he took a seat across from them, leaned forward to deposit his carrier bag.

'Being buying anything new?' Marjorie asked brightly.

'Hoping to sell, actually.' Douglas's eyes flickered, as if he were uncertain that this was allowed. 'Got to keep my room from getting too cluttered,' he added in a rush, 'And I've learned all I need to about the basics of coldwater and tropical tanks.'

'So you're selling the books?' Simon prompted.

Douglas nodded. Marjorie smiled at them both.

'Yes. I thought I'd mention it to the organiser, see if he has any objections...'

'I think it's a good idea,' Marjorie said.

Douglas smiled at her. She smiled back at him. Simon felt his nails curl in to touch his palms almost involuntarily. Still he kept his voice jokey, light: 'You'll soon have outgrown this club, then?'

'No, I want to learn about mari... '

Douglas cut himself off mid-word, and coughed awkwardly, 'Want to learn about less hardy tropicals, about breeding methods,' he said.

'I'd like to know more about improving ones water quality,' Marjorie added nervously.

All three looked up as several more men hurried through the door.

'Cold!' they said, 'Not a night to be outdoors.'

Simon smiled as he recognised John and Michael amongst the six men walking towards them. John said 'Hi' and Michael nodded at everyone as he took his seat.

'That medication working?' he asked Simon.

Awkward question. Simon turned to Marjorie who nodded and looked away.

If only he could get Michael and Marjorie together, let him see how sweet and loving she could be. The shopkeeper probably had the impression that she ate men like him for breakfast. Simon sighed inwardly at the analogy. In truth it had been years since she'd even had a snack...

John started telling one of the older men about some Apple Snails he was breeding.

'Got any exciting new stock?' Simon asked Michael, hoping he'd name some fish familiar to Marjorie so that she could join in.

'In the tropical line?' Michael started to reel off a list of names. Simon glanced at Douglas who was eyeballing Marjorie's breasts. Marjorie had gone pink, was frozen with self consciousness but was pretending not to see.

Fish types and behaviours and habitats and foodstuffs and mating habits. Simon's mind wandered as the speaker for the evening got underway.

At the coffee break, Douglas, Marjorie, a woman in her fifties and himself shared a table and Douglas succeeded in selling the older woman his books for her son. Marjorie somehow brought the conversation round to a keep fit teacher she'd seen on TV, and they all agreed that they'd avoided sports since school.

'It would be interesting to study the correlation between fishkeepers and more cerebral hobbies,' added Douglas. Both the older woman and Marjorie looked impressed.

'Last orders, please!' shouted one wag, and Douglas winced slightly.

'According to the prospectus we get a film on Catfish now,' he said.

'It does rather seem to be focused on tropical, doesn't it?' added the woman.

'I'm glad—I've a tropical tank,' Marjorie replied.

'You can keep certain catfish in a coldwater aquarium, though it helps to have a heater just to take the chill off the water,' said Douglas, 'In winter the goldfish appreciate that too.'

'I read that—that sudden changes of temperature could affect them,' Marjorie added.

Douglas smiled at her and she looked as if she'd won a prize.

'Back to work,' joked Simon as people began to leave their tables and walk towards the rows of seats in front of the slide projector. He wondered if he was the only one who found these little gatherings awkward and tense. Still, they'd gotten through it and Douglas hadn't asked Marjorie for a date or anything. At least, not yet...

'I'm thirsty now,' she said, looking at Simon and Douglas as the evening ended.

As if unwilling to commit themselves, everyone headed for the door. Simon brightened as Michael came level with them.

'We were thinking of going to the pub,' he told the shopkeeper, 'Want to come?'

'Love to, but I've to arrange next months Discus Show with the organisers.'

'Another time,' said Simon, turning to his flatmate with a shrug.

'How about you, Douglas?'

Marjorie sounded wary, none too hopeful.

'There's a decent bar just over the back of the cinema,' Douglas agreed.

'Good, I could use a drink,' added Simon and they both looked at him impatiently.

'Enjoy yourself!' Michael grinned, starting to hurry ahead.

At the door, he turned back, and winked at Douglas.

'Bought any jellyfish yet?'

'No,' muttered Douglas, flinching. And as Simon stared at him, the funeral director blushed and hung his head.

CHAPTER THIRTY SIX

Rain outside and a television screen filled with romances. Even her confessions magazine largely centred around male and female relationships. *I Cheated On Him And Lost His Love* was this week's main story. She'd never cheat...

Had no one to cheat on, she acknowledged sadly. Had this rented flat, a flatmate who suddenly wanted to play gooseberry, and a few ailing fish. Douglas hadn't made plans to see her again after the last *Fish Are Fun* evening. She crossed her cold fingers and prayed it was only Simon that was putting him off.

The air was cool in here yet somehow stagnant. She lumbered over to the window and opened it a quarter of an inch. Her stomach rubbed against the lower window frame, felt bloated. She breathed in, out, in, monitoring the tight feeling in her chest. Went over to her nearest inhaler, the one she kept on top of the coffee table, and used it twice.

The pressure eased slightly. She walked to the phone and dialled.

'Can I see Dr Ashford today?'

A slight pause.

'He's not here.'

'Not here?'

'He'll be on holiday for the next fortnight.' The receptionist's voice was coolly familiar, 'You can see a relief doctor, though.'

She said that was fine, secretly hoping it wasn't a lady doctor. She didn't like lady doctors. They made her feel awkward, almost ashamed. They might ask about her most recent employment and she'd have to admit it had just been a cleaning job. Well, two...

Even her work in an office hadn't been demanding or exciting. Compared to them she'd done so little with her life.

But a man was different. A man didn't judge you on the same terms—at least she hoped he didn't. She'd take time to blow dry her curls to give them extra body and bounce, wear her best dress and those new tights that were free with her latest magazine. She might even polish her shoes!

Feeling better for making the appointment, Marjorie showered and dressed and made her hair look pretty. The receptionist had said that the doctor could see her at midday. They had a cancellation then.

She walked to the surgery, shivering. Rain drove against her face, felt strangely grainy. She had to keep her eyes half-closed. A girl stood on tiptoe to kiss a boy as she passed them at the bus stop. A woman hurried by, smiling down at her small, tail-wagging brown dog. Further along a teenage couple were holding each other and laughing beneath a golf umbrella, his hand in the back pocket of her jeans.

Walk on. Walk on. She forced herself to walk faster. They were probably wondering why someone her age didn't wear a wedding ring. Men and women looking into each others eyes on posters for champagne, for gold, for coffee. Couples shopping for carpets, for children's toys, for food. Her throat felt raw, her nose itched, her breath seemed caught and held as if in a vacuum. She couldn't cope.

When she gave her name to the receptionist, her voice sounded reedy.

'Are you alright?' asked the woman. She looked displeased.

Marjorie nodded with difficulty. The boy standing next to her was staring. She didn't want to make a fuss. She hated the thought of being singled out with everyone looking. The small queue waiting to collect repeat prescriptions would notice her if she was led away.

Walking into the waiting room now. Others looking up, looking at her. Then waiting, waiting. Not enough room, despite the name. Other doctors from the practice called other patients. Breathe, she told herself. Breathe. Breathe.

'Miss Milton?'

He was young, dark-haired, good looking in a thin sort of way. She stood up, and for a second clutched the chair back and feared she would fall. *Walk. Walk.* She followed him out of the room, and down the corridor, through the door which still bore Dr Ashford's name.

'Now, what can I do for you?'

'I can't breathe properly.' The words came out in half-gasps, sounded reluctant.

He immediately left his chair and knelt by her side.

'I see you're asthmatic. Are the symptoms the same as usual?'

'They're getting worse.'

Even as she spoke, the constriction in her chest began to ease and she exhaled less painfully. His eyes were a warm brown, caring, close.

'Recently,' she added proudly, 'I had such a bad attack that I almost died.'

Now he was really interested in her, eyes widening further.

'You were hospitalised?'

'My mother called for an ambulance. Yes.'

She hoped she looked small and pale as he stayed beside her, stretching out for his notes.

'If you'd like to stay here for a while today in the nurses room so that we can keep an eye on you?'

'No, really. I feel better now, rarely have two attacks in the one day. I just—I'm not sure if my new inhaler's right for me. It seems to take longer to work.'

Stronger medication. A referral to a new Asthma Clinic. He talked for long, compassionate moments. He touched her arm.

'If you feel bad at any time during the day or night get help right away.' He paused, 'Do you live with anyone?'

'I have a flatmate.'

She was so glad she had a flatmate. She tried to look brave as she stood up to go.

'Good.' The doctor smiled at her gently, 'Try not to be alone overnight.'

As she left he was writing furiously in her records, had obviously realised how serious her case was and had mentioned the likelihood of repeat visits to the Asthma Clinic. Feeling better than she had in ages, Marjorie hurried home.

CHAPTER THIRTY SEVEN

Purple eye-shadow, a matching skirt, legs in tan nylon that she spreadeagled on a mattress in a darkened room. She'd bared herself for him, made him a proper man. He wanted her again. Wanted her now!

He reached for her breasts but they blurred into another's breasts, which said something about a party. A party in the park. They'd lain down together behind some bushes, groping, holding. She'd been noisy at first, but had learned quickly. He'd like to see her again too, if she kept quiet...

The alarm clock startled its sound round the room, bringing with it full consciousness. Damn, he'd been having such nice half-dreams. If he could just stay in that twilight area for a few more moments, just recapture the essence of what he'd lost.

But it was Friday: a work day, a responsibilities day. He awoke more fully, sat up in bed, reached for his dressing gown, wished his joints didn't feel as if they'd been made to run miles and miles. Even in his terry towelling bed socks his feet felt chilled. Yet he hated slippers, refused to have them in the house.

Spring always got to him like this: made him feel dislocated. The early morning sun, laced with cold, sent out conflicting signals, further irritating him. It was too cool to rely on his jacket, too warm for a coat. His stomach begged for toast, scones: a feast of carbohydrate. Pity he'd gone to the pub on Wednesday night instead of doing the weekly shop.

Still, he'd wanted drink more at the time: still did, come to that. He'd been mad at that Simon, tagging along with Marjorie like some over-protective dad. Coming with them to the bar after *Fish Are Fun* and hogging the conversation with his publishing jokes. He'd thought of his own work, dismissed it, ignoring Simon's attempts to find about the funeral trade. Women didn't like to hear about how bodies atrophied, how they were despatched.

Well, Marjorie didn't anyway: she never asked him about his day to day duties. But she normally sat and smiled and nodded, made him feel confidant as he talked about fish. Some weeks before he'd even told her some facts about Australia and she'd seemed interested, impressed.

'It must be nice, eating outdoors with friends,' she'd said, and there had been hope in her eyes.

Eat, eat... He reached for his biscuit tin and found some cheese-flavoured crackers. Ate six whilst waiting for the kettle to boil then had another four with his tea. He and Marjorie had shared a bag of crisps in the pub: he'd noticed that her nails were painted. She looked clean and wholesome, if a little large.

Simon hadn't eaten any crisps, had sipped at his whisky.

'Driving?' Douglas had asked, feeling wild.

He'd said no, that they'd walked: he made Douglas feel lazy, greedy. Even Marjorie had looked down at the table, and her bosom had fallen forward, revealing the crevice between her breasts.

Big breasts, attractive breasts. A pulse in his groin fluttered as he remembered them. Walking over to the wardrobe, he pulled out a shirt and tie. Until recently he'd ironed his clothes the night before, then laid them out on a chair after ironing them. Now it seemed too much trouble: they'd do.

He peered out into the corridor: no Eleanor. Dashed into the bathroom and emptied his burning bladder. Sod the bath. He wasn't really dirty anyway, could have one tonight instead. It would give him something to do after the pubs closed. He hadn't been sleeping well. He needed to sleep less and less.

At night, at any rate. The mornings were different—hazy. When the alarm went off he usually wanted to throw it across the room. Work wasn't enough any more: was a prelude to life, not the whole of it. There had to be more...

There was. He was just tying his shoelaces when the phone in the hall went. He heard Val's slightly tinkling voice, then she knocked on his door and called 'It's for you.'

Reevon's, he thought: wanting him to get a move on. Grabbing his jacket, he locked his door and hurried to the phone.

'Hello?'

He forgot to breath and his stomach contracted slightly as he heard the caller's name and position. His consignment of Cones had arrived in the country—success! He cleared his throat, concentrated on sounding like Reevon did when he made an important business call: 'I'm inundated with work at the moment. I'll arrange for a delivery service to pick them up.'

After putting down the receiver, he leafed through the Yellow Pages and found a private carrier service. When could they deliver? What did they charge? He'd have his Cones that very night—a quartet of carnivorous creatures. He wondered if they'd eat dead flesh such as tinned sardines or if he'd have to buy them live minnows or similar tiny fish.

He had a momentary vision of the handler being spiked through the holding box, collapsing at the airport. But the aquarists would have labelled it as *Livestock: Handle With Care*. He wasn't going to handle it at all: he wasn't stupid. But someone might...

He must have walked to work but he couldn't remember making the journey.

'Morning after again?' Shelley asked.

He blinked, shrugged.

'Isn't he a little ray of sunshine?' she added in her falsely-sweet tone. Reevon looked at her with his intense unsmiling eyes: 'We can't all have your sensitivity, my dear.'

Someone was on his side. Douglas shrugged off his jacket and walked towards his coat hook. Once such a comment would have cheered him, but now it was no longer enough. So what it people stood up for him sometimes? He was still an object of pity, a figure of fun. Oh, they asked about his Christmas—but he'd still spent the entire period alone. No, they went through the motions, displayed their social skills, salved their consciences. He was still on the outside, looking in.

Damn Alice. Damn Paul. They'd ruined his chance of a normal life. All those years of mocking him, turning him into a sullen creation: half-adult, half-child. By the time they'd emigrated it had been too late: he couldn't communicate. Could only relate to the selfless acceptance of the dead.

Or the almost dead. He shuddered, remembering his morning dream, and Reevon touched his arm and pulled his mouth into a sympathetic line.

'Don't mind her,' he said, 'Got out of the wrong side of the bed as usual.'

'Mmm? Oh, I don't. It's just her way.'

If only he'd had a man like this for a father, he thought sadly. If only he'd had a father at all.

But you had to live for now, make the best of things. By tonight he'd have a new pet to add to his hobby, or, as Alice would have put it, another string to his bow. Imagine owning a creature that could hold someone prostrate. Not that he'd ever do such a thing, but it was exciting, having that power.

Cot deaths, pensioner deaths, suspicious deaths. All that day he dealt with corpses that the coroner had finished with, whilst his mind felt tremblingly alive. The coroner had to do a post mortem unless the person had been seen by a doctor within the last seven days.

Adrian worked with him, mind and hands active, talking of his latest venture into Tai Chi.

'The instructor was honest—said not to believe all that New Age crap. Said they hold back on teaching you the kicks that could maim your opponent. You know, for insurance purposes, in case they're sued.' He nodded and Adrian continued. 'So it's not guaranteed to work in self defence.'

What was the man on about? He agreed again, made a couple of neutral comments. He'd never been able to loosen up at sport.

'Doesn't your wife mind?'

If he had a wife, he'd stay home with her. No he wouldn't, he corrected himself as the image settled. The thought of someone there all the time, talking, moving, made him feel nauseous, trapped.

What did he want? What could he get? He could feel his stomach twisting up again. Too many headaches in the morning, too many gnawing nights awake after the pub.

'Going to the old watering hole tonight?'

The guys had commented on his hungover state a couple of times and he'd given the impression a group of them went to the pub together. Well, it was true occasionally, after *Fish Are Fun*.

'No, not tonight.'

He had to wait in for a parcel, a very special parcel. He looked at his watch again and wished that its hands would race round.

CHAPTER THIRTY EIGHT

Round, round—was it really still moving? He sat on his bed and stared at his alarm clock: it read 6pm. The courier service had said they'd deliver sometime between six and eight: he'd left early. Now he'd been home for almost an hour. At the briefest tinkle of the bell he'd leap into action. He didn't want Eleanor Denning getting there first.

Keep calm, calm. He looked again at his gloves, wished it was still Winter. That way he could wear them to answer the door, pretend he'd just come in. But in April this would look strange, cause the man to remember him. And he felt more comfortable when no one gave him a second glance.

Soon, soon. He looked at his marine tank, ready and waiting for its decorative occupants. He'd had to move the furniture around for the only available space had been visible from the door. The last thing he wanted was his neighbour marching in to inspect his purchases so he'd pushed his bed along towards his PC and fitted the tank in the space near the other two tanks.

Better than having the Cones next to his divan. Contemplating, he felt colder than ever, pulled his knees up under his chest. Imagine if the glass was pushed outwards and he woke to find a heavy rough shell on his face preparing to attack him. Some books said the Cones had a siphon, others mentioned a specially sharp tongue. Whatever, the creatures could eject a poisonous spine into their victims. This was how, in the wilds, they caught their prey.

Caught divers hands, too, if they brushed against them by accident. He'd read in *Marine Toxicology* about the ones who'd been paralysed after grabbing a handful of sand which contained a Cone. Some had died, others had eventually come round after being comatose for up to ten hours. *Up to ten hours.*

Douglas stared at the empty, waiting waters. Had anyone ever been stung at repeated intervals, say every second or third day? Would the body die or would its defences partially rally? In other words, could you keep it paralysed for the rest of its life?

The doorbell, arrowing through the house, caused him to recoil then scramble into an upright position.

'I'll get it,' he called, and started towards his door. Went out onto the landing, praying no one else would beat him to it. Took the steps two at a time, not even bothering to hold onto the rail.

'Parcel for Tate.'

A biker stood there, holding a well-taped cardboard box under his arm. Douglas inhaled sharply: he hadn't realised the Cones would come by bike.

'I'm Tate. Where do I sign?' He motioned the boy to put the box down on the doorstep.

'Here, and here. Cash on delivery.'

He paid.

The Cone was his—his! He watched as the biker turned away, then stepped into the house and picked the box up by its top string. Carried it away from his body, taking the stairs slowly now. He didn't want to die suddenly: the bladder and bowels could open, discharging their contents. No dignity, lying in your own waste matter on the stair.

'Was that a delivery man?' He heard Val's voice behind him but kept on walking.

'It was for me,' he called back, 'Mail order plants for my fish.'

He'd already decided on that story in case he met Eleanor Denning. It explained all the *Handle With Care* signs, the sticker about livestock on top of the box.

'Lucky fish.' Her voice sounded giggly, as if she was flirting with him.

He thought of asking her up to see them but this wasn't the time.

Handle With Care. He put the box down on the floor and stared at it for a moment. Got the big scissors from the writing desk and cautiously cut the tape.

Opened the box, half expecting something to hop out at him, realised that he was being stupid. These creatures didn't leap into the air but propelled themselves along the ground with a muscular foot like other aquarium snails.

Careful, careful... He put on his leather gloves, pulled out masses of padding to find four heavy plastic pouches with zip fastenings. Unzipped one to see nothing but wet cotton wool. Walking over to the marine tank, he agitated the material, shaking it out over the water. Watched as a Cone fell from its temporary home into its new des res. Three to go. Moving carefully, he repeated the process. Turned the pouches inside out when he was finished to make sure there was nothing living left inside.

Intricate markings in strong, bright colours. He thought the Geography Cone was the reddish brown, somewhat oblong one, got the book he'd bought just to make sure. Yes, that was it—ten centimetres long with a reticulated pattern. One of the most deadly molluscs in the world!

As he watched, the Cones, as if by tacit agreement, buried themselves in the sand, leaving only their syphons protruding. Presumably this allowed them to breathe.

He stared at them for a while, all lying there, just filtering water. Could they attack each other? There was no one he could ask. Well, there was Michael, but the man would start to become suspicious if he asked another poisonous creature question. He'd already made that jellyfish joke at the club.

Douglas stretched out on his bed and folded his arms behind his head. Tomorrow was Saturday, so he could spend all day thinking and observing his Cones. He closed his eyes, imagining Shelley coming by to sort out some administrative error or arrange his overtime. Grinned, picturing how her face would change as he plunged it into the water, held it there. Imagined the Geography Cone sliding imperceptibly towards her. His skin prickled with pleasure: almost anything could happen from now on.

CHAPTER THIRTY NINE

Time on his hands again: his watch said 11am. It was Saturday. He hated going to the pub this early: it was an admission of defeat. No friends to visit, no family to see, no shopping that you cared about. He took the cherry brandy from the wardrobe and slugged some straight from the bottle, gasping as it went down, down, down.

Sweet warmth suffused him, spread through his belly. Downstairs, he heard Val giggle. Heard Eleanor calling some last comment to their landlady as she trekked up the stairs.

So, it was an all girls together kind of weekend. Val's boyfriend seemed to have left: leastways he hadn't seen the man, or heard his deep laughter, for several weeks. She must get lonely sometimes in that large flat which had once housed a husband. And she'd flirted with him, Douglas, last night...

Ask her up to see the fish. Offer her a brandy. He'd concentrate on pointing out the beauty of the coldwater and tropical tanks. Not that it mattered if she preferred the pretty Cones—she wouldn't know the marine snails were of a venomous nature. Even if she only stayed for twenty minutes, it would be something. He was tired of keeping his hobby to himself.

He was halfway out of the door when he realised he'd forgotten to comb his hair or wash his face and hands. He backed into the room, stared into the mirror above the sink, noting that the glass needed a good clean. Everything seemed to take more effort nowadays, required an energy he found hard to summon. He wondered if he was simply getting old.

Val would make him young again—even if she was a more mature woman! As an afterthought he grabbed his jacket and shrugged into it: it made him look more of a man. She'd have had her breakfast by now, so he wouldn't be disturbing her. That reminded him, he really must eat something soon. Lack of food frequently hurt his head, numbed his thought processes. Drinking on an empty stomach always made things go a bit unclear.

Reaching her door, he steadied himself against the opposite wall for a few seconds. No voices. She definitely appeared to be alone. He knocked twice, waited a moment, knocked more loudly. Heard a light tread coming down the hall.

At first when the door swung open he only took in the tousled wet hair, droplets hanging from her curls then splashing downwards. Then he saw the towel, the cleavage, the bare and dripping legs.

'As you can see, I was in the shower, just home from my morning aerobics.'

She smiled. She seemed pleased enough to see him. He stared back.

'I've bought new fish,' he said, 'I thought you might like to see...'

See her tits, her big red nipples. His head seemed to dip slightly closer though he didn't instruct it to, brain and eye signals not quite connecting, feeling dulled. The towel pushed more closely to the teasing flesh. He licked his lips.

'I... not now.' Val's voice had gone colder, harsher. He pulled his gaze away from her body, looked at her face. Blushing—she was blushing, her lips set in an unyielding line, as if she hated him. 'If you'll excuse me,' she said, and slammed the door. He stood there, swaying slightly, listening as she shot two bolts into place. Heard her bare feet moving quickly away.

Bare feet, bare legs, bare everything. He'd wanted to reach out and grab her, wanted to... A teenage girl came hurrying down the stairs and frowned at him slightly. He stared after her, feeling too weak to move.

Eat, eat. He hauled himself slowly upstairs again. Went into the kitchen and rummaged in his half of the breadbin for a remaining roll. Nothing. He'd eaten them yesterday or the day before that. When had he last gone shopping, cooked a meal rather than had a pub lunch?

'Help yourself to my bread. I've got plenty.'

He jumped, feeling guilty, as Eleanor Denning came in.

'No.' He started automatically, then changed it to 'Well, it'd make things simpler. I'll pay you back.'

'Too much in a loaf for one—we should come to an arrangement.'

He shuddered, and took six slices back to the toaster in his room.

Food, drink: he munched the buttery crunchiness, had

another then yet another swig of cherry brandy. Fuck Val! God, he'd have liked to. Hungered to slide between these warm wet legs. Ease the towel off and palm breasts that were ripe for the touching. Cup that pert little backside and thrust in, in, in.

He was throbbing now, hard, but touching yourself was disgusting. Paul would get you. Paul could punish little boys. Yet it was little girls who were bad, who needed to be punished. Girls who caused you sexual tension, who teased.

The Cones seemed to mock him with their predatory brightness. They had colour and power: he was drab and had none. Just his maleness, crying out for attention. Just his sadness, crying out for release.

Going into his pocket for change, he walked to the phone like an automaton. Was aware that he could hardly focus, hardly think. Still, his voice came out fine, as it usually did in a crisis.

'Marjorie—it's Douglas. I thought you might like to come round.'

CHAPTER FORTY

A date—she had a date. Marjorie put down the phone and grinned at herself in the hallway mirror. Went back and picked up the receiver to phone Sue's house and give Simon the news.

And stopped, her finger poised at the right page of her address book. He might not be pleased to hear from her—he'd been mad the last time she interrupted him at work. And he and Sue might be... well, anything! After all, the girl had a flat to herself.

As she considered what to do, she inked a little drawing on the telephone pad. Stood up and began to walk towards her wardrobe: she'd surprise him with all the details of her burgeoning love life when he got home.

Assuming he got home first—she might be at Douglas's for ages. They'd have so much to talk about, what with his tanks and her getting to see his room. He'd probably show her round the whole house—she might even meet his neighbours. Maybe they could watch some TV together in the communal lounge. She could tell him about her visit to the doctor the other day, how worried he'd been. How they'd be keeping a closer eye on her from now on.

Maybe Douglas would want to go out for a drink or two. There'd even be time to see a film after lunch—or in the evening, if the date went especially well. They could go for a drive if he had a car. There was so much about him that she didn't know, wanted to know.

Obviously he felt the same way: hence the urgent phone call. She hugged herself as she took her best velvet jacket from its hanger and dusted it down. He must have felt increasingly attracted to her during all these meetings of *Fish Are Fun*.

What to wear? April was still acting like March, with winds that made her skirts billow out and embarrass her. Yet she didn't suit trousers, looked too big in the hips. A heavy dress would be best: she settled on a print of brown ferns on a lime green background. Knowing Simon wouldn't approve, she looked out her far-from-sensible gold high-heeled shoes.

She'd bought them in a sale—wishful thinking, really. When did she ever go to dances, to restaurants? Still, she'd worn them to Simon's nights out, to her mothers at Christmas. Each time she saw them in the wardrobe she felt hopeful that she'd go out someplace nice again.

Now yesterday's new tights, her prettiest briefs... she took all her clothes carefully into the shower room. Peeled off her dressing gown and nightdress, stepped into the sprays of hot water and got seriously clean. Normally she had a bath: the refuge of the lonely. It took longer to prepare, to luxuriate in. You took a lot of baths when you were on your own in the house all day and much of the evening. Not that she'd mind Simon deserting her after this.

Go! Go! Douglas had said to come round as soon as possible. As she waited at the bus stop she looked at the piece of paper upon which she'd written down his address all those weeks before in order to send him a Christmas card. He'd said that the house was a maze, just to ring the bell of the outside door and wait. He'd come down to let her in.

It must be exciting to live with several others—very sociable. There would always be someone around to talk to, something she'd never had. Mum said the same things all the time, usually negative. Simon could be great company when he wanted to, but there were so many demands on his time.

Douglas and Marjorie. Marjorie and Douglas. The bus arrived and she sat on the front seat, thinking of how their future could be. Mrs Marjorie Tate would be the wife to end all wives. An hour from now their lips might meet for the first time. Her stomach fluttered as they passed a street sign with a similar name to the one in which Douglas lived. Almost there...

She should get off here in case she went past her turning. He'd given her instructions but he'd sounded tired: they'd been slightly vague. She walked along, not minding the breeze or the light grey clouds that were gathering. She didn't even mind that she'd miss her favourite lunchtime programmes and the afternoon film.

Douglas, Douglas... for once all the street signs were clear and she didn't become lost or walk in circles. Within a few minutes of alighting from the bus she found the rooming house. Patted her hair and tugged at her dress hem, hoping he wasn't watching from a window. Moved her lips into a smile and rang the bell.

'Hello.'

She jumped and blushed a little. He must have been behind the door, just waiting to open it.

'That was quick,' she said, and he blinked. They stood there for a second. She'd forgotten to smile, must look grumpy. She tried again, said: 'I found you easily.'

'Come in. This way.'

He sounded slightly robotic, like a bad actor reading from a script. Was she too early? Too late? Too dressy? He turned his back, and, walking slowly so as not to trip in her sparkly shoes, she followed him up the stair.

To a large room that smelt as if it needed airing. The window was closed tight. He shut the door behind them as soon as she entered and she fancied she heard a lock click shut. The dryness of the atmosphere suggested the radiator had been on full for days.

'Voila!' said Douglas, and swung his hand in a semi-circle towards the tanks.

Marjorie drew nearer. 'Oh, that little black one's cute!'

'He's a Moor. That's my coldwater tank.'

'Are these real plants he's nibbling?'

'Elodea. Yes.'

'I had to move to plastic, couldn't get mine to grow properly. The leaves kept going brown.'

She waited for Douglas to suggest she should have used an iron fertiliser. She'd found that out later, when *Fish Are Fun* distributed leaflets on aqua plant care.

'Never mind them,' he said, and she noticed the crumbs clinging to his shirt front, 'Come and see this.'

Pink buds with orange centres, like half-opened chrysanthemums. She stared at the mass of colour and smiled.

'That's beautiful! Is it... What is it?'

He followed her gaze.

'That? That's coral. But I meant the shells.'

'Coral's marine, isn't it?'

She felt glad that *Fish Are Fun* had had a speaker on the cost of a new marine set-up. She'd seen the various invertebrates that went to make up a typical tank.

'Marine it is,' Douglas said in a monotone. She wondered if he was bored.

'Isn't that expensive?'

She moved ever so slightly closer to him. He gestured at the waste paper basket with its empty bags and boxes.

'Receipts are in there. See for yourself.'

He sounded so cold, so distant—did he think she was being mercenary? He'd been pleased when she asked questions at the club before.

'A thermometer, too.'

As she read it, her calves itched and her hairline felt clammy. Could the high setting of his aquarium thermostat have anything to do with the general warmth of the room?

This wasn't like she'd imagined—she wanted him to be nice to her. Passionate, even, undoing a button or two of her favourite springtime dress.

'Marjorie. I've wanted you for ages,' he'd groan as they did in the magazines.

'I know,' she'd whisper, as he bent his head to her breast.

'I've never seen coral this close before,' she said now, to break up the silence.

'See what else is in there too?'

She squinted uncertainly. He pointed to a shell almost buried in the sand. Yes, now he mentioned it she could see several such shells, near the bubbles from the airstone.

'You haven't put any fish in yet?' she asked, eyes examining the sand.

'These are better than fish, much more beautiful.'

'Lovely markings,' she said dutifully, thinking that they didn't seem to do very much.

'You can hold one of them. That one there—the reddish one. I've had it the longest. It's not so shy.'

'It's alive?'

The way he spoke, plus the air bubbles, made her think it must be.

'Like a mussel or a scallop. It's harmless. It'll... it'll change colour due to the heat of your palm.'

'Really?'

She'd never heard of that before. Trust Douglas to find something unusual. Even Simon the sophisticate would be impressed.

'See. I'll take the hood off the tank. You can just put your hand in.'

Marjorie grimaced: 'Won't I get electrocuted? Shouldn't you turn off the power?'

'No. I'll hold the lid up here—the fluorescent tube's well away from the water.'

He seemed to slur the word *fluorescent*. She wondered for the first time if he was drunk. Maybe nervous about their first date: that was understandable. She winced inwardly as dampness continued to spread beneath her armpits, adding to the heavy scent of the room.

Calm down. Calm down. No wonder you don't get asked out often. Listen to the man, smile, say intelligent things.

'Just put my fingers in like...?' The water was warmer than she'd imagined.

'Lucky you're wearing short sleeves,' Douglas said.

The phone rang through the house: it seemed to come from the stairway.

'Ignore it,' Douglas almost shouted. There was a startled pause then someone knocked on his door.

'Back in a mo.'

As she pulled her hand from the tank, he let the aquarium hood down noisily. She watched as he crossed the room in a few strides, opened the door a little and slipped through. He'd been so stealthy. Who'd been standing there that he didn't want her to see? And why? She walked to the other side of the large room and turned her ear towards the door.

'Thanks,' she heard him say in answer to a female voice. Was there someone here who fancied him? Who he fancied? She shivered: what about a former wife? Or maybe that was an ex-girlfriend phoning, trying to get him back?

In the romantic novels things never went as planned, especially for the heroine. There was always an ex-lover, a would-be lover in her hero's bachelor past. But she'd thought Douglas was like her—inexperienced. She'd hoped they could learn together, that they'd be kind to each other, pleased not to be alone any more.

Now she'd irritated him or bored him. She had to try harder! She had to fully appreciate these shells. They were probably exotic, imported all the way from the Pacific Ocean or the Great Barrier Reef or something. Maybe there was only a few like them in the world.

'Who was it?'

She smiled at him as he came back: wanting to show she was interested.

'Mmm? Work.'

His hands were clenched by his sides. His face looked pale and pinched.

She waited for his explanation, but he just walked over to his wardrobe and pulled a large black coat out.

'What did they want?' she prompted.

'Old man died at home. Daughter wants him off the premises now.'

'Oh!' she pulled a sympathetic face, 'So you have to give up part of your weekend to collect the body?'

'Twenty four hour standby, every day of the year.'

He sounded like a machine on automatic as he walked over to the mirror and put his black tie on.

'I'll leave...'

The words seemed to jolt him. 'No! Stay!'

'But... how long will you be?'

Scary, yet exciting to be left in his room on her own. She could at least open the window, get some air. And look at his books and tanks, find out more about him. Only...

'Promise, I'll be quick.'

'Okay.' She sat down on the edge of his bed, looked over at the other tanks. Mum would hate... Her excited brain remembered. *Mum*. She stood up again: 'I forgot— mum always phones me today. She'll be worried.'

'Simon'll tell her.'

'He doesn't know, yet. He's at Sue's.'

Picking up her shoulder bag, she found her purse and removed some change. 'I'll just use that coin box on the stair.'

She started to walk towards the door, conjuring up exciting and romantic descriptions of the day she'd have with Douglas, trying to second guess what her mother would say.

'Hang on.' He sounded over-stressed now, running his fingers through his hair as if he was pruning it. Still it couldn't be easy working all week then having to go in on a Saturday as well.

She'd found it so tiring even working a nine to five shift. She'd found... She blinked as Douglas said something. He was standing in front of her, smiling.

'Sorry?' She muttered, 'I was miles away.'

'I was saying you were just about to hold the... shell when we were interrupted. I think you'll be surprised by the weight of it.'

'Oh, right.'

She didn't really want to do this, didn't even like putting her hands into her own aquarium very much. Mum was always on about diseases and even though she knew there was no risk...

'See the reddish one? Just put your hand in, open your palm. That's right—make a cupping movement. It's quite a robust covering. See that pattern?'

She saw it, duly admired it. He obviously loved these coloured shells.

She smiled at him before letting her arm down by degrees into the warm salty water. Picked up the shell which felt slightly rough to the touch. She looked at Douglas and smiled. He was staring at her.

'Did you buy these from Michael?' she asked.

He shook his head, still staring.

'Lift it out of the water if you like—just for a few seconds. It'll not do any harm.'

She started to raise her hand slowly. Something slid out and pricked at her palm.

'Ouch!' She dropped the shell back onto the substrate, feeling her face go red, her heartbeat quicken, 'There was something in there! It...'

'A marine snail. Didn't I say? Nothing to worry about.'

He was staring at her. Staring, open mouthed.

Looking away, she wiped her wet hand on her jumper. This wasn't her fault. She'd just done what he said.

'You should have...' warned me, she wanted to add, but her lips felt tingly, fuzzy. As if she'd burnt them, as if...

She brought her palm up and stared at it, looking for signs of a puncture wound. Shiny flesh blurred into a fawn-pink mass and she looked up to see the tank had faded to a smudgy oblong.

'Douglas,' she whispered, 'My eyes...' She turned towards the man, seeing his outline become indeterminate. 'I... can't see,' she cried.

'Lie down.'

She felt him push her back onto the bed, felt the mattress give a little.

'My inhaler... handbag... doctor,' she said.

'Beautiful.'

She heard him breathing, felt him touch her hair, tried to identify his features.

'Now!' she lisped more urgently, feeling her lips pulse and swell. Didn't he realise this was an emergency? *Urgent.* She felt his weight leave the bed, heard him leave the room to dial. Heard him come back, stand somewhere to the left of her: 'Doctor's on his way.'

Marjorie gave up trying to see, let her lids close. She'd be fine in a minute. That shell thing must have triggered a particularly bad asthma attack. Keep calm, she told herself: in a few days this'll just be another tale to tell Simon. Yet something felt wrong, very wrong.

'You—don't—know—who—my—doctor—is.'

Thinking the words was easier than saying them. They came out slowed down, like when you put a record on the wrong speed. She tried to sit up, but her spine felt as if it had been liquidised. Move your feet... find the floor... She tried to swing her legs off the bed, but her thigh muscles seemed to have disappeared.

'I have to go out for an hour.'

His words sounded magnified, as if spoken directly into her ear via a loudspeaker. She tried to open her mouth, ask if he'd phoned an ambulance, but her voice wouldn't work.

'When I come back we'll have such fun,' he said more gently.

Fish are fun. Douglas wasn't fun. Douglas was... *changed*. She listened to his cold, sure voice and realised things were worse than that. Douglas was mad.

'You're so perfect like this—so ready. I'll fuck you for hours. We can just do it to each other all night.'

Doctor... ambulance... Simon... anyone. He wasn't going to get help, was leaving her to die alone in this suffocating room on this narrow, crumpled bed. As she strained to speak, to move, to breathe, his voice got quieter, smaller. The last thing she heard was the front door slam.

CHAPTER FORTY ONE

'You took your time!'

He stared at Reevon as he entered the funeral parlour. Looked at where his watch should have been, realised he'd forgotten to put it on. How had he got here? He couldn't quite remember the journey. He must have walked...

The older man was still staring, as if expecting an answer.

'Sorry.' His mouth felt dry and furry, 'Missed the bus.'

Reevon nodded, then handed him a memo with an address on it. As Douglas squinted at the letters, he snatched it back again.

'On second thoughts, I'll drive. Get yourself a bottle of mineral water from that shop over there then help me load up the hearse.'

Shop. Water. Minerals. He did as he was told, came back clutching the plastic receptacle.

'Now drink it,' said Reevon grimly.

Douglas did.

Leaned against the bonnet of the car whilst he finished his drink, then stood there clutching the bottle. Reevon took it from his fingers, put his hand on his back and steered him towards the area of the parlour where they kept the coffins and body bags.

A few minutes later he opened the hearse door and Douglas got into the front passenger seat. His throat and mouth felt cleaner, but he'd give anything for a black coffee, a neat brandy, something to fully clear his head.

'Douglas,' his boss looked at him as he started the engine, 'Any time it's not convenient, you can always bow out of the weekend roster. You know, swap your shift with someone else.'

He nodded at the older man. Someone else...

Someone was waiting at home for him, wanting him. Someone was lying on his bed, her eyes closed in the raptures of desire.

'The woman who phoned was in a right state,' said Reevon, negotiating a roundabout, 'Yet her father was diagnosed as terminal six months ago.'

Denial, Douglas thought: he'd read about it. Reevon was looking at him expectantly, so he nodded again. Once this would have been a longed-for trip, which made him feel important. Made Alice and Paul recognise his worth, the fact that he was so indispensable he could be called out any time of the day or night. Now, though, he wanted to get back to his girlfriend, his almost lover. Wanted to push her legs apart and plunge into her.

'Here we are.'

Reevon carefully nudged the hearse into a narrow driveway. He must have blanked out again, couldn't remember being driven here at all. Rubbing his head, Douglas followed his boss from the vehicle and up a path noisy with little stones. As they reached the welcome mat, a woman opened the door.

'I just left the room to make some tea.' It was obvious that she'd been crying, 'And when I came back he was... gone.'

Here today, gone tomorrow. Douglas felt the laughter bubble up inside him. Win some, you lose some. Luck of the draw...

'He's through here.'

They followed the woman into a single guest bedroom. The man was lying in a single bed.

'You said the doctor had been?'

The bereaved daughter nodded, handed over the death certificate.

'I didn't feel I could go to sleep with dad in the house. We—that's my two sisters and I—we've all been sitting with him, taking shifts, like. You get used to staying awake.'

'I understand. Several of our clients have said that. We'll take him to our Chapel of Rest.'

Hurry up, thought Douglas: get the man into a covered stretcher, get back to the parlour.

'You can visit your father tomorrow afternoon or thereafter, if you like,' Reevon said.

The woman passed her handkerchief from hand to hand. 'When I can think straight I'll phone you. Now, do I have to put it in the papers, in the Deaths?'

'We can do that for you.'

Reevon steered her back into the lounge and made her a cup of tea, got her settled in an armchair. When her colour evened out to normal he pressed their standard booklet, *Services For The Bereaved*, into her hand. Douglas sat and listened as he went through the familiar list of services available. He wanted to be free of this place, home.

'About visiting,' said the woman, 'I could just sit with him for a while? I wouldn't be in the way or anything?'

'Of course not. We have a small private Rest Room where you could say goodbye privately, and a larger one where the entire family can pay their last respects.'

Respect my right to be with Marjorie, thought Douglas dazedly. Reevon nudged him a couple of times until he looked out the required documents from the briefcase and added a few kindly words.

At last it was over and they took their leave, drove back to Reevon's with their cargo and off-loaded it.

'We'll sort it all out tomorrow,' Reevon said shortly, 'You look like you need to sleep it off.'

Had he been drinking? Just a swig or two of cherry brandy. But that had been ages ago, before... before Marjorie came.

'I'm going on to my brother's house, but I could drop you off halfway.'

Halfway house. His brain searched for sense.

'I...' His bladder gave an odd little twitch, but Alice hadn't liked him using the word toilet, 'I'll just stay here for a bit... have a... em... a coffee. I've been restless these past few nights, may take a detour home.'

'Take it easy, then.'

The older man put his hand on his, Douglas's, arm for a second. Strange, being touched in a way that wasn't sexual or punitive. He wasn't used to it.

As Reevon set off towards the outer door, Douglas took his pressure-filled bladder to the bathroom. Came out again just as Reevon drove away in his own personal car.

Which left the hearse free. The thought came to him in an adrenalin rush—he could be home in minutes, back to Marjorie's wanton, willing flesh. Pocketing the keys, he hurried out to the sleek black vehicle. Started the engine, which was still warm and sweet.

Warm. Sweet. All work and no play. He'd never be dull again. Never be a boy, either, come to that. His forever lover awaited him on a narrow bed in a room that he had the keys to. Douglas pushed his foot down on the accelerator and drove fast. An old woman looked at the hearse and crossed herself. Paul in a headscarf! He laughed out loud.

And felt God-like. He could do anything. Had a job, a home, a hobby, a compliant cunt. A few moments from now he'd be inside her, taking her. Discharging endless pleasure throughout the ensuing night.

Soon. Soon. The word sang through his veins, beat a pulse in his forehead. Once 'soon' had been the stuff of daydreams: today it meant 'almost now'.

'My girlfriend,' he whispered, and for a moment her name escaped him. What did it matter? She had buttocks and breasts and lay motionless and didn't cry out.

Or even speak. He screeched the car to a halt outside the house and let himself in, letting the door slam behind him. Raced up the stairs, unlocked his door, locked it behind himself again.

Turned slowly, terrified that she'd have gone—but she was still lying there.

'I came as quickly as I could,' he said.

No reply. He walked over to her, sat on the side of the bed, touched her neck. It was a casual gesture which failed to find the expected pulse. The flesh was cooling. But so soft—so silky! His fingers walked down, down: he watched them intently. Saw them undo the top button of her dress, the second, the third.

A pretty pastel pink bra. He squatted on the bed above her face, pushed her up, and got his knees behind her. Nudged her into a sitting position, edged the bodice of the dress down as far as the waist. Undid the clasp of the bra and pulled the cups away from their cargo. Put his palms on her nipples and began to...

The knock echoed round the room. Marjorie fell forward.

'Just a minute,' he shouted. His voice sounded nervy, high. *Think. Think.* With effort he got half the duvet out from under her, pushed it over her body. Ran his hand over his hair and face and walked jerkily to the door.

'Val's coming to unplug your sink.'

The messenger of bad tidings—Eleanor Denning.

'I... I told you. I fixed it. Bought a plunger from the store.'

'Anyway she's coming up. Says it's best to make sure these things are done properly. Seemingly the last tenant put broth down that sink and choked a pipe.'

'Well, she'll need to give me twenty minutes. I've aquarium plants in that sink at the moment.'

'I'll tell her. She wants me to come too.'

She glared as if daring him to challenge this. He realised she hadn't once flirted or smiled; his chest felt leaden. What had Val insinuated or said about him that meant they had to enter his room in pairs?

'Twenty minutes,' he said again as she turned away from him. Shut the door, raced back to Marjorie, took the duvet away.

Cooler. Much, much cooler. Unusual for a temperature to drop so rapidly when a young person died. Still, it was a cold day and she was now stripped to the waist.

Fumbling, he put her breasts in her bra, tried to get the

hooks and eyes to meet and stay in. Succeeded on the third attempt, did her buttons up. He could take her to work but the others might show up there. He couldn't put her in a coffin as the paperwork wouldn't be right. After all, there were always two of them sent to collect a body. There was a death certificate issued by the doctor. There was...

His head felt enlarged by thoughts, all rushing round, all random. He picked her up in his arms like a groom about to take his bride over the threshold, and walked towards the door. Of course—he could take her to her own house. No one would ever connect it to him if she was found dead in her own little flat.

Please, please keep Eleanor Denning away. Leaving his door slightly open he set off down the stairs carrying Marjorie. If they came out he'd have to say she'd had too much to drink or that she fainted or had some sort of epileptic fit. He started to breathe more easily as he made it out into the afternoon drizzle. Hurried with her to the coffin space at the back of the hearse. Put her in.

Started the ignition. Then stopped. Christ—where did she live, exactly? He'd walked her to her bus stop once: what service had that been? No matter, she had a handbag, somewhere—had arrived carrying it. He raced back up the stairs, found it just inside his bedroom door, brought it back to the car. Opened the clasp and located a small red diary. Checked the Personal section, which had all the details he required.

This belongs to... he knew the area well, noted the phone number. And a medical section which said she was asthmatic and carried an inhaler at all times. She could have died at any moment then, he thought numbly. Everyone died.

Get to her house—and fast. He put his foot down, felt

a sense of *deja vu* as the hearse once more leapt into life. Through familiar and less familiar streets to her tenement. He stopped at the block next to hers. She'd said Simon was out. Still...

Sweating and shaking in turn, he walked up the road to the pay phone, dialled the number in her diary. No answer. If he could just get her up the stairs, he'd be fine. Luckily most people were in town at this time of day, or in the main shopping centres. Those who were at home were enjoying lunch.

Too excited to feel overwhelmed by her weight, he carried her up the communal stairway. Found her flat, rang the bell just in case. The house stayed silent, unthreatening. Fishing out her key, he let himself in.

Walked down the hall, found the lounge first time, lowered her into the armchair and put her shoulder bag beside her. Only then did he register his parched, parboiled lungs, taste the copper in his mouth. Gasping in lungfuls of air, he made sure everything was buttoned up properly. Walked down the hall just as the doorbell rang.

Freeze. Walk backwards slowly. Look. Listen. He side stepped towards a door across from the bathroom, slid it open soundlessly, found himself facing a cupboard with a vacuum cleaner and two wood-based brooms. Creep in, shut the door quietly. He exhaled as he stared ahead into the unbroken dark.

'Marjorie—it's me-eee...'

He prayed he wouldn't sneeze or cough or shuffle. It sounded like someone was shouting through the letterbox, rattling its flap. Then he heard them turn a key, heard the door creak inwards. Heard and felt footsteps pass by his door and into the lounge. A seconds silence. He winced into the darkness. Then a high pitched wail.

'Oh no! Oh what... Oh why?'

Sounds like running up and down, then a voice.

'Daughter... Cold. She always phones me on a Saturday. That's why I went round, to see...' A nervous sniff, 'No, except... suffered from... suffers from asthma. Her name? Marjorie. I'm her mum. Milton. Yes.'

Then the address, voice shooting up and down the scale again. He had to get out of here before the ambulance arrived. The driver might notice and comment on the hearse either at the time or later. He listened as she put down the phone, as her footsteps faded away. She was presumably back in the lounge again, trying to bring round her dead daughter. Was she still in time to resuscitate her? Cold weather could preserve brain function and if the woman knew mouth-to-mouth...

He had to flee now, whatever happened. Providing she didn't come out to use the bathroom, he could get out of here. Slowly he began to push open the broom cupboard door, remembering how he did it when Paul might hear. Putting his hands against the wall to steady himself, not exerting too much pressure on one particular piece of wood. Opening the door centimetre by centimetre, placing each foot equally over more than one board at a time.

Slow, slow... in the hallway now, with nowhere to run to if she made an appearance. But facing the outer door, facing the route to freedom, ready to run. Slowly, slowly. Right foot, then left foot, then right foot. That ambulance would be gaining on him all the time.

He reached the door, opened it, swung out more quickly than he should have. Forced himself to pull it closed quietly, letting the lock take with a barely perceptible click. Then he raced down the stairs and out to the still quiet street, to the waiting vehicle. Got in, roared back to Reevon's. Parked and walked quickly away.

CHAPTER FORTY TWO

'Dead?'

Simon stared at Mrs Milton. This was ridiculous. He'd seen Marjorie on Friday morning, and she'd been fine. Standing in the doorway of the lounge, he felt increasingly disorientated, moved so that he was leaning against the nearest wall.

'I thought I'd better come back to... wait here to tell you,' Marjorie's mother said in a peculiarly expressionless voice.

His legs were going to give way. He grasped the back of the settee for comfort. Sank down into it, clutching the familiar lemon cushions with their embroidered pansies design. She'd bought the cushions but they'd chosen the settee together. It was the one thing they both half-owned in this flat. He looked more closely at her mother, sniffed the air for alcohol. The old bag must be playing some stupid trick.

'Start at the beginning.'

He tried to make his voice cool, dispassionate, the way it had been at the staff dance when one of the junior typists had been jilted and had started to scream abuse at her retreating mate.

'She usually phones... didn't. Dialled and dialled her. Then I came round.'

He wished the woman's voice wasn't so sterile, so different. He wished her face wasn't so stage-makeup white.

'And?'

She was rocking back and forth again in her daughter's armchair. 'She was here.' She touched the seat, 'Dead.'

Pills? Booze? He looked around for the means—he should never have stayed at Sue's overnight or could at least have come back first thing this morning, instead of now—after tea.

'How long had she been...?'

The woman opened and shut her mouth, spread her arms out and lifted her palms up. Let them fall to her sides.

'The ambulance men didn't say—just put her on a stretcher. They had their machines but it was too late. They took her away.'

Breath coming fast now, threatening to turn into a wail: he tried to hold back her panic. 'They actually told you she was dead?'

A nod. 'Not right away. They said they were trying to revive her. Took me into a little room. Just me...' She was staring ahead now, 'Funny little place. Not as much as a picture on the walls. And all those leaflets about tooth decay...'

'Mrs Milton. Did they say what she'd taken?'

A half remembered article: sometimes paracetamol

could lower the temperature so much that it appeared you were dead when you were only comatose.

'Taken?'

The woman looked at him blankly.

'To kill herself.'

'My daughter wouldn't kill herself!'

Like a slow-motion picture she came at him, crossing the short space between them in seconds. He watched her bend at the torso, close in on him, all twisted cheeks and beating fists. Caught her thin wrists in his hands and held her off for long shocked seconds. Moved over and lowered her onto the settee.

'Mrs Milton, lie down, please. I didn't mean it!' Her body felt rigid, as if no longer made of blood and flesh.

'Aaaah...' She exhaled as if exorcising some demon then her hands went to her face, fingers splaying out over eyes and cheekbones. When he was sure she wasn't going to sit up again, he moved himself over to the armchair, took a deep breath.

'What... what killed her, then?'

'The asthma, of course.'

'You found her with her inhaler?'

The woman looked confused.

'No. I... I suppose she didn't have time.'

But no asthma attack overcame you that fast—she'd have at least reached for the inhaler on the coffee table, and if it had failed to work she'd have started towards the bedroom cabinet. She had the damn things all over the place. And she'd known her mum was at home, that he was at Sue's. Knew that they'd phone an ambulance the second they heard someone wheezing on the line.

'There'll be a coroner's report?'

He couldn't believe he was saying this. He sounded so

clinical. Felt as if he was in a play—this wasn't for real.

'I don't think...' Mrs Milton seemed to be struggling to keep awake now, 'I said I didn't want her... cut up. They said she didn't have to be seen by the coroner's office as she'd seen a doctor just yesterday.'

'Yesterday?'

'Turns out she'd been given an emergency appointment. They had her records at the hospital. She'd been having an asthma attack in the surgery.'

'So she's still at the hospital?'

Mrs Milton's eyes were rolling back now: obviously the medics had given her a tranquilliser.

'She's... no, they gave me a card somewhere. Said to phone...'

The phone—could it be out of order in some way? Marjorie had failed to phone her mother earlier as promised, had failed to phone anyone when the asthma symptoms intensified. Mrs Milton had rung in whilst her daughter was presumably in the house, yet no one had gotten through.

'Excuse me.'

He stood up and backed into the hallway. Marjorie's mother responded with an incoherent reply.

The phone was fine. He dialled the speaking clock then phoned the recorded weather report. Put down the receiver, and saw the drawing on the telephone pad. Well, a sketch, really. A sketch of a smiling fish and the initial D.

D for Douglas. D for Dwarf Gourami. D for Dying. So Marjorie had been thinking about fish—talking about fish?—as she chatted on the phone. Could she have inhaled some fish medication? Died of some rare fish-carried disease?

Deciding to ask Mrs Milton what plans Marj had had for yesterday, he walked purposefully into the lounge. Stopped, and looked down at the sleeping form, skin and hair looking even more dried than he remembered them from moments before. Went into his room and fetched his duvet, covered her with it as far as her lightly-haired and poorly defined chin.

Then sat there by the fire, as if waiting up like a worried father. Sat there and tried not to think about anything in particular, guarding the old woman in what was now his solitary home. At one stage he went to the phone and called Sue to tell her what had happened. Said he wouldn't be in work for a few days, that presumably the funeral would be held on Tuesday or thereabouts. Said that, no, he didn't want company, that she should just go to work as usual. He'd be in touch.

When he finished talking to her, he looked at the fish drawing, and, after a moments hesitation put it in his pocket. Then he went back into the lounge and lay down in Marjorie's chair.

CHAPTER FORTY THREE

Fish eyes, fish scales, fish vents, fish fins, fish everything. Simon woke with a start as lidless black eyes closed in on his. Sat up, confused, saw Mrs Milton asleep on the settee across from him, mouth gaping in a silent snore. Lay back in the chair and shuddered, trying not to think.

Floaters swam behind his sleep-crusted lids like break-away dots of jelly. Perhaps his subconscious was reminding him to feed Marjorie's fish? He opened his eyes again with effort, leaned forward, prised himself out of his all-night chair, wincing at how seized-up his back muscles felt. Walked, stiff-legged, over to the aquarium and stared unfocusedly through the glass. Feed the fish, feed the fish, feed the fish. He'd watched Marjorie do so one evening. Remembering the drill, he dropped some flakes through the designated opening in the hood.

'There you go.' He felt better for doing it, felt he was achieving something. Marjorie would be—*would have been*—pleased. Soon Mrs Milton would wake up and they'd have to talk about the funeral. She was supposed to phone someone. He'd better take care of all that.

Fin and tail flashed at the surface of the water, frightening the gravel-scouring occupants. Today Marjorie would normally... well, quite often be making a trip to Michael's shop. He opened on Sundays, was within walking distance: though she usually didn't buy much, it helped her pass the time.

He felt ashamed again, remembering. Typical to think about someone more in death than you'd ever done in life. After all he'd said, after all the promises he'd made to himself following Jo's suicide, and he'd left his flatmate to draw pictures on a pad and die alone in her chair.

Marjorie dead: he still couldn't believe it. She'd loved life deep down, was just a little afraid of giving it her all. She would have fought hard to breathe, to tell someone. Something she couldn't handle must have gone on...

He walked over to the still sleeping woman, decided to let her rest for now. Walked over to the window. Walked back to his chair. Staying in like this wasn't achieving anything. He wanted to keep moving, going on and on and on. Fingers and toes over-energised, Simon pulled on his shoes and jacket then left the flat intent on a tension-ebbing walk.

CHAPTER FORTY FOUR

'Another three from the hospital.' Reevon's voice came faintly at him down the receiver.

'I'll be with you in twenty minutes,' Douglas said, going to fetch his coat. He was glad of the call—it would give purpose to this dragging Sunday, and the overtime money would come in useful too. He'd been spending lots recently, what with alcohol and pub meals. Not to mention the cost of the marine tank, the Cones.

He knotted his tie, put on his shoes, combed his hair quickly. He'd gotten into trouble for being late yesterday. Today he'd be there in time, make Reevon happy. Unwilling to spend the money on a taxi, he broke into a half-run. You could claim cab fares back from the firm if you used them to help you do emergency overtime, but Shelley didn't put your refund through till the end of the month. Hurry. Hurry. A boy sitting on a wall grinned as he pumped his arms to increase his speed. His white shirt clung to his underarms like velcro. He joined Reevon, breathless, in the hearse.

'You'll end up in the back at this rate,' Reevon said, snorting his disapproval, 'If I'd known you'd get in this state I'd have picked you up at your house.'

'I'm fine.'

It was a house rule never to drive the hearse on unofficial business. He wondered what he'd done wrong now.

A few pleasantries, a few jokes—death jokes. They waved goodbye to the mortuary porter, carried the body bags from the hospital morgue and drove them back to base. Unloaded them and took them into the Prep Room. Unzipped each bag.

'Not much to do here.' Reevon was referring to the fact that the hospital always did the laying-out. The older man looked at the name tags. 'We'll log them in, then phone.'

Phone the relatives and arrange the date of the funeral, find out if they wanted to see their nearest and dearest for the last time on this earth.

'Brown, Billy,' said Reevon, and Douglas countersigned the book. 'Milton, Marjorie. Eppingdon, Steve.'

Marjorie. He prayed he hadn't blushed, shown some emotion. She'd been with him yesterday, and they'd almost... he'd touched her breasts. Reevon went out to attend to some work in the office. Left alone in the Chesting Area, Douglas stared at Marjorie's cold white face. So young to be dead: Paul would have said it was God's punishment to die before your three score years and ten were out—which meant she must have been wicked, a temptress. There must have been evil behind that half-shy hopeful smile.

'No answer at Mrs Milton's house. I hope she hasn't

gone to stay with relatives. Better get the body chested in case she's on her way here now.'

He heard Reevon's words, as if from a distance. Anything was possible where the bereaved were concerned.

'Take her top side.'

Obeying the older man, he helped lift the body from the table onto the trolley. Wheeled it through to the smallest Chapel of Rest. As he'd done hundreds of times before, Douglas helped his boss lower the pallid limbs into the oak-effect display coffin. Mrs Milton could choose the burial one when she arrived.

'Young girl,' said Reevon. He always sounded genuinely sad when the dead were under forty. Douglas couldn't imagine feeling so sorrowful for anyone at all. 'I'll go phone the other two,' added his employer, hurrying off back in the direction of the office.

Douglas stared down at Marjorie's lifeless flesh, stroked her cheek, felt his fingers drawn to her neck to check her carotid pulse, her life pulse. Though the funeral directors weren't medically trained, they ran a series of checks to ascertain the person had truly entered the realm of the dead. But in this instance the hospital would have done that, determined all vital signs had gone.

He checked nevertheless. She was cold, motionless. Didn't appear to be breathing. Had no visible heartbeat, circulation flow. No warm breath.

Yet she didn't feel dead to him—he could usually sense such things. He ran his fingers over her breasts, her throat. Smoothed her hair out, where the body bag had mussed it. Found the tiniest flicker of a beat behind her right ear.

Calm down. Calm down. He forced himself to remain

remote, dispassionate. Checked that the pulse wasn't in his own finger: many a nervous young doctor had made that mistake. But no, there was the merest flicker of life, of biological continuation. She was simply comatose. A man could do anything he liked...

His for the taking. Now he had to get rid of Reevon so that he could have her to himself for hours—forever. Could he do a variation of what he'd done last time? Borrow the hearse and bring her to his flat?

Coffins weren't usually nailed down till the day of the funeral which mightn't be till midweek at the latest. He'd have to make very sure he was the one who did the final nailing of that lid so that no one else had a chance to peek inside. Would fasten it down over a body-sized weight of chunks of rock to fool the coffin-bearers. He'd have to find a quarry or a builders yard...

Or he could re-inject her here with his marine snail if she showed any likelihood of coming round, of getting noisy. Could sleep beside her at the funeral parlour with his Geography Cone wrapped in wet cotton wool in its little bag. Put her—wrapped in a sack, say—in a cupboard on the day of the funeral. Fill the coffin with a heavy substance, bury it, then come back.

To take her home—his ideal woman, his eternal lover. In time she'd probably learn to lie there of her own accord. Let's face it, she probably didn't like the injections: they seemed painful. And if someone hurt you enough you did what you were told.

He smiled, glad he lived in these times, in modern times. Once, the corpse would have been watched from death to burial, around the clock. The family often paid an old woman to sit there, night after night, knitting beside the body. That way if the person came round there was someone in attendance to offer them water, warmth.

No more, though. He smiled again. God, but he knew his subject. Though it was a crime in Scotland to disturb a body once it was buried, it wasn't criminal to carry off or steal it before it was interred in the ground. Not that someone like that Simon would see it that way, but then what he didn't see wouldn't hurt him. He'd never know...

'It's just you and me, now, Marj,' he whispered. And, from habit rather than desire, moved an exploratory hand over her uncomplaining cold nipples through the yielding lime green dress.

CHAPTER FORTY FIVE

Someone was shouting—no, just speaking. Marjorie's brain swum back to consciousness. A male voice, a familiar voice, her friend... No, not her friend. He'd hurt her, made her joints go heavy and slack, made her lips go numb.

She had to tell someone about him—anyone! He couldn't be allowed to treat people like that: she'd been hugely, overwhelmingly afraid. She tried to open her eyes, found the lids no longer seemed hinged to anything. Instructed her lips to open, but they wouldn't obey.

Speak. Speak. The place at the back of her throat which formed sounds was out of commission. *Move an arm, a leg.* The signals went from her brain but weren't carried out. Oh, Christ, how long would she have to stay like this, in his room, a prisoner of her body? What was he going to do with her? Would she be raped?

She might already have been. There was no feeling down there... anywhere. Why was he doing this? Was she clothed or unclothed? He had said it was just him and her, now—but mum would report her missing, or Simon would. They'd notice her absence within hours, alert the police...

'Still no Mrs Milton.'

Another male voice, an older voice. So he had a co-conspirator. At least they both thought she was still unconscious: she'd better keep it that way. Funny, though, that the other man had got her prefix wrong—Douglas knew she wasn't married. She listened, trying to work out where each of them was in the room. Listened for the phone ringing, for a neighbour or the landlady to go past or knock on the door. Her thinking had never been so focused, so perfectly clear.

'Billy Brown's brother and sister-in-law are coming down to the office now. I offered to go up there. But they've the decorators in, said the whole place was a mess.'

'You'll do the forms?' Douglas's voice, sounding hopeful.

'Got writer's cramp, have you? Alright, you can tidy up in here.'

Office... what was this about coming down to the office? Bringing other people here. It was mad.

'All going to the Crematorium, bar Milton, who wants a burial,' added the stranger's voice.

Marjorie felt panic shoot through her head like a bolt. *Burying her. They were talking about burying her.* That meant... Her mind wanted to close down, go to sleep, crowd out the thought. Douglas must have brought her to his workplace, to his blessed funeral parlour. This was her funeral they were talking about.

She wasn't ready to die—she just wasn't. She'd never been abroad, never helped a child with its homework and seen its worried face clear. She wanted to find a best friend, to see the Pyramids, to plan someone a surprise party. She wanted to... she wanted to live.

A man's voice was saying something about making her presentable. Was she already in a coffin or in a mortuary drawer? Images flickered inside her head as reality crept relentlessly closer. Weren't funerals almost always held within the week? Many took place after two days—she'd been to some. An elderly neighbour, a work mate buried with undue haste. Even as she lay here, the gravediggers were doubtless enthusiastically excavating. She was going to be buried alive.

CHAPTER FORTY SIX

Death was so final. Simon increased his walking speed as the stale but true statement clogged his mind, made his chest feel hollow. Christ, to die so young.

He looked right, then left, decided to stroll uphill. If you got ill you adjusted, settled for different pleasures. Embraced the hot water bottle and chicken soup instead of the five mile run. Your limbs flagged, you feasted on the many pleasures of the brain: reading, expressing, solving. Enjoyed the golds and greens of growing plants, the warm lightness of morning sun upon your face.

But death—you went from maybe having everything to having nothing. No sight, no sound, no taste, no sense of smell. Marjorie had loved her home cooked meals, her much-fed fish, her TV programmes. He didn't want to think about her dying, wanted to walk till he dropped.

Blank it out, blank it out. He kept seeing her getting up from her chair, walking to the phone, dialling the *Stella* number. Saw her proudly holding out her container of pond pellets: 'Michael says they're suitable for tanks too!'

Saw her putting on her heart-shaped pendant to attend the *Fish Are Fun* club. Saw her... saw her very much alive.

It was no good. He had to face up to this. He had to view the body. Pace slower now, Simon turned towards home again to ask Mrs Milton where Marjorie's corpse was being stored.

CHAPTER FORTY SEVEN

She'd moved! Her finger had moved! He'd have to... negate her. Douglas stared across the Chapel at Reevon, who was sitting on one of the two seater settees filling in a form.

'... wait for the Brown sister to phone back. Her brother said she'd only be about twenty minutes. Sweep up these rose petals, will you Douglas, before someone arrives?'

Rose. Petals. Sweeping. He forced his gaze away from Marjorie's tell-tale digit.

'Uh... right.'

He swept the petals into his left hand rather than going to the cupboard in the hall for a brush and pan set. Reevon frowned at him slightly. He couldn't leave Marjorie for a moment, not a solitary second—never again. If the paralysis in her throat wore off she would speak—would shriek.

She'd sit up, flail out, accuse: everyone would hate him. He had to get Reevon out of the room and permanently silence her before it was too late.

CHAPTER FORTY EIGHT

Mrs Milton—I'd like to go and see Marjorie, pay my respects. Simon rehearsed the line in his head as he trundled up the stairs. The woman was an unknown quantity. He had to woo her, to appease her. Maybe *pay my respects* was too vague a term? He paused outside his front door. Mrs Milton might say that it was too late for that, that he hadn't bothered to respect the girl when she was alive.

Try another tack. *Mrs Milton, I have to say goodbye to Marjorie.* Surely she'd understand that, understand the need to see for yourself, to fully know? People always said they'd give a great deal to see the dead person one more time, to commune with them. Simon put his key slowly into the lock.

This was a death house. He closed the door carefully, quietly, tiptoed towards the lounge with its sleeping occupant, its surviving host. He'd wake her up gently, bring her tea and biscuits, offer to take care of any paperwork at the mortuary or wherever, sort things out.

'Mrs...' He sidled into the lounge—and stopped: the

settee was empty. The duvet wasn't there any more: it was as if she'd never been. Was he dreaming? He rubbed his eyes, backed out of the room, went into the hallway. The duvet was neatly rolled outside Marjorie's door.

For a second hope flooded him—Marjorie had been tidying! She'd revived, come back, sent her grateful mother off home. Half expecting to hear her voice, he knocked softly on her door then rapped more loudly. Waited, walked in. Empty as before.

Where was everyone? He corrected himself: where was Mrs Milton? He turned and walked into the kitchen, which looked lonely and unused. Moved on to his own room, then to the bathroom, finally walked dazedly to the phone. And saw the note: gone home. Mrs Milton's initials, and a number. He dialled, listening to it ring and ring.

Bad timing on his part. She must have left recently, must still be on her way there. He couldn't follow as he didn't have the woman's full address. Not that Marjorie was going anywhere... but *he* wanted to be going somewhere. He could phone the hospital. They'd tell him if they still had Marjorie at their mortuary or had sent her body elsewhere.

Fumbling with the heavy telephone book, he looked up the number, dialled. Realised he didn't know which department he'd have to be connected to. Exactly when she'd been admitted. Anything.

'Can I help you?' asked a female voice. It sounded remote, if professional.

'Um, my flatmate was brought in on Saturday.' He thought fast, 'Morning or lunchtime, I think. She... was declared dead almost immediately. Now I need to know where she's gone.'

'Her name?'

'Marjorie Milton.'

'Hold on one moment.'

He held and held and held.

Rustling noises as someone approached the phone.

'Hello, Mr..?'

'Brent. Er, Simon.'

'Her mother has that information. If you get in touch with her.'

'But I can't contact her. She's gone out.'

Another pause, muffled voices. He heard a woman's tone going up and down, sounding querulous. More rustling. Crackling on the line.

'Not a relative...' he heard in the background. Gritting his teeth, he hung up, dialled Mrs Milton again. And this time she answered, and gave him the details of where Marjorie was.

'It was the ward sister who mentioned it—I asked her to choose someplace nice for me. She said they weren't allowed to make recommendations, but someone else said that this place was big and had branches everywhere.'

Reevon's. The name sounded familiar—but she'd said they were a large company. He dialled, fingers drumming an unrhythmic hollow on the table, but the line was engaged, engaged, engaged. They were there, though, on a Sunday—at least that was something. He could be there himself in double quick time.

Simon walked nervously to his car, opened the door, closed it quietly. His fingers felt thick and oddly numbed as he tried to click his seat belt into place. What exactly would she look like, feel like, smell like? Strange that he knew so much more about birth than death. Knew to boil water for hygiene purposes, help the mother pant, cut the umbilical cord and tie it close to the child's body. Didn't know what happened to that same child's body when it ultimately died.

Buses. Cars. Motor bikes. A lorry. The third vehicle in a row overtook him. Everyone seemed to sense his exhaustion today, his lack of fight. I've come to see Marjorie... He saw an oncoming driver staring at him and realised he'd been muttering to himself. This still felt like being in a film or a play.

Yet in real life people were dying strangely all the time: reacting badly to peanuts, contracting some blinding disease because they didn't wash their fingernails after cleaning out the dog's basket. Hardly a week went by without some youth collapsing after inadvertently inhaling shoe cleaning spray, some old woman found burned to death from the inside.

The traffic lights hit red and he braked again: the third set of lights in a row that had turned against him. Lucky he wasn't in a hurry, wasn't exactly rushing towards this meeting with death. Still, he was doing the right thing—maybe once he saw Marjorie he could accept what had happened. Grieve, even. Let the bereavement process begin. He nosed the car on again as the lights turned to green, getting in line between the optimistic picnic-goers and zoo-trippers. Hemmed in by the pleasure drivers, the Sunday-lunch-in-town leisure crowds.

Normally he hated the fact that they all drove at twenty miles an hour as if being shadowed by a police car. Usually he sighed and rolled his eyes as they stopped to let each pretty girl cross the road. He looked at his watch, found he wasn't wearing it. He hadn't been to bed at home so must have left it at Sue's. The car clock must be wrong: he felt he'd been trapped in here for at least an hour. Yet it had only moved on ten minutes since he'd driven away from the flat.

Could he have a flat? The car slowed down, his foot still pressing firmly on the accelerator. Don't you give out on me, he thought, not really believing it was likely to. The car coughed and almost stalled. Impossible—he'd had it serviced recently, had everything checked or changed. The vehicle should be damn near invincible. He put his foot down further and the engine died.

No petrol. The gauge was showing no petrol. He and Sue had gone to a barn dance in Fife on the Friday night. Thinking back, he realised he'd driven for miles, taking several wrong turnings. Had meant to go out on Saturday night to replenish the fuel. Then he'd come home and heard the news about Marjorie and every other thought had gone out of his head.

A taxi. He could walk all the way whilst keeping one eye out for a taxi. Or, failing that, catch the infrequent Sunday bus. Looking behind and before him every few minutes, Simon began to stroll through the busy springtime streets.

CHAPTER FORTY NINE

'Billy Brown needs some cosmetic work.'

Marjorie listened more intently.

'Oh, I thought he was a natural causes?'

'Was left lying face down. Bad hypostasis. Should really embalm.'

'I'll leave it to you.'

Papers being shuffled or moved, footsteps retreating again. Was that madman staring at her, touching her numb limbs and openings? *Don't leave me with Douglas again. Don't! Don't!*

What time was it? What day was it? They'd said they were burying her on Tuesday. She'd gone to Douglas's on Saturday morning, and he'd... Time became a blank. Had he brought her straight here or kept her in his room for hours? Days, even? How long ago had she been pronounced dead?

How long till she was buried alive? She'd seen several TV programmes which featured it. They were usually on at Hallowe'en or to coincide with some ritual like the Mexican Day of the Dead.

She'd seen a historical programme once on death in this country. They'd show how cholera victims in days of yore often appeared to have expired. So the overworked nurses would put them in rough wooden caskets, nail the lids down. Leave them in a room ready for the graveyard truck to come round.

Only often the patients weren't dead—only insensible. Revived to find themselves in a crudely stapled box. Banged on the lid, and screamed and cried and begged to be let out again. Begged and begged and begged.

But the nurses, coarse from drink and poverty and overwork, pretended not to hear them. After all, as the commentator had said ghoulishly, the nurses knew the patients were going to die anyway within a few more days. Madness to break open a good coffin lid just to give them further access to that ever scarce resource, a bed.

She'd felt the horror then, those poor men and women suffocating slowly. Lying in the fetid darkness, unable to curl into the foetal position like one usually did when one was afraid. No quiet, peaceful death: the last words a curse, a cry for clemency. The last movements not a palm going to a weary brow, but hands tearing like claws against cruelly smooth wood.

No purchase there, and not enough space to pull your legs up and kick out. A few splinters beneath your nails for your trouble. That was it. And ah, the exertion would use up more of that dwindling air—your last air. Breathing in the stench of your own fatal fear.

Worse, though, to wake after the coffin went into the earth, after the tons of soil came down upon it. You could scream and scream but if it was evening there'd be no one around. It had happened throughout history: she'd read the records. Bodies were dug up and coffin wood found in their mouths, in their scratched and torn palms. The eyes would be fixed with horror, fingers possibly clutching a pendant or ring with which they'd raked at the wood. The mouth was often open in an eternal scream.

Yes, medical men had often pronounced the merely-comatose as being dead, had consigned them to the graveyard. People who were still alive could be cold and blue. Could be stiff to the touch, heartbeat and breathing so poor that they couldn't be felt. Was that how she looked now to this innocent stranger whose voice she could periodically hear? Did she look dead to Douglas, too, or did he know the truth?

One man had invented a bell that went above ground, was attached by a cord to the corpse's hand as he lay in his coffin. Then, if he revived, he could signal help. Problem was, the bell rang when the wind blew, when the body jerked due to shifting fluids and gases. Many a corpse had been dug up, only to be repronounced dead.

Most of the boys had grinned at the idea of that bell when they discussed it in school History lessons. But she'd thought it was worth a try even then. Would give almost anything for one now: one that rang at the lightest touch, the faintest movement. She'd need one even more when they lowered her into the earth...

At one stage it had been common practice to leave bodies above ground till they began to rot or show other unmistakable signs of decomposition. But more medical knowledge, a fuller understanding of disease had put paid to that. So, she'd be buried... She amended the thought: so *some people* were buried alive today, in order that the others might live a healthier fuller life untainted by the corpses stench.

Were they digging her grave even as she mused? The

door burst open again: her hearing was amplifying every sound, bringing it right into her brain like a Walkman on top volume. Her mind tensed up. She wondered if her feet and hands did too. They normally did when she was anxious. But nothing was normal now.

'When will the Brown corpse be ready? Just in case the brother wants to see him whilst he's signing the papers next door.'

That was the other man again. Then a pause, a loud creak. Had Douglas been touching her and jumped back when the other man got closer? She couldn't tell unless he murmured something about how soft her hair and skin was, how fine her...

'Um, I'm just... Not long.' Douglas said. He sounded laboured and confused.

'Not long is a relative term.'

The stranger had a sigh in his voice, sounded weary. Was he still reading his newspaper or some business report? One set of footsteps leaped at her out of the black. The surrounding silence accentuated Douglas's persistent tread. What was he doing now, and why? He sounded as if he was walking further into the centre of the room.

Move an arm, a leg—anything. Croak a word, a sound, summon up a sneeze, break sweat. Stretching, straining— and absolutely nothing happening. Praying, pleading, a world of silent beseechings in her head.

'I'll embalm the Eppingdon corpse in a couple of hours. He's to be flown out to the states—Kentucky.'

She was going to be left with Douglas again, all alone! If he didn't believe he'd done so already he might use this opportunity to kill her. Or could he slay her with this man in the room, right here? He might just prick her with a syringe, with another of those poisonous creatures.

Sending out desperate signals from her brain to her body, Marjorie thought she felt a tremulous pulse of power returning to her lower lids.

CHAPTER FIFTY

Her eyelids had twitched. Douglas stared from Marjorie's flickering features, back to Reevon. Had he noticed? He was facing them both, still chatting away.

'New hair style coming up,' he said, walking into the centre of the floor so that he stood between her body and Reevon. His employer's lips gaped open, eyes narrowing yet staring: 'Douglas, the hospital took care of all that. You're not yourself these days.'

Not himself? Then who was he? Who was anyone? What was the point of it all? The point for a while had seemed to be lust, but now he wasn't so sure. Lust made you feel better for a few moments of releasing, pulsing ecstasy, made you feel worse the next day. It was like snatching something you'd coveted then later feeling guilt as if you'd been caught stealing. He looked back at Marjorie and realised all desire had died.

If she would just die, too, it would be over. He didn't want any more women, just wanted to sleep and sleep.

Maybe later he'd get a small dog for companionship, buy some new books, go back to a quiet kind of a life.

But for now, he had to get her into a coffin below the ground and keep her there. Preferably an iron one, he thought wildly, not the kind of structure from which you could easily escape. They'd had them in past centuries: the cemetery could charge a higher fee for one of those. Full metal jacket—or, in her case, metal dress. Problem was, it took longer to break down, took up space for decade after decade. And the ground was supposed to belong not just to the deceased and the currently living, but to generations to come.

Future generations. He'd cared enough not to inflict life on future generations. He sighed and Reevon walked towards him, a growing frown between his eyes. Disused burial grounds were sometimes made into recreation areas where people could sit and rest and enjoy the flowers. The idea was that the needs of the living should have priority over consideration for the dead.

But should they? He looked at Reevon as he started some talk about Douglas taking time off for a holiday. The dead were more wise...

'Well, you know where I am,' Reevon finished heavily.

Douglas stared. The man was right before him. Here. Of course he knew where he was.

'Anything you say will be in confidence, of course,' added his employer.

Douglas turned away, saw Marjorie's right hand tremble back to life.

'Yes. I'll... I'll let you get off,' he said desperately to Reevon. The second the man left the room, he could overcome the girl. *Stop the movement—stop, stop, stop.*

He'd suffocate, smother, keep pushing, holding, crushing until the last flicker of life expired. He'd be quick and sure, professional. First gasps, then muffled half-breaths, then a final childlike sigh.

The phone trilled through the parlour. Reevon looked at Douglas and raised his eyebrows, then stared in the direction of the office.

'Got to polish,' Douglas muttered, desperate to stay here. He realised belatedly that the polish was... somewhere else. Somewhere outwith the Chapel which contained Marjorie. He couldn't leave her now, with her right thumb twitching back and forth.

'Won't be a mo...'

He fished a pastel pink tissue from his sleeve and started to scrub fixedly at the side of the coffin.

Reevon sighed—'I'll get that'—and strode out of the door.

What to use? What to use? He gazed frantically around the pretty room, seeking a weapon. Started to take off his jacket then saw the little lace-trimmed cushion on the furthest away chair. Cushioning her from the blows of life, cushioning her from fear, from future uncertainties. Douglas picked up the suffocating promise in both hands and advanced.

CHAPTER FIFTY ONE

At last. Simon walked up to the funeral parlour and was raising his hand to knock when a man in his fifties came hurrying out of the door and almost cannoned into him.

'Oh! I was about to get my briefcase from...'

From the hearse, Simon thought, swallowing hard.

'I'm sorry to... I rang. You were engaged.'

'If you'd tried one of our extensions. Someone's just rung in about some papers so...'

'I was just given this one by Marjorie's mother. Marjorie Milton—that's who I'm here to see.'

The funeral director nodded. 'I'm Wallace Reevon. We've just placed her in our Chapel of Rest. I'll show you to her then go and collect these papers. It's the third door along.'

He'd have to look death in the face, in the body. He'd have to say sorry before he said goodbye.

'Is she...?'

What? Happy? Peaceful? The man couldn't know.

It was a stupid question. He was half-afraid, stalling for time, flushed with guilt mixed with a little fear.

Looking suitably sad, Reevon pushed the door open, moving his arm forwards in an on you go polite mute gesture. And both men stared at Douglas, his face red with concentration or rage or excitement as he bent over the coffin, holding a floral cushion over the corpse's face.

CHAPTER FIFTY TWO

'What the...!'

He heard the words and looked up, watched as if through a long lens as Simon came through the door in a forward kind of gait with Reevon close behind him. Simon lurched all the way up to the coffin but it was Reevon who took the cushion away.

'Mr. Tate, if I can see you in...' Reevon's cheeks were pale as death, eyes dark with shock or anger.

'Douglas!' Simon muttered, clenching his fists.

Everyone was displeased with him. When people got angry with you, you had to stay really still, totally soundless. He locked his knees, his calves, made his shoulders freeze, arms by his sides. Reevon was still clutching the confiscated cushion. 'You two know each other?' he asked, blinking.

'Marjorie and Douglas go... went to the same social club for people who keep... kept fish.'

Reevon stared at him even harder. Douglas looked

at the walls, as if the answer lay in their neutral shades: solution in pastels.

'She's... just here,' Reevon said heavily.

Douglas watched Simon's feet edge closer to the coffin stand. She'd made little snuffling noises as he edged her towards the next life with his little cushion. Had the pressure been hard enough? Had he been in time? He wanted her to stay, stay, just as perfectly preserved as a Tussaud's waxwork. Sensed rather than saw Simon lean forward, heard the man's hard holding-back sniff.

Silence. Good. Then...

'She... oh Christ, she moved!'

He saw Reevon shake his head. 'Sir, gases can redistribute...'

They both bent over the corpse, which had once been his corpse. Douglas stared at her downcast eyes and saw them open more, more, more.

'My God.' Simon turned to Douglas. 'You... you were suffocating her.'

Reevon staggered back as if he'd been struck.

After that, a lot of words, lots of looks in his direction. He didn't like people looking at him, so kept his eyes on the floor. Then phone calls and footsteps and ambulance men and policemen. Someone put their hand on his arm and he flinched.

Hands behind your back. Step this way, please. It was encouraging that they said *please*: friendly, respectful. Someone put their palm flat over the top of his hair, said 'Don't bump your head.' He did as he was told, concentrated fully on each word—well, instructions really. *Sit there. Listen. Anything you say...*

Seated in the back of the van he practiced staying silent. Let his tongue remain inert against the floor of his mouth, half-closed his eyes. Folded his arms on his lap and concentrated until he made each limb motionless. Paul, he thought proudly, would be pleased.

EPILOGUE

'The usual?'

Marjorie nodded at the newsagent, and he picked up her gossip magazine. Not that anything had been usual these past few days. First there'd been all the hospital tests, the police statements. And now mum and Simon were treating her as if she was a fragile glass figurine.

She smiled to herself. She was, superficially, more fragile looking than she'd been a couple of weeks ago. She'd lost ten pounds in weight since then. *Recommended: The Cone Diet.* She shuddered at her mind's strange sense of humour. Or should she blame her shrinking girth on hospital food? Thank them, rather—already she was feeling so much lighter and fitter, had no intention of going into the ungiving ground.

She appreciated the sun, now, didn't mind the damp, the rain. Found even the colder evening breeze refreshing, though she'd shivered and complained about it before. To have lost all that: walks and shops, the changing skyline.

Different plants, trees, colours, the familiar beloved programmes on TV.

As ever, she stepped towards the confectionery section after choosing her magazine. Let her hand hover between a bar of chocolate and bag of mints. Her fingers stayed by a new oatflake bar and she stopped to read the label. Saw that it didn't contain chocolate, was about to move on.

'It's supposed to be healthier and lower in calories,' the shopkeeper said chattily, 'It's selling well.'

Healthier. She wanted to keep getting healthier. And slimmer. She'd already made a surprise start.

'I'll take it,' Marjorie said, turning away from her usual high sugar choices, 'Time for a change.' She stopped, looked at the display behind the man's head which was advertising a slimming magazine, 'And I'll take one of those, too.'

Reluctant to go straight home and miss out on the pale but increasing sunshine, she walked to the corner, sat down on a bench to read her impulse buy. Women much larger than herself had shed several stone, said that it gave them new zest, the confidence to learn to drive, try different jobs. One had gone abroad on holiday for the first time. Another had learned to dance.

She read on. Many had taken up exercise after losing that empowering first stone or so and swore it helped burn off further fat. Admitted that they felt silly at first in their larger size shorts and T-shirts, but that the rest of the class were so nice... Everyone at the hospital had been nice. So had her neighbours. Even the aloof couple on the ground floor had recently started to say hello.

****

Three days later Marjorie walked through the park towards the Community Centre: she'd taken cookery lessons there once before. She'd go round to mums after she'd been, tell her that she'd just joined the beginners aerobics class. Mum would shake her head, of course—but by then it would already be a *fait accompli*. Mum would say it was dangerous on medical grounds but a suntanned Dr Ashford, fresh back from The Gambia, had said it was okay. Then Marjorie would have two places to go of an evening: keep fit and *Fish Are Fun*.

Douglas would never be back at *Fish Are Fun*, would never be anywhere other than a cell or high security hospital for decades. The police had arranged for her to see a psychologist to talk about it, talk about the hours spent on the mortuary slab. Maybe she'd tell him about dad dying, about the man who'd flashed, about the kids at school and the things they'd said and done to her. Maybe it was time to talk.

Spirits lifting, Marjorie smiled without thinking at a passing jogger and the girl smiled back. Perhaps one day she, Marjorie, could run through open parkland like this in an emerald tracksuit. It must be great to feel your limbs moving in unison, feel the warm breeze rushing through your hair.

Dr Ashford had said that both losing weight and taking moderate exercise would improve her general health, even help with the asthma. After a month or so of aerobics she could ask him if she could try table tennis or badminton. They were the kind of hobbies she could find time for even if she started working. Bag swinging out before her, Marjorie broke into an awkward half-run.

Acknowledgements

My grateful thanks to the Institute of Aquaculture at the University of Stirling for responding quickly and helpfully to my requests for information. Thanks also to individuals within the funeral industry for giving of their knowledge, insights and valuable time.

About the Author

Carol Anne Davis was born in Dundee and was everything from an artist's model to a dental nurse before going to university and gaining an MA. She then took a postgraduate course in Community & Adult Education at Edinburgh University before beginning to write full time.

Her novels include the psychopathic *Safe As Houses*, killing-the-neighbours-from-hell *Noise Abatement* and male rape *Kiss It Away*. She has also written three true crime books, *Couples Who Kill, Women Who Kill and Children Who Kill*.

Carol currently lives in south-west England and her website can be found at www.carolannedavis.co.uk.